Rings clattered as I shoved aside the striped plastic.

A scream welled up from deep inside me, clawing its way through the lump in my throat. There, hanging by the neck with a brightly colored scarf around her throat, slumped a woman. A small wooden stool lay at her feet. The showerhead had pulled away from the wall. The scarf hung on the edge of the plumbing, while the woman's knees rested on the stained fiberglass floor.

Penny

Other mysteries by Cynthia Hickey

Fudge-Laced Felonies

Don't miss out on any of our great mysteries. Contact us at the following address for information on our newest releases and club information:

Heartsong Presents—MYSTERIES! Readers' Service
PO Box 721
Uhrichsville, OH 44683
Web site: www.heartsongmysteries.com

Or for faster action, call 1-740-922-7280.

Candy-Coated Secrets

A Summer Meadows Mystery

Cynthia Hickey

HEARTSONG PRESENTS MYSTERIES

First, I want to thank God to whom all glory goes. Without the gift of imagination He's given me, this book would never have come to be. Second, to my husband, Tom, and his unfailing support and encouragement. I couldn't do this without him. My awesome agent, Kelly Mortimer, who believes in me enough to give me a kick in the pants when one is deserved. My wonderful editor, Susan Downs, who is entertained by my character's wackiness. To my parents, siblings, and children, who eagerly await my next book, and to the wonderful readers of Summer's first adventure, *Fudge-Laced Felonies*, who can't wait to indulge in another of Summer's crazy mishaps. To my critique partners, the Crit-Critters, who make sure I stay on the right track.

ISBN 978-1-60260-185-7

Cover design: Kirk DouPonce, DogEared Design
Cover illustration: Jody Williams

Our mission is to publish and distribute inspirational products offering exceptional value and biblical encouragement to the masses.

Printed in the U.S.A.

A horn blared. I heard a crash. A shrill shrieking, like metal on metal. Then I felt a vibration beneath my feet.

"Earthquake!" Aunt Eunice ducked beneath the kitchen table.

I shot her a look. "Please. In Arkansas?"

Another blast of the noise a shattered trumpet might make.

"That sounds like an elephant." Aunt Eunice crawled from her hiding place and glanced at me, her brow furrowed.

In Mountain Shadows? "It can't be."

The trumpet screamed again.

Aunt Eunice tossed into the sink the cucumber she'd been peeling before her dive under the table. She whipped off her apron, sending it in a yellow-checkered parachute to the floor, and then headed toward the living room.

"Race you to the window!" My aunt was game for anything. We dashed to the front of the house. I planted my feet on a throw rug and slid to the door first. I hit it with a thud. "I won!"

"You cheated!"

Truly, my cairn terrier, barked in a fit of frenzy. Aunt Eunice dodged by Truly as we rushed outside onto the porch. The screen door slammed behind us.

A diesel rig in garish colors had collided with another trailer and lay diagonally on its side across Highway 64. Tires spun as smoke poured from beneath them. The acrid odor of burnt rubber assaulted my nostrils. Other brightly painted trucks pulling trailers idled beside the road.

Men darted around our yard, herding escaped animals: sheep, miniature ponies, and a pig. Cries of alarm and cursing filled the air. I never would have believed such a sight had I not seen it.

A horse whinnied, a lion roared, and an elephant trailing a length of frayed rope thundered past the cars and across the front lawn.

"My roses!" In my usual fashion of acting before thinking, I grabbed an umbrella from a stand beside the door. "Hey!"

Opening and closing the makeshift weapon in rapid succession, I waved it in front of me as I flew into the yard. The elephant blasted a warning and turned toward me. *Horror.* Gone was the cute Dumbo of my childhood. Instead, I faced several tons of a frightened giant who rose to stand on two legs. Doing what any sane person in my circumstances would, I whirled and dashed around the corner of the house. Then, peering into the front yard, I watched in anguish as the elephant stomped through the roses I'd grown for the county fair. So much for my hopes of a blue ribbon.

Aunt Eunice took a step off the porch in my direction, and then obviously decided against being trampled to death. She turned and scooted into the house. "Summer, get back in here this instant!" she yelled through the screen door, as if the mesh could protect her. "No use dwelling on uprooted dreams. You'll get squashed." My heart thundered as loud as the beast's massive feet. I cowered beneath my still open black-and-white polka-dotted protection. *God, save me.* How do I get into these messes?

"Ginger! Down, girl."

I peeked around my umbrella. A massive woman waddled toward the raging beast. A sunny yellow muumuu with teal and green flowers stretched across the woman's girth. Fluorescent flip-flops adorned her feet. Wavy black hair, tied with an emerald ribbon, hung in two pigtails. In her extended hand, she carried a rod that she tapped against the animal's front legs. The elephant quieted and lowered to its knees.

"You can come out now." If I didn't know who'd spoken, I would've thought a child had. The woman had a shrill little girl-like voice. I stood, keeping my protective covering between Ginger and me.

"She won't hurt you none." My new friend patted Ginger's trunk. I loved the woman for saving my life. "She just got a little scared when the truck fell over. It's probably your overalls she's attracted to. Ginger likes pink."

With the speed of a waltzing turtle, my heartbeat returned to normal. I took a step forward and extended my hand. "I'm Summer Meadows."

"Big Sally, they call me. I'm Ginger's trainer. Had her ever since she was a calf. We're with the carnival." She waved toward the tangled vehicles. Her actions were strangely graceful despite her bulk. "Had us a bit of trouble."

I dropped the umbrella. No longer afraid for my life, I was ready to help. "Anyone hurt?"

"No. Just some frightened ponies, one elephant escapee, and an angry lion." Big Sally giggled, an infectious childish sound that elicited the same response from me. Her dark eyes disappeared into the folds of her face. "Our lead driver got spooked by a black cat crossing the highway. Man's always been superstitious. Took a turn too sharp, and the rest is history."

"Here you are." Aunt Eunice joined me as I turned to survey the mess. "You disappeared. Thought maybe you became some circus animal's dinner."

"Really, Aunt Eunice. You tend to exaggerate. If something had tried to eat me, the people in the next county would have heard me scream."

A thin black man led several shaggy Shetland ponies and tied them to the split-rail fence bordering one side of our property. Other characters in all shapes, sizes, colors, and manners of dress mingled among the diesels. Not a single vehicle sat in a straight line. One cab lay separate from a massive carrier. Ginger's, no doubt. The air stank of fuel.

Something told me to keep my mouth shut, but in true Summer-like fashion, I forged ahead. "What can I do to help?"

"You're a real sweetheart." A gleam appeared in Sally's eye. "We've got to get these beasts to the fairgrounds. I could use help keeping Ginger in line." She leaned in as if to share a secret. "She seems to like you. The sweetie doesn't take to many people."

Was the woman serious? I'd seen *America's Worst Animal Attacks*. I knew what an elephant this size could be capable of. I swallowed against the lump rising in my throat.

"You'll have to walk her." She shoved the rod in my hand. "The carnies will take care of the others." Big Sally giggled. "No one wants to be around Ginger. She's a bit pushy."

The fairgrounds was a mile away. The thought of "leading" something of Ginger's bulk had me telling God He could take me home right now. Anything to spare me the results of my good intentions. I could just imagine how Ethan, my boyfriend, would react. After I'd sort of made him a promise to stay out of trouble, he'd be livid.

Just say no, came to my mind, but how many opportunities like this came along in a lifetime? It might be fun.

"But I don't have a clue what to do."

"Just go. She'll follow you. Tap her with the rod if she slows or gets out of line. I'll be just a few yards back. If we get too close, Ginger might bolt. I'd go myself, but I have a hard time getting around."

With those encouraging words, Big Sally lumbered to a waiting truck. The vehicle listed to one side as she squeezed in and called one more bit of advice. "Just talk to her. She likes that." They backed off, leaving carnival workers wandering in and out of idling trucks and me babysitting.

To the left of the porch, a water spigot stuck out from the wall. Ginger wrapped her trunk around a tin bucket beside the water hose and tossed it in the air. It landed with a clatter on the porch, sending my dog into a shrill yipping bark.

"She's thirsty." Aunt Eunice folded her arms.

"What do I do?" I sent a pleading glance toward my aunt. "You can do this."

"You know I can't. My knees would never hold up. Chin up, girl. It's just an elephant. Think of her as a big cow. If you're skittish, don't do it. Wait for someone with more experience."

My aunt picked up the pail and handed it to me. "I bet when you woke up this morning you didn't think you'd be leading a carnival parade down the highway." She handed me a small box of chocolate-covered peanuts. "Here. Who could resist these?"

Not in a million years would I have imagined this scenario. I stuffed the box of peanuts inside the bib of my coveralls, set the bucket beside the hose, then filled it. Ginger plunged her trunk inside, slurped disgustingly, and sprayed the contents in the air.

Ewwww! Now I was frightened out of my wits and splattered with elephant boogies. Anger welled, threatening to overshadow my fear. "Stop that!" Ginger's answer was another spray. "Stop or I'm going to whack you." I raised the rod, then lowered it when Ginger trumpeted at me.

My heart leaped into my throat. This was it. The final moment. I would die under the feet of an enraged elephant. Ginger shoved me, almost knocking me to my knees. If I wanted to spare myself a gruesome death, I'd have to get moving. I retrieved the candy and held it enticingly in front of her. She grabbed the box, dumped the nuts into her mouth, and pushed me again.

"Fine." I spun and walked toward the road, hunching my shoulders as my new buddy sauntered behind me. I didn't need the rod. Ginger seemed to get a perverse pleasure out of nudging me in the back with her trunk. As long as I kept moving, so did she. And, being out of candy, I kept up a brisk pace.

What a sight the pair of us must've made, hiking down Highway 64. Me, wearing royal blue overalls with fuchsia flowers, drenched, with an elephant shoving me from behind. Not a common sight in the Ozarks. Horns blared as cars zoomed past, and Ginger quickened her pace until she paced beside me.

I shivered in my wet clothes, growing angry all over

again at Ginger's showering me. I would've loved to whack her with the rod. She draped her trunk over my shoulder, bearing down on my five-foot-two, 115-pound frame. "Now you love me?" I swatted her away. "I don't even like you. You smell."

She didn't really. Except when she belched. She smelled of mud and earth, and something wild. Not a bad scent.

A *whoop-whoop* had me stopping and cringing. Ginger skipped sideways. *Horror*. My cousin Joe, Mountain Shadows's chief of police, pulled up beside me in his squad car, lights flashing. A grin split his face.

"What are you doing, Summer?"

"Walking an elephant." *Duh*. "Why'd you turn on your siren? Do you want to get me killed?"

Ginger's trunk found its way around my shoulders again.

"Why?"

"Didn't you see the commotion in front of my house? Of course, you had to pass by there, didn't you?" I flung her off me. "They had no way to get Ginger to the fairgrounds, so they asked me to take her."

"Right. We're clearing the highway now. You do know how dangerous this is, right? Oh, I forgot. I'm talking about Summer here." He laughed and twirled his finger in a circular motion beside his head. "You and your big mouth. Is that the trainer following?"

I drew myself up to the pinnacle of my height. "Elephants may be unstable, but her people are close by in case of trouble." Ginger's trunk snaked around my shoulders again. Sighing, I flung it off. "She's very tame. Not frightened at all by the traffic. What do you want?" Ginger nudged me.

"As much as I'd like to stay and watch you play, I'm on

my way to the fairgrounds. I want to make sure everything runs smoothly. When should I expect you?"

I wanted to smack the grin off his face. "About fifteen more minutes."

"Oh, wait." He rummaged around his seat, straightened with his cell phone in hand, and snapped a picture. "Ethan will never believe this. It might make him have second thoughts about marrying you." His laugh floated out the window as he drove off.

"Big oaf." He was right, though. The two were going to have a great laugh when Joe sent Ethan the picture. "Come on, Ginger, we're almost there." The truck carrying Sally passed us with a honk.

We walked onto the grounds as if a disheveled woman and an elephant were a common sight. The midway resembled an anthill as workers scurried here and there, many burdened with planks of wood or boxes.

Empty rides spun and twirled. Tinny country music blared from speakers. I was glad I'd volunteered to walk Ginger. I loved the carnival. Now I had an opportunity to see a side of it I'd never witnessed.

Joe stood near the entrance, next to his squad car, speaking to a middle-aged man wearing a cheap suit and sporting a handlebar mustache. I gave a cheery wave and glanced around for Big Sally.

She shouldn't have been hard to spot, yet she was nowhere in sight. Nor was the vehicle she rode in. Vividly striped tents were popping up everywhere. Food stands were being rolled into place. Rusty metal trailers, obviously the workers' living quarters, lined the perimeter of the fairgrounds. "Come on, Ginger. It's time to knock on doors."

Ginger chose that time to abandon me and lumbered away to a large barn riddled with woodpecker holes. I sighed, feeling a bit sad that she'd so easily desert me. After all, she'd covered me with the contents of her nose. We had a relationship.

Where could a woman the size of Big Sally hide? To my left sat a trailer with bright crimson curtains blowing from the windows. It was as flamboyant as Sally. Just her style. Amidst wolf calls and howls from carnival workers, I made my way through the bustling fairgrounds to the trailer. My face most likely burned as bright as the fabric flapping in the breeze.

"Hello?" I pushed the partially opened door, trying to peer through the gloom inside. "I've brought back Ginger. Hello?" Heavy incense assaulted my nostrils. Born with the gift of nosiness, I stepped inside. A floor board creaked.

The only light filtered through curtains. I stepped into a combination living room and kitchen. Dishes littered the counters and dust covered every surface. I wandered down the hall to my left. A door revealed a bedroom decorated in the same garish red of the living room curtains and the obvious location of the incense. An aromatic haze hovered in the gloom. A water bed took up most of the space. A bathroom branched off to my right, and I peeked inside.

The absence of a window left the room in darkness, and my hand searched the wall for a light switch. A flick of the switch dispelled the gloom, and I blinked against the glare.

A shadow behind the shower curtain caught my eye. "I'm sorry." I stumbled backward. By the silhouette, I could make out a fully clothed, kneeling person. Was he or she hurt?

"Are you okay? Do I need to call someone?"

When no irate voice demanded I leave, I gnawed my lower lip and reached toward the curtain. Goose pimples rose on my flesh. Every nerve ending tingled, warning me to run away.

Rings clattered as I shoved aside the striped plastic. A scream welled up from deep inside me, clawing its way through the lump in my throat. There, hanging by the neck with a brightly colored scarf around her throat, slumped a woman. A small wooden stool lay at her feet. The showerhead had pulled away from the wall. The scarf hung on the edge of the plumbing, while the woman's knees rested on the stained fiberglass floor.

I grabbed my cell phone from my pocket and punched in Joe's number.

2

Footsteps pounded outside. I dashed to join them, certain that whoever approached had to be better than a dead body. Joe rushed up, his hand on the handle of his pistol.

"Summer?" He glanced past me, then grabbed me by the shoulders and ushered me to a nearby patio chair. "Stay here. Don't let anyone in." He whipped his cell phone from his pocket and ducked back into the trailer.

A crowd gathered. People jostled for position. Big Sally shoved people aside as she made her way toward me. Her chest heaved as she struggled to regain the breath she'd lost from her dash across the grounds. "What is it? This is Laid Back Millie's trailer. Somebody tell me what's going on."

No match for her, I stepped aside. What I'd witnessed sunk in, and I slid to the ground, raising a cloud of dust around me. Mr. Handlebar and a younger version of him, minus the mustache, dashed up. The older man hurried inside, his clone following. Within minutes, the younger man reappeared.

"Come with me, miss." He kept a tight hold on my elbow and led me to the larger of the trailers skirting the fairgrounds. "I'm Eddy Foreman. That's my father, Rick. He owns this fair slash carnival. Pretty slick idea, isn't it? Combining the two attractions? That was my idea. Foreman's Fair and Carnival. Has a nice ring to it." Eddy pulled up a straight-backed chair and lowered me into it. "I'm sorry. You aren't interested in hearing about my brain scheme."

Was it possible I'd imagined seeing a dead woman? This was a carnival, after all. *Please God, let it be an illusion.*

"Are you okay?"

Nodding, I removed my hands from my eyes. "Who is she?"

"Laid Back Millie." He pulled up a chair across from me. "I don't understand why she'd kill herself. She seemed happy enough."

"Who said she killed herself?" I was thinking like my cousin. After I successfully solved a murder and diamond theft earlier in the summer, that thought pleased me. As long as I didn't look like him, everything would be fine. My cousin Joe stood around six feet two inches and easily weighed two hundred pounds.

"Didn't you notice the knocked over stool below her? What else could it be?"

Narrowing my eyes, I took a closer look at the man in front of me. Thinning russet hair swept across the spreading bald spot on top of his head. Gray eyes beneath bushy brows. Thick lips and. . .did my eyes serve me right? He wore a shiny polyester shirt with tight blue jeans. Had I stepped back in time when I'd entered the fairgrounds gates? The shirt came complete with buttons left undone, revealing ample chest hair and several gold chains. A close-to-forty-year-old trying to relive the good old days.

He leaned forward, placing a sweaty hand over my folded ones. Then an expression of what could be sorrow dropped over his face. "Now that Millie's gone, God rest her soul"— he paused in a moment of silence—"the carnival will have a job opening if you're interested. I saw you with Ginger. I know you own this land, but you'd be a natural. A great attraction. Never enough pretty ladies around here."

"What was Millie's job?" Despite feeling I'd been insulted, my curiosity got the better of me. Did it matter what the poor woman did? I pulled my hands free. "I'm sorry. It's none of my business."

"Officially, she ran the ringtoss. Unofficially, she—"

Joe barged in. "Summer, I told you to stay by the trailer. It's a circus out there." His face reddened as he apparently realized what he'd said. "Sorry. No pun intended."

"Carnival," I corrected and stood. "Sorry, Joe, but Mr. Foreman came to my rescue. It's not every day I see a dead body."

"Good grief." He grabbed my arm and pulled me outside. He stared into my eyes. "Stay. Out. Of. It." A muscle in his jaw twitched. "I don't want Ethan coming home to a dead girlfriend."

"Stay out of what?" If Joe thought there was something to stay out of, something big must be happening. My investigative antennas went up. "You don't think it was suicide, do you? Why?"

"Don't go picking my brain, cousin. It won't do you any good." Joe pulled me along until we reached his squad car. He opened the passenger door. "Get in and behave yourself, or I'll put you in the back."

"You wouldn't!" Everyone knows what kind of germs are in the backseat of a policeman's black-and-white. Plus, with my damp clothes, I might slide off the plastic seat.

"Try me." The door slammed in my face.

Of all the nerve. I folded my arms and slouched back to watch fair life pass by the car windows.

Ginger plodded the perimeter of the fence around her paddock like an overgrown cow, to use my aunt's words. Carnival workers tossed feed to goats, lambs, and rabbits.

Part of the petting zoo, I imagined. Fat ponies grazed, tethered in a grassy area. Long tails swatted at flies.

The sound of striking hammers switched my attention to the right. Men in overalls nailed rails in a makeshift rodeo ring. The rodeo ran the first weekend of the carnival. Ethan won a blue ribbon in the horse-breaking event last year. Everyone expected him to do the same this year.

Shouts were bandied back and forth as workers scurried like mice on the scaffolding. The empty Ferris wheel spun like a forgotten toy. The whir of generators filled the air. And among it all—a dead woman. Her life snuffed out in an instant. And not by her own hand. I didn't believe that for a moment. What bothered me was that more people didn't seem concerned.

Big Sally moaned outside a trailer. Her wail increased as a silent ambulance rolled through the carnival gates and came to a stop in front of her. Joe glanced in my direction. Probably to make sure I stayed where he'd put me.

Catching a glimpse of myself in the side-view mirror, I groaned. *Horror.* I met people looking like this? Dark auburn hair plastered to my head. Mascara ringing my eyes, and my blush completely washed away. I looked like something from a nightmare.

A slight man, barely the size of an average sixth grader but a little taller than me, darted past the car and threw himself into Big Sally's folds. He practically disappeared when she wrapped her arms around him.

I leaned forward for a better look. Seemed there might be a strange love story here. My heart lightened seeing the tenderness despite the shadow of death hovering over the fairgrounds.

Joe got in the car and glanced at me. "What are you smiling at?"

I pointed at the couple. "Look how cute they are together."

"Are you serious? It's like a mother and child. That woman is massive." He turned the key in the ignition.

"I like her." I put my seat belt on. "Despite having walked her elephant down Highway 64 for a mile. In flip-flops. I've got blisters."

"About the elephant, Summer. Rick Foreman is beside himself with the possibility you could've been hurt and would sue them."

"Tell him he has nothing to worry about. It ended up being kind of fun. I thought of the danger, but not the liability." Silly me. Chalk one more thing up to the rash actions of Summer Meadows. I turned to him. "Ready to tell me what happened?"

Joe stared through the car window as the crime scene investigators pulled onto the grounds. "Nothing to tell. And if there were. . ."

"I know. You couldn't tell me, anyway."

I stared out the side window. It didn't matter. I'd be back tomorrow to see if I could set up a booth to sell my candy. Just a formality. My family owned the land the fairgrounds sat on.

~

The water cascaded over my head and shoulders like warm liquid heaven, washing away the odors of the carnival. But it couldn't erase the vision of a woman dangling from a scarf. Or that someone unsuccessfully tried to make her death look like a suicide. If she'd wanted to kill herself, there were other places to do so. Hanging from the Ferris wheel, for example. Definitely high enough her knees wouldn't have dragged.

If the showerhead hadn't pulled from the wall, they would have left what, two or three inches between Millie's feet and the bottom of the shower? A person would have to be very small to pull suicide off in that way.

Stop it, Summer. This doesn't involve you. I lathered my hair with my favorite shampoo and inhaled the sweet scent of floral and citrus. Why would Foreman think she'd tried to commit suicide? And what about Joe's evasive answer? And what was the woman's unofficial job with the carnival? I couldn't help it. Questions swirled in my mind like a whirlpool.

I shook my head to clear it and stepped beneath the spray of water to rinse my hair.

"Summer!" My aunt's voice rang from the other side of the door.

I jerked, causing soapy water to run into my eyes. "I'm in the shower." I forced my eyes open to wash the shampoo out.

"Ethan's on the phone."

Ethan! Forget the burning. I reached for the faucet and turned it off. "Be right out. Tell him to hold."

"He's calling from Mexico."

"I know where he's calling from." I stepped over the lip of the tub and opened the door, hiding behind it. "Here."

"You can't talk to him while you're naked." Aunt Eunice's horrified whisper echoed in the tiled room.

"Shhh. He doesn't have to know if you keep quiet." I slammed the door, grabbed a towel, and wrapped it around me. "Hello."

"Sweetie." My heart melted at the sound of his voice. "We must have a bad connection. I could have sworn your aunt said you were. . .without apparel."

"Uh." Heat crept up my neck. "We do have a bad connection." The line *was* filled with static, so it wasn't a lie. I didn't do that anymore. Not after making a deal with God back in July. "How are you?"

"Tired. Missing you. What have you been up to?"

Wow. Where to begin? I decided to save the elephant story until I saw Ethan, and I'd skip the part about finding Laid Back Millie. No sense in worrying him. "I've decided to sell solid chocolate carnival characters at the fair. I'm renting a propane-powered refrigerator. Do you think my candy will sell well?"

"With your pretty face behind the counter? Yep. Besides, people line up to buy from Summer's Confections." Since I'd opened the doors to my dream of owning a candy store, I'd been blessed with regular customers and growing Internet orders.

I left the bathroom and stretched my body across my bed. I hugged a pillow, my insides warming at his words. "You're sweet. You're still coming home in time for opening night, right?"

"About that. . ."

"Ethan!" My whine would have put a two-year-old to shame. "Can't someone else build the house?"

"I made a commitment to chaperone the youth group on this trip." Ethan sighed. "Would you rather I came home to take you to a carnival, or build a house for someone who doesn't have a decent place to stay?"

"I miss you, that's all." Great. Now I had guilt. *Forgive me, Lord.* "I know you have to stay. What about the rodeo?"

"I'll be back in time for that. Anything exciting happen over there?" Ethan laughed. "I got an interesting picture on my cell phone."

"Oh?" Darn my cousin. I'd make him pay dearly next time I saw him. I'd spend the evening devising evil plots of revenge.

"How in the world did you end up herding an elephant?"

The story seemed hilarious as I told Ethan, and I giggled along with him. With my flair for description, he swore he could see Big Sally and the other characters. His laughter washed over me like a fine rain in May. Made me want to offer my services again to the colorful people of the fair. Almost. He stopped laughing when I let slip about Millie, and how Foreman offered me her job.

Ethan cleared his throat. "Is your aunt going to cover the store while you run your booth?"

"I'm thinking about closing for the week. There probably wouldn't be many customers anyway. The fair's a big deal. Everyone will be there and can buy from my booth. Aunt Eunice has pickles and vegetables she wants to enter in the competition. She'd kill me if I did anything to prevent her from doing that."

"Uh-huh. Speaking of killing and Millie. . ." Ethan went silent.

"Ethan?"

His sigh vibrated through the phone. "Joe told me you found her."

"Yes."

"Summer. Please, stay out of it."

3

The next morning dawned sunny and warm. A perfect day for another visit to the fairgrounds. I dressed in faded blue jeans and a flowered T-shirt. Aunt Eunice decided she would go with me to "scope out" the competition for the canning contest. Her hand rested on the top of her floppy hat as she thundered down the stairs in her steel-toed boots.

She darted past me, hefted a cardboard box from the table, and squeezed out the front door. Her hat flew off her head and landed in the gravel. I bent to retrieve it.

"I'll drive!" Aunt Eunice set the box in the bed of her truck, then apparently thought better of the idea. She picked it up and thrust it in my arms.

Great. I get to babysit her pickles. I plopped the hat on top of the jars.

"Oh." Aunt Eunice fairly skipped to the passenger side. "Let me get the door for you. I don't want anything to happen to my babies. Today's the last day to bring in entries." She opened the door and, with a bow, waved me inside.

"Why did you wait until the last minute?"

She looked at me as if I'd asked the most ridiculous question in the world's history. "I had to see what Ruby and Mabel are entering. It wouldn't do to put in the same thing."

"Of course."

She bustled back to the driver's side and slid behind the wheel. "A person needs to scope things out to decide the correct way to proceed."

This definitely didn't sound like my aunt talking. Where did she learn to speak such proper sentences? With the box secured in my lap, I settled back. I'd bought the *Dolt's Guide to Private Investigating* during the summer and successfully solved a murder. I knew all about scoping things out. Besides, I didn't know there was a "wrong" way to proceed when entering vegetables in a county fair.

"Isn't that the point of a competition? To see who has the best?" I glanced at my aunt.

"You obviously don't know nothing about it." Aunt Eunice backed the truck out of the drive, thrust the gear-shift into place, then roared down Highway 64 toward the fairgrounds. "That might be why you've never won anything in your life."

Ouch. She didn't need to be so mean. "What's got you so riled up?"

"You."

"What did I do?"

"You went and found a dead body."

"Excuse me?" Now I *knew* my aunt had lost her mind.

She swerved the truck to the shoulder and stopped. She turned to glare at me. "I promised Ethan I'd keep you out of trouble. And here you go, finding a dead woman. Since your uncle Roy decided to join Ethan on this trip, it's up to me to keep you out of trouble."

"That wasn't my fault, Aunt Eunice. Besides, Joe said it was suicide. Well, he didn't exactly, but there are clues pointing to that not necessarily being the case. . . ."

Aunt Eunice steered back onto the highway. "Last time you thought you could solve a murder, you got kidnapped and almost killed."

Thought? "I *did* solve the murder."

"Whatever. You just got lucky. Next time you might not get off as easy."

Had I mentioned a desire to get involved? No. So why was everyone on my case? If I didn't have a box full of pickles in my lap, I'd have crossed my arms and pouted.

"Summer's gone and got all mad, do-dah, do-dah," Aunt Eunice sang. "Won't say another word all day, oh how I hope and pray."

"Very funny."

"Cheer up. We've only got your best interest at heart."

A sign declared Arrow County Fair ahead of us. Aunt Eunice sped onto the grounds. A cloud of dust rose and drifted through the Chevy's windows. I endured, trying to hold my breath until my aunt opened my door, retrieved her pickles, and the dust settled.

"I'm off. See you in an hour." She fairly sprinted toward a squat, rectangular building, her arms stretched around the box. She kept the hat in place by squashing it with her chin.

I slid from the truck. More amusement rides spun with gay music and no screaming passengers. Workers scurried from one attraction to another. A steady stream of farmers and women in country clothes trailed from the building my aunt had disappeared into and from a large barn next door. Last-minute entries to floral, vegetable, crafts, and livestock, most likely.

Usually our county fair offered only rides, rodeo, freak shows, and contests. This year we'd hired a company that aspired to being a circus. Well, Eddy Foreman said carnival, but it all looked the same to me. The only thing circuslike was the elephant and animals. Well, maybe some of the people. The fair committee must have gotten a good deal on hiring this group. I shrugged. The change could've been nice, if death hadn't gotten in the way.

Yellow crime tape encircled Millie's trailer, and I couldn't help but hope it would be gone by Friday. The tape wouldn't be a good sign on opening night.

"We meet again." Eddy Foreman stood next to me complete with gold chains, heavy cologne, and shiny polyester shirt.

"Oh, hello. Nobody seems very concerned about Millie's death." I breathed through my mouth and wanted to spit. The fumes from his scent hung heavy in the air.

"The circus must go on. Or the fair, in this case."

My dislike for the slimy little man increased. "Could you point me in the direction of my booth?"

"I'll take you there myself." Foreman tucked my arm in his. I felt like a child who needed some cootie spray. "Have you thought more about taking Laid Back Millie's job? I'd be your first customer." His eyes traveled over me. Okay, make that a giant can of cootie spray.

"I already have a job running a chocolate business. But thank you." I pulled my arm free. This guy was too smarmy for my taste. I wiped my hands on my jeans.

"Oh, I like a feisty woman. You and I are going to get along just great."

Not if I have anything to say about it. What was with me and guys? At least Nate, the diamond thief I'd helped catch a couple of months ago, had been good looking. "I can find my own way. Thanks for the help."

"Catch you later." Foreman cocked his fingers, pointed at me, and winked. Something told me this was going to be a long week.

My booth faced the midway and sat opposite the

Scrambler. Great. Fair attendees could eat my chocolate, ride the dizzy ride, and throw up all my hard work.

No, the candy booth should be considered more of a craft than a food. Despite the shivers that ran up my spine at the thought, I'd have to speak to Foreman about moving me.

A shadowy figure cut between two game booths. I squinted to try and make out who it was. The form looked hairy. Hairy? I stared harder. I shook my head and continued, deciding I imagined things.

Ahead of me loomed a fun house. From its size, it was obviously a huge hit with the fair attendees. A giant clown head wobbled over the entrance. This would be one attraction I definitely wanted to miss.

My slimy little friend leaned against the Ferris wheel talking to a voluptuous, platinum blonde. I took a deep breath and stepped forward. "Mr. Foreman."

"Eddy, please." He turned toward me, a smile across his smooth-shaven face. "Miss me already?"

"I'd like to request that you move my booth."

"Really? The ones along the midway get good traffic." He swatted the other woman on the rear and turned back to me. "Where do you wanna go?"

"The arts and crafts building."

"Sure. I'll see what I can do. With my connections, I ought to be able to get anything a pretty little thing like you wants."

I swerved to avoid his touch.

From the corner of my eye, I caught another glimpse of my fur-covered friend. "Do you have bears here?"

"Yes. We have a bunch of circus animals, and one's a black bear."

"Could he have escaped?" The shadow disappeared

behind the Toboggan Ride.

"Possible, but not probable. Besides, Samson's very friendly. He likes to greet visitors with a kiss."

Wonderful. The last thing I wanted was a kiss from a bear. "Does he ever get loose?"

"Scared?" He leered.

"Maybe." Yes. Definitely.

As we passed the animal paddock, Ginger lumbered along the fence, keeping pace. Her trunk snaked out and nuzzled my hair. Ugh. I brushed her away. If she went for the water trough, I'd be out of there.

"We'll put you in the middle of the arts and crafts building. Next to the quilts." Foreman opened the building's door. "You'll still have a lot of traffic, but you'll be away from the hustle and bustle. You might regret this decision."

No way. The building had to be cleaner than the dirt-covered midway. "It'll be fine. Can you get someone to move my refrigerator in here?"

"Washington!"

A reed-thin black man rose from where he knelt behind a partition. Foreman clapped a hand on the man's shoulder. "This is Washington Bean. Washington, Summer Meadows." He gave Washington the number of my booth and informed him I'd be moving. "I'm pretty sure there's a vacant spot we can set up for her."

Washington's teeth flashed in his ebony skin. "I'll get right on it, Miss Meadows."

"Summer. Thank you, Washington."

I turned to see a red-faced Aunt Eunice rushing toward me. Her chin quivered with indignation.

"Did you get your pickles entered?"

"Ruby Colville entered her bread-and-butter pickles. That sneak." Aunt Eunice crossed her arms. "She waited until today to register."

"Isn't that the same thing you did?"

"She ruined my plan." She glanced over the cubicle they'd assigned to us. "This our spot?"

"Yes."

"Better get to work then." She strode toward the exit. "I can't believe how devious some people can be."

Before exiting, I peered outside, fully expecting Samson to be waiting with puckered lips. Instead, someone in a gorilla suit stared at the building. When I stepped out, he or she darted behind the restrooms.

Aunt Eunice took one look at me and clutched my arm. "What is it?"

"Since we've been here, I've felt like I've been followed. I thought it looked like a black bear."

"A bear?"

"Yeah. But it isn't a bear. This time I saw someone wearing a gorilla costume." I gazed at her face. "It's clear someone is following me. I'd like to know why."

Her grip tightened. "Oh, no you don't. You ain't going chasing off after nobody in a costume."

"It does seem fishy, doesn't it?"

"This is a county fair with a carnival attached. There're bound to be strange things." She tugged at me. "Come on. We've got candy to make and only three more days to make it."

We marched to the truck, but I couldn't help myself. I had to glance over my shoulder. My gorilla friend stood in the shadows.

Watching.

4

With a box full of chocolate tigers, lions, clowns, and hot air balloons on the seat beside me, I drove to the fair. The midway still resembled an anthill with workers striving to finish before opening night. I parked in front of the arts and crafts building and gathered my wares.

Not being buff, and having ditched my resolution of working out, I could only handle one bulky cardboard box at a time. The chocolate weighed about thirty pounds. To have enough to sell, I figured I'd be making a couple of trips a day from the candy store to my temporary new home—at least for this week.

The carnival looked different as the hues of a summer sunset cast the first shadows over the grounds. Like a fairyland with the rides outlined in colored lights.

The drone of the generators vibrated around me. A lion roared. Must be feeding time. The box slipped and I had to stop to get a better grip. My gaze roamed over the gaily lit fairgrounds searching for my gorilla shadow. The tightness in my shoulders relaxed when I couldn't find it.

Someone had propped open the door to the arts and crafts building, and I sent another thanks to heaven. The dusk cast the cavernous room into a gloom of shadows and gray-tinted light. A quick glance didn't readily show a light switch, and with the box growing heavier, I decided the light was good enough to see by. At least until I deposited my load. To not run into anything, I slid my feet inch by inch along the concrete floor until I arrived at my cubicle.

My arms ached with relief as I set my box on a folding table. The hum of the refrigerator assured me it worked. As I withdrew my chocolate treasures, I thought of how much I missed Ethan, and again asked for forgiveness for my selfishness. God sent him to build houses for the homeless. Who was I to complain of my need to have the man I love close to me?

Yet my stomach churned with longing for his company. Desire to speak with Ethan spurred me to move faster so I could call him. Thank God for the modern miracle of cell phones.

I yanked open the refrigerator door—and screamed.

The beady eyes of a dead armadillo stared up at me. A scrap of paper hung from a tooth. With trembling fingers, I reached for the paper, held my breath against the rotting odor, and read, *This is what will happen to you if you stick your nose where it don't belong.* I released my grip on the handle. The door slammed with a muffled thud.

The beat of pounding feet rushed toward me, echoing through the building. Harsh fluorescent lights blinked on, blinding me. I'd seen dead animals before. Living in the country guaranteed that, and I didn't usually shriek. But having one in my refrigerator had to be a first. I wasn't involved in anything, yet everyone warned me to stay away.

"Miss Meadows?" Washington Bean sprinted to my side. The whites of his eyes and teeth shone against his ebony skin.

I pointed, and thought of Joe. "Don't touch anything." My fingerprints were already on the refrigerator. My cousin would be livid.

Washington used his shirttail to open the door and whistled through his teeth. "That critter's been dead awhile.

You're going to need a new refrigerator, Miss Summer. No amount of cleaning will take that smell out. Let me take care of that for you." He melted into the shadows and disappeared.

"Summer!" Eddy Foreman appeared by my side and placed one sweaty hand around my upper arm. He glanced in the open refrigerator. "I'm beginning to think you're a magnet for dead things. Are you all right?"

I pulled free. "Didn't anyone check the refrigerator before placing it here?"

"Of course, my dear. We had it cleaned and ready for you." Foreman urged me away from the space. "That was not in the refrigerator when we plugged it in."

Then why is it here now? My knees weakened, and I slumped into a nearby chair. After finding Millie hanging in her shower, I'd done nothing as far as investigating her death. I'd been willing to leave things as a suicide. On one hand, my family warned me to stay out of things, yet someone seemed to be trying to draw me in. Why? Fear pricked the nape of my neck.

The crunch of gravel outside pulled me to my feet, and with heavy steps I headed out of the building. As I suspected, Joe stood with crossed arms next to his squad car.

With a deep breath, I squared my shoulders. "Who called you?"

"Doesn't matter. I was already here asking questions. Why didn't *you* call?" He motioned toward his cell phone.

"I would have. As soon as the shock wore off. Give me a minute, Joe. I just found the thing." I crossed my arms. We resembled two roosters squaring off. "I haven't done anything to warrant someone putting a dead animal in my fridge."

"Uh-huh." He pushed away from the car and marched into the building.

Twilight fell with crimson beauty, increasing the vibrancy of the amusement ride lights. Fewer workers scurried between buildings, choosing instead to join in the fun of carnival life without fair attendees. Laughter floated across the midway.

"You all right?" Big Sally startled me, coming up behind me in amazing silence despite her bulk.

"I'm getting used to surprises."

Washington wheeled a dolly carrying my new—and hopefully unoccupied—refrigerator. He gave a jaunty wave, called out a greeting to Big Sally, and vanished from view.

"A good man, that one. Been a carny most of his life." Big Sally moved to a nearby bench and patted the small amount of space remaining beside her. "Come. Sit."

With a glance toward the building, I joined her. Holding on to the edge of the tilted seat prevented me from sliding into her. A sour odor wafted from the folds of her skin. Would her feelings be hurt if I gave her a gift of scented body powder? Diverting my attention, I hoped things would move quickly before I had a melted lump of chocolate in a cardboard box.

Sally put a plump hand on my leg. "Eddy Foreman said you were thinking about taking over for Millie. That's mighty nice of you, but I hadn't figured you for the type. A nice girl like you, I can't imagine your parents allowing it. I had a son once. He was murdered. The last thing I'd want was for him to have this kind of life."

No, my parents would've been shocked. "I'm sorry about your son."

She clapped a hand on my shoulder, almost knocking

me off the bench. "Don't worry about little Richie. Justice will be done."

"My mom and dad are. . .dead." I blamed myself for their accident, and the last thing I wanted was to talk about it. "I don't understand where Eddy got the idea I want to work here. I have no desire for carnival life. Or operating a game booth. Foreman assumed, since he found me in Millie's trailer, that I wanted her job."

Sally's laughter escaped in a wheeze. She clapped me on the back, almost knocking me from the bench. "Sally did more than run the ringtoss, girlie. She was employed in the oldest profession in the book." She giggled. "You are priceless. Why else do you think that weasel Eddy Foreman is all over you?"

I would like to think it was because of my attractiveness. Now, I felt dirty. Mortified. Astounded. Angry. Ethan's stunned silence on the phone made sense. Obviously, he and Joe had had a good laugh at my expense, and they both had a lot of explaining to do. I bolted to my feet and stalked into the building, Sally's gasps of laughter following.

Washington had already unloaded the fresh appliance and strapped the armadillo's General Electric coffin to the dolly. Joe stood next to Eddy Foreman, laughing at something the greasy little pervert said. I glared at Foreman then grabbed Joe's arm and pulled him to a vacant corner of the building.

"Had a good laugh at my expense, didn't you?"

"What?"

"You, Ethan, and Foreman." I spit Eddie's last name. "I just found out what Millie's 'unofficial' job was. You're the sheriff. How could you let this sort of thing go on?"

"Summer, that's why I was headed out here the day you babysat that elephant. I'd heard rumors the carnival ran a side business of prostitution and came here to shut it down. Turns out, someone else did."

My antennae shot up. "So you *don't* think it was suicide!"

"Shhh." He shoved me out of the building. "Stop putting your nose where it doesn't belong. Ethan will be home Saturday. I'd like you to still be breathing. Then you'll be *his* problem."

"I haven't done anything. I promise. Someone in a gorilla suit followed me yesterday. I mentioned it to Foreman. I thought maybe a bear, but Foreman said it wasn't likely Samson, who's a bear, could get loose. I am fairly certain it *wasn't* a bear." *Please, God, don't let it be.* I'd watched the Discovery Channel. I knew what bears were capable of.

Joe rubbed his chin. "Now a dead armadillo."

"Want to know what I think?"

"Not really."

I leaned closer. "I think something is going on here, and someone is afraid I'll find out. The newspaper had a huge write-up on my involvement with the diamond theft and murder last summer. My face is recognizable."

"You aren't famous, my dear cousin. And if you think a quarter of a page in the middle of the *Gazette* is a huge write-up, then you go ahead and suffer your delusions." Joe chucked me under the chin. "Take care of your candy. I'll follow you home."

"Don't you have to call April or something?" I marched ahead of him. Upon reaching my table, I opened the box and discovered unmelted chocolate. At least my work, if not my time, hadn't been a waste.

I paused as I reached to open the refrigerator, then I smiled over my shoulder at Joe and opened it. Blessedly empty. To keep it that way, I'd have Washington install a lock.

Fifteen minutes later, lock installed, I drove down the highway toward home. Joe followed. He wouldn't be able to convince me someone wasn't afraid of my digging up information. My gut feeling told me I was onto something. I just needed to find out what that something was.

Joe honked as I pulled into my driveway, and then sped past the house. The welcome glow of lights through the windows greeted me. Truly's head poked above the windowsill, her triangular ears perked. Coming home always sent a warm rush through me. What would it feel like when Ethan and I were married and we came home to each other?

Aunt Eunice exited the kitchen, drying her hands on a dish towel. "You've been gone quite a while. Did you decide to stop by the store?"

"Let me get a soda, and I'll fill you in." I brushed past her. "How'd you get home?"

"Caught a ride with Ruby." She pursed her lips. "You were right. I shouldn't let a thing like pickles come between friends."

The ice clinked into my glass, and I prepared for the lecture sure to come. The soda's carbonation tickled my throat. I placed the drink on the table and pulled up a chair.

Aunt Eunice frowned, tossed the towel on the counter, and joined me. "What did you do now?"

Why did everyone always think the worst? "Nothing."

After filling my aunt in on everything that had transpired within the last hour, I lifted my glass to my lips and watched her face as she digested the information.

She remained impassive. Only the slight frown line between her eyes indicated she was mulling things over. "Somebody thinks you're onto something."

I leaned forward. "That's what I told Joe. Either he doesn't think I'm right, or he doesn't want me to think he believes me."

"Probably the last." Aunt Eunice got up and paced the kitchen. "It's the gorilla that bothers me. Dead things can't hurt people."

Truly barked from the front room. I rose and headed out of the kitchen. "That's probably Joe coming to rib me some more about hanging out with the carnies."

When I reached the living room, Truly scratched at the front door. Her barks had turned into whines. I peeked out the curtains. "Aunt Eunice?"

"Yeah?"

"Take a look out the window." Although our visitor stood in the shadows, it was clear the hairy creature that stalked me now watched our house.

She joined me. "The gorilla you've been talking about? He ain't very big, is he?"

"Big enough to scare me." Our visitor melted into the trees in back of our house. I reached for the phone.

5

My mind's focus on making a mental list of who might fit the "small" gorilla description woke me the next morning at six thirty. Eddy Foreman looked small enough. So did Big Sally's love squeeze. On my next visit to Foreman's carnival, I'd have to keep my eyes peeled for other carnies of the right size and build. Nothing said the gorilla had to be a male.

I smiled remembering Aunt Eunice's demands during my previous case-solving. She'd told me to ask God who should go on my suspect list. I'd do that much sooner this time. No waiting on consequences to become life-threatening before calling on His help.

My gaze fell on the *Dolt's Guide to Private Investigating* lying on my nightstand. First piece of advice I'd taken was to establish a suspect list.

My nose for crime-solving had gotten me into trouble once before when I'd placed Mabel Coffman and Ruby Colville, Aunt Eunice's best friends, at the top of my list. Their unexpected downpour of riches had come to them honestly. The widower they'd both been chasing had died, leaving Mabel his Cadillac, and Ruby his deceased wife's jewels. Their shrewlike attitudes had made them suspect enough in my book.

Chuckling, I tossed aside the blankets, covering Truly, who slept at my feet. The fair would start tomorrow night, and I still had a lot of chocolate figures to make.

My cell phone rang, playing the "Candy Man" from *Willy Wonka and the Chocolate Factory*. *Clever*, I thought, considering my profession. Caller ID showed Ethan. "Hello, sweetheart."

"Hey, babe. I'll be home early Saturday morning. Not the first night of the fair, but not too bad. I won't miss the parade and can still ride in the rodeo Sunday afternoon."

"I miss you." I fell back onto the bed. Truly scooted closer and laid her head on my stomach. My fingers twirled the long hair on her ears.

"Ditto." He remained silent for a minute before continuing. "Joe called and told me about the armadillo."

Why couldn't Joe keep his big mouth shut? "Just a practical joke, I'm sure."

"Don't go back to the fair alone." A touch of steel hardened Ethan's velvety words.

"I've got to take another batch of carnival figures."

"Have Eunice go with you. I'm serious, Summer. I'll be back soon and can stay by your side the whole time."

"Don't be silly. You'll be bronc riding in the rodeo." And he looked good doing it. Tight jeans, flannel shirt, scuffed boots, and a cowboy hat pulled low over blond curls. I couldn't wait. I conceded. "I'll get Aunt Eunice to go with me." With both of us asking questions, we could cover more ground.

"And no snooping. Gotta go. I love you."

After letting the phone fall to the quilt, I pushed Truly aside and rose, reaching for the black pants and cranberry sweater I'd chosen to wear. Not exactly carnival clothes, but I wanted to head there right after work. A woman needed to look good at all times, right? You never knew when you'd have to make a good impression.

The aroma of brewing coffee spurred me, and I skipped down the stairs. Aunt Eunice had just poured the first cup. She smiled. "Roy, Ethan, and April are coming home Saturday."

Getting myself a mug, I grinned back. "I know. It's been too long." I sniffed in appreciation before savoring the first swallow. Ooh, hot. I fanned my mouth. "Ethan wants you to go with me tonight when I drop off the chocolate."

"Okay. I'd like to do some more scoping of the competition."

"I'd hoped you could help me ask questions." Not start World War III at a county fair.

She waved a hand in the air. "There'll be plenty of time for both." Aunt Eunice sat in a chair at the table. "After the fiasco the last time you went and tried to solve a crime, I figure I'd better help you. And—" she peered over the cup's rim. "—I've already prayed to God about it, considering how long it takes for you to get around to doing that. We don't want you to die unmarried."

My aunt sounded like that would be the worst thing in the world. And I definitely looked forward to marriage and had no intention of dying anytime soon. Not if I could help it. "Come on, Granny Gloom. There's work to be done."

The day passed quickly. Almost before we knew it, five o'clock arrived and we closed the store. Five boxes of candy were loaded into the trunk of my Sonata. Tomorrow we'd pack as many one-pound boxes of assortments as we could, and we'd be ready to make a killing at the fair. I flinched. Bad choice of words.

Aunt Eunice chattered during the drive. I tuned in enough to know she was talking about her odds of beating out Ruby and Mabel for a blue ribbon. She seemed to think it a sure thing. Although despondent at having to start over again with my roses, I wouldn't miss the stress of competition. Destruction of the flowers for the second time, a few months ago by someone searching for diamonds, and now Ginger, might be God's way of telling me entering them wasn't going to happen.

My gaze focused outside on the signs of summer's end: leaves with just a tip of red and gold. I could already feel the hint of a chill in the air during the mornings and evenings. I'd contemplated an autumn wedding for the sheer romance of falling leaves, but I had my heart set on a strapless, long-trained wedding gown. With no shawl to mar the effect.

"Hello?" Aunt Eunice waved a hand in front of my face. "Earth to Summer."

Oops! Heat rose to my face. "Sorry. Daydreaming."

"Oh, look. There's your new best friend." She pointed toward the paddock where Ginger lumbered up and down the fence.

"I think I'll go say hello once we've got this candy unpacked." I reached into the glove compartment and pulled out a box of chocolate-covered peanuts.

"Go ahead. I can handle this. You know I have a knack for arranging things artistically. I'll play around for a bit."

"Thanks. See ya later." I pushed open the car door and slid out.

"Okay, but you'd better be inside before it gets fully dark. Ethan will have my hide if I don't babysit you."

I rolled them so far, my eyes probably disappeared to the back of my head. Aunt Eunice giggled as she headed toward the arts and crafts building. Ginger trumpeted as I strolled closer. It felt nice to be welcomed. Like she was a big hairless dog with a long nose.

With one foot propped on the lowest rail of the fence, I rested my folded arms across the top plank. Ginger ruffled her trunk through my hair then nosed the box. "Don't go getting me all messed up, girl." I swatted her away. "I bet you see everything that goes on around here, don't you? Any idea who my primate friend might be? Or why someone would've killed Millie?"

She bumped me with her head, almost sending me to the ground. "Not speaking, huh? Well, that kind of information could land you in the same situation as me." I held out a palm full of the candy I'd brought from Summer's Confections.

"Talking to the animals?" Foreman stepped up, standing close enough for our shoulders to touch. "Should I call you Dr. Doolittle?" The oaf guffawed at his wit. He turned and leaned against the paddock. "The fairgrounds looks pretty at night, doesn't it?" He scanned the area briefly before turning his attention back to me. His creepy roaming gaze up my body made my skin scrawl. "Not as pretty as you, of course." He reached up as if to tuck away a stray strand of hair.

I slapped his hand away. *Night?* Aunt Eunice would kill me. The sun had set. The only illumination outside was the lights around the rides. Beautiful, but lots of shadows where my gorilla friend could hide. "Sorry, Mr. Foreman, but my aunt is waiting for me."

"Please, call me Eddy. I believe I saw her in the livestock building arguing with a couple of old ladies."

"Thanks." I couldn't get away fast enough. The cologne he'd bathed in threatened to overpower me, clinging to my skin and the fibers of my clothing.

The livestock barn stood to the right of the arts and crafts building, its recesses cast in muted shadow. Snuffling and low bellows greeted me as I ventured inside. Halfway down the straw floor lined with animal stalls, I still hadn't seen anyone. "Aunt Eunice?"

I jumped at a loud snort and bang. My heart rate accelerated. "Hello?"

Every B-rated horror movie with a too-stupid-to-live-heroine flashed through my mind. There was absolutely no way I'd take another step forward. A chain saw-wielding gorilla could be hidden behind one of the stalls. I inched backward.

A squeal rang through the barn. I stopped and peered through the gloom.

The largest pig I'd ever seen rushed me. It grunted with the effort and moved much quicker than seemed possible for something with its bulk. My scream bounced off the rafters. I spun to dash out of the building.

My shrieks continued as the squealing behind me increased. I darted across the midway looking for a place to hide. One glance told me the door to the arts and crafts building was closed. Not enough time for me to fight with the latch and open it. I hadn't yet had the opportunity to find the restrooms.

Grunts continued behind me as I made a beeline for the closest ride, the Tilt-A-Whirl. The heel of my shoe caught on a power cord, tripping me. I slid belly-first across the dirt-packed ground. Pebbles dug into the palms of my hands. Sobs caught in my throat. I imagined the huge beast leaping on my back and sinking its teeth into my neck.

Ever since I'd watched *The Wizard of Oz* as a child

and seen Dorothy snatched from the pen of a bunch of snarling swine, I'd been deathly afraid of the hairless animals. Like a child. I'd fallen into a pigpen at the age of six, in my own imitation of the Dorothy thing. Hogs symbolized everything horrific. Nothing had happened. Those pigs had seemed nice. They'd been babies, after all. Kind of cute. However, giant swine should be outlawed. I felt an unreasonable stirring of resentment toward my aunt. She was supposed to be watching me!

Uncle Roy told me pigs didn't attack unless provoked. Well, now I had proof otherwise. I'd done nothing to aggravate this animal. But an angry pig is a mean pig, and this one sounded infuriated.

I pushed to my feet and crawled into the first car of the ride and cowered on the floor.

6

I covered my ears with my hands and mumbled "save me" prayers to God.

The crunching of gravel interrupted my frantic thoughts. I immediately stopped covering my ears. With all certainty, I knew the monster stalked me.

"Her coming around here puts a kink in the plan. You flubbed Millie's death. No one believes it was suicide."

Pigs don't talk. My ears perked. I opened my mouth to call for help until I made out the words murder, money, and that nosy Summer Meadows.

"That doesn't mean you can stiff me from my portion of the dough."

Someone laughed. "Letting that crazy sow go was hilarious."

"Yeah, but what're we gonna do about that nosy Meadows broad?"

"I'll think of something. Don't worry. I'm the brains of this outfit."

"And don't let my sweetie get hurt."

"As if anyone could hurt *her*. Look at that pig rooting around the rides. I ain't catching her."

"Neither am I. Let's go before someone orders us to."

Whose sweetie? My heart beat so loudly, my unseen conspirators must hear it over their conversation. So intent was I on overhearing them, I forgot to be frightened until their footsteps faded away. I rose from my hiding place and came face-to-face with The Beast.

There wasn't enough steel between me and the pig.

If the ride shifted, she'd see the opening and in she'd be. Right within biting distance of me.

She snorted. I screamed and fled, heading toward the highest ride in the fair. The Ferris wheel. A carny leaned against the railing. I scrambled into the first car.

"Are you here for the test ride? I just finished the repairs."

"Yes. Yes. Just go." I slammed the lap bar across me and gripped the sides of the car. The pig had disappeared. Most likely hiding, waiting to devour me when I least expected it. But I hoped by the time the ride stopped, the swine would've given up on me.

"I've got to go to the restroom. You can ride until I get back. About ten minutes."

With a lurch, the Ferris wheel rose. It stopped at the top. Peeking over, I gasped. The car perched like a nonflying creature on the face of a giant cliff. A slight exaggeration maybe, but every bit as frightening. My gorilla friend waved and held up the power cord. I choked back a sob as the lights went out. He turned and darted toward the carny trailers.

Below, I could make out the form of my aunt, hands on her hips, turning in a circle. Her mouth opened and from far away, I heard my name called.

"Aunt Eunice. Up here!"

What little bit of breeze the night carried blew my voice away. I choked back another sob. Stuck. On top of the scariest ride in the world. Why did our fair have to boast of having such a tall Ferris wheel?

She continued to stride toward my car then leaned against it. I looked around the floor of my prison for something to throw. Nothing. Clean except for rust spots.

What to do? I had absolutely no way to alert anyone to my presence.

Aunt Eunice pushed away from the Sonata and stalked back to the arts and crafts building. *Don't go!* If she would've been where she belonged in the first place, I wouldn't have gotten chased by the hog from Hades.

I crossed my arms and flounced back in the seat. My movements caused the car to sway, lodging my heart in my throat. What happened to the ride operator? How long did it take to go to the restroom?

Someone below would have to notice a swinging car on a motionless Ferris wheel. I increased my movement, stopping when nausea threatened. Suddenly, the Ferris wheel didn't seem as frightening as spending the night in the dark, millions of feet above the ground. And the night grew cold.

Other lights around the fairgrounds blinked out until I found myself cast into the darkness of a quarter moon. Normally, a dark night didn't frighten me, but these were extenuating circumstances. I broke into a cold sweat and wiped damp palms on my dirt-streaked pants.

Think, Summer. I dug in my pocket for my cell phone. No bars. When would I start remembering to charge it? You'd think after all I've been through in the last few months, a fully charged phone would be a priority.

What would any normal, red-blooded, almost thirty-year-old woman do at this point? I screamed until my throat hurt. When Aunt Eunice drove away, I cried. Huge, quarter-sized tears complete with hiccuping sobs. This counted on my scale as being worse than when I'd been locked last summer in Richard Bland's musty car trunk. A simple act of taking out the garbage had warranted me a knock on the head and a greasy rag stuffed in my mouth. Diamonds or not, I'd wanted that particular mess to be over. Now, mere months later, I found myself trapped again. I never should have given my aunt a set of keys to my car.

Once I'd cried myself dry, I wiped my eyes on my sleeve and rose, keeping a death grip on the gently moving car. I surveyed the world from my perch. Lights flickered on from trailers around the perimeter. Okay, I'm not alone.

You're never alone.

Okay, God. Once again I forgot who was in control. I'm sorry.

Moving at a snail's pace, I curled myself into a ball on the seat of the car and prepared to wait. Away from the terror of realizing I was suspended above the world. It wasn't long until a full bladder called to be emptied. Where was the carny who operated the contraption?

Visions of him murdered in the men's room rose in my mind. I couldn't come up with any other reason for him not to return. My thoughts definitely did not spin in comforting circles.

What now, Lord?

The wind increased and whistled through the iron bars of my prison. I peered again over the edge. How high could it be? I'd climbed plenty of trees in my youth. The bars of the Ferris wheel crisscrossed, providing plenty of hand and foot holds. The carnies probably scaled it all the time. I couldn't possibly be the first person to ever be stuck on the top of this ride, could I?

With a deep breath, I got to my knees, wiped my hands once again across my thighs, and slung my leg over.

An increasing wind buffeted my back and I shrieked, plastering myself to the bars. *Oh God, I am so stupid. Your Word says You protect the foolish. Well, I'm queen of the foolish. What was I thinking?*

The thought of returning to the relative safety of the ride beckoned. I turned my head. A thin ladder stretched about twenty feet from me. The feat was accomplishable. Even for me. My spirits rose despite the breeze that caused me to shiver. My teeth chattered. With knees shaking, I inched my way across the iron beam. *Don't look down. Don't look down.*

If I'd known I'd be clinging like a locust to the side of a metal structure, I would have worn white. Even what little moonlight shone would have cast off me, making me easier to see. Maybe someone would've noticed.

My Sonata, driven by Aunt Eunice, pulled into the parking lot followed by Joe's squad car. Aunt Eunice gestured wildly with her hands. Giddiness caused me to lose my grip. I squealed and hugged the beam. Continuing to clutch my lifeline, I turned my head. "Help! Aunt Eunice. Joe!"

The weak beam of a flashlight illuminated me. I craned my neck farther and thanked God that Joe had better hearing than my aunt. He ducked into his car and pulled out a bullhorn.

"Stay where you are!"

And where, exactly, did he think I would go?

"I'm calling the fire department!"

Horror. If Mabel or Ruby found out, my picture would be across the front of the newspaper. Thank goodness I hadn't wet my pants. Yet.

Carnies swarmed from the outlying trailers and

gathered below. The ride operator approached Joe. Music blared from the loudspeakers, and Joe had to keep busy with crowd control. They were all having a party at my expense. Probably wishing I'd fall. One death this week didn't seem to be enough for this bloodthirsty crowd.

Aunt Eunice yanked the horn from Joe's hand. "Are you all right?"

How could I answer her? She wouldn't see my nod. I waved, and slipped, hooking my arm over the nearest bar. The crowd roared. Never in my life had I been this popular.

"Keep. Your. Hands. On. The. Ferris wheel!" Aunt Eunice's voice boomed.

I rested my forehead against my arm. Good grief.

What seemed like eons later, a fire truck pulled up and extended the ladder. It moved in slow motion toward me. With a peek beneath my crooked arm, I cringed. Bill Butler, a high school not-so-good friend, grinned up at me. And far below, Mabel and Ruby stood, one with a camera, the other with a notepad.

"Got yourself in a fix, didn't you?" Bill slipped an arm around my waist. "Relax, Summer. Grab ahold of my neck, and I'll pull you over. You'll be down in a sec."

My face flamed, but I kept my mouth shut. Anything I said would be printed in tomorrow's paper. Flashbulbs exploded as we descended.

Aunt Eunice ran up to us, bullhorn still held to her mouth, and blasted my eardrums. "What were you thinking? Ethan is going to kill me."

Joe reached over and shut off the horn. "No more need for this." He removed the horn from her grip and tossed it through the open window of his car. Then he leaned with folded arms and glared at me. Much worse than a lecture.

Aunt Eunice would make up for that. "Tell me how you managed to get up there, hanging like a fly on the wall?"

I sagged against the car. "Thanks, Bill." Then I turned to my aunt. "A fly on the wall is pretty apt, actually. I heard some very interesting information while in the Tilt-A-Whirl. And, I *really* need to use the restroom."

"Don't change the subject."

"Fine." I crossed my legs. "After you disappeared, I went into the livestock building to look for you. The biggest pig I've ever seen charged at me. A carny gave me a test ride on the Ferris wheel. Only he went to the restroom and never came back." Someone handed me a bottle of water. My bladder screamed.

Joe's lip curled. "He said someone locked him in."

Mabel ran to me, a microphone clutched in one hand, while Ruby continued to blind me with flashbulbs. I held up a hand to shield my face.

"Why did you try to kill yourself?" Mabel barked. "How close to jumping were you?"

Joe pushed away from the car. "She wasn't going to jump, Mabel. She was on the ride, unbeknownst to anyone else, and they turned it off. It's that simple."

"Well, that isn't news." Mabel frowned and clicked off the microphone. "That's just Summer getting into trouble." She turned to Ruby. "Come on, Ruby. We have all we need for the paper. I'll make something up. Summer won't mind."

Actually, I would, but I had more important things to talk about. Once Mountain Shadows's nosiest were out of hearing range, I turned back to Joe. "Two men were talking about Millie's death. How they'd bungled making it look like a suicide, and how they needed to get rid of that nosy Summer Meadows. How's that for sleuthing?"

"Not much considering you could've been killed. But not bad, either. Did you see their faces? Would you recognize their voices?"

"No to both. They were kind of filtered through the sides of the Tilt-A-Whirl. Plus, I had my hands over my ears for part of the conversation." I gulped some more water.

"Why did you? Oh, never mind." Joe turned to Aunt Eunice. "Can you get her home in one piece?"

My aunt nodded. "I'll tie her up if I have to."

"Doesn't either of you care about what I heard?"

"Yes, Summer. I care. And I'll check into it." Joe rubbed a hand across his buzz cut. "It's kind of difficult to do an investigation when I have to keep saving you. Man, I'll be glad when Ethan gets home."

I agreed with his thoughts of Ethan getting home. If I lived that long.

The picture of me dangling from the Ferris wheel graced the front page of the newspaper. My rear end looked huge. Not a good angle. I skimmed the article. Without coming right out and saying so, Mabel alluded to the fact that, although unconfirmed, it appeared I had a death wish. She quoted my cousin as agreeing.

Like it or not, this case concerned me. I couldn't hide in a closet just because someone was out to hurt me. God tells His children not to fear, and I didn't intend to. I may be taking the words out of context, but regardless, it helped calm me.

My Dolt book lay open on the table in front of me. My newest acquisition, *The Handy Dandy Guide to Spying*, lay next to it. Last night, burrowed under the warm blankets of my bed, I had skimmed through the contents, searching for something that would help.

The fair officially opened tonight, and first on my list for the day was a trip to the closest electronics store to buy a wireless camera to stash in my rented space. No more surprises in the refrigerator. I had the perfect duffel bag in which to hide the camera. No one would suspect a thing.

"Don't tell me you're reading that again?" Aunt Eunice joined me at the table.

"I need some tips on grilling the carnies for information."

Aunt Eunice grabbed a slice of toast from a nearby plate. "We could crash the masquerade party after the fair tonight."

"Masquerade party?" I straightened so quickly, I

spilled coffee on a place mat and grabbed a napkin to dab at the spreading stain.

"Yeah, I heard some of the vendors talking. They do it opening night everywhere they go." Aunt Eunice spread butter across the warm bread. "Of course, since we're vendors, it wouldn't exactly be crashing, but that makes it sound more fun."

"If we want to hear anything of value, we'll need really good costumes. We can't be recognized." The idea definitely had merit. I wonder if Aunt Eunice could hear my wheels spinning.

"I've always wanted to be a giant Hershey's Kiss." Aunt Eunice stood and modeled for me. "I've already got the right shape." She cackled with glee.

Leaning back in my chair, I gnawed my lower lip. If we drove twenty miles, we'd be able to visit a costume shop. What disguise could I wear to make myself unidentifiable? I'd just need to keep my mouth shut long enough to listen and not be heard. It would be tough, but I had faith I could do it.

I slapped the table and jumped up. "Let's drive to the Costume Corner. That should leave us time to stop by work and pack candy boxes."

"I'll get my purse."

I grabbed my own from the counter, slung it over my shoulder, then dashed out the door to my car. Not wanting to spend a half hour having every bone in my body jarred from riding in my aunt's 1952 Chevy truck, it was imperative I be behind the wheel of my Sonata with the engine running.

Aunt Eunice frowned as she opened the passenger door. "You know I like to drive."

"My car gets better gas mileage. We need to do our part to save the environment. Go green." I turned the wheel in a circle, drove onto the highway, and headed east.

"Since when do you care about the environment?"

"It's never too late to start."

"Hogwash." Aunt Eunice crossed her arms and pouted. "You can think about saving the earth in silence. I'm not speaking to you until we get there."

Thank God for small favors. I turned up the volume on my radio. Worship music filled the car. Sometimes I felt older than my aunt.

She perked up when the costume store came in sight. She opened her door before I'd turned off the car.

"We should find costumes that go together." Aunt Eunice grinned like a child. "This'll be fun."

I could only imagine what she'd come up with.

Only a few patrons inhabited the store, and we made a beeline for the adult sizes. Aunt Eunice grabbed a white square of fabric. "Look at this. I could go as a bar of soap, and you could go as a shower." She held up something else. "Or a roll of toilet paper and a toilet."

No way. I shook my head.

"Well, we can't go as something ordinary. Where's the fun in that?" She slammed the costumes back on the rack. "I suppose we could go as a donkey. I'd be the head and you'd be the—"

"Stop right there! I will not go as a donkey's behind. Aunt Eunice, get real." I riffled through the hangers. "Why don't you go as a queen, and I'll be a ninja. Your royal bodyguard."

"Not very original."

"Maybe not, but the ninja costume will hide my face."

Thirty minutes later, we weren't speaking again. Who would have thought finding a costume would be so stressful? There had to be an easier way to eavesdrop. If Aunt Eunice didn't become more cooperative, I'd have to think about getting another sidekick. Did Nancy Drew have this much trouble? I could go solo like Miss Marple.

"We could go as geisha girls. There'd be a lot of makeup." Aunt Eunice broke the silence.

I giggled. My aunt would look hilarious.

"Or I could be a madame, and you could be one of my 'girls.'" She guffawed.

"How did you find out about that?" Joe most likely. For an officer of the law, the man had loose lips.

"Big Sally mentioned it. Wouldn't Ethan be fit to be tied?"

"Definitely." In my mind, I could envision the muscle ticking in his jaw as he clenched his teeth. "Maybe we could just go as clowns. We'd blend in."

"Boring, but all right."

The full pants of my costume, held wide by an expandable hoop, made maneuvering through the door of the huge tent difficult. I tripped and landed on my knees. Not exactly an unobtrusive entrance. Face flaming beneath my makeup, I pushed to my feet. Aunt Eunice's brightly striped, baggy, one-piece suit looked easier. She ditched me right away.

Lights twinkled from the ceiling. Costumes of every variety added color. Several ninjas and many clowns mingled with kings, queens, and, one misshapen horse.

Hands lifted in greeting as I made my way through the crowd. I congratulated myself on the choice of costume. No one would guess my identity.

Aunt Eunice laughed from beside the buffet table with Washington Bean dressed as a mime. I'd recognize his lanky frame anywhere. There were also three gorillas. One stood over six feet with broad shoulders. The other two looked the right build. I veered away from them. They'd have to move to where I could overhear their conversation and stay hidden at the same time.

Eddy Foreman carried a whip and wore a top hat. Apparently he fancied himself a lion tamer. Next to him, dressed as a sultry lion, stood the platinum-haired woman I'd noticed a couple of days ago.

Country music blared from speakers, and a small crowd danced the latest craze in a Western line dance. Obviously several of them had already visited the beer keg in the corner. They leaned heavily on their partners. Joe and another police officer watched with stern faces from the sidelines. Talk about party crashers. They hadn't even bothered with costumes.

Big Sally sat in a high-backed chair draped with colorful fabric. A tin crown rested on her head, and she held a scepter in her hand. The queen of the fair. I sidled closer, pretending to watch the dancers.

A diminutive woman climbed into a chair next to the large woman. "Why so sad, Sally?"

"Just doesn't seem right to hold this party. Not so soon after Millie's death."

"So tragic for someone so young." The woman's voice sounded like a child's. I hovered near them to hear more.

"She was unhappy. More so the last few weeks. But no

more than me, I suppose. But I've got my eye set on the person responsible for my distress. When I can catch her unaware—" Sally noticed me and waved me over. "Be a sweetie, would you, and get me a drink?"

I nodded and headed for the buffet table. She hadn't seemed to recognize me. Only a willing servant to fetch her majesty something to quench her thirst. My steps faltered at the sight of two gorillas. I switched direction and headed around the other side of the table.

"Do you think she heard anything?"

"I don't think so. If she did, what could she have heard? We didn't mention names, did we?"

"We said hers."

"You worry too much. If I'd known she was on that Ferris wheel, I'd have left it running all night. Would've made her sicker than a dog. You're too nice."

"Not my fault they found her hanging there. You weren't even very convincing."

"No, but you had to go and wave around that cord. If Foreman would've found her like—"

I gasped and switched direction again. Sally would have to get her own drink. I spotted a nearby potted plant and tried to duck behind the large green leaves. No way would the foliage hide all of me. Maybe the two conspirators would think I occupied myself by watching the dancing.

Crossing my arms, I tried to act nonchalant. I leaned against the wall. The hoop of my pants flew up in the front and smacked me in the face. I choked off a groan and lifted a hand to check for blood. I smeared my makeup and knocked off my foam clown nose.

"Opening night went well, didn't it? We made a

bundle off those new wristbands you came up with."

"Yeah, I stole the idea from another fair I worked for. We're going to make a killing off this town. The last night, we'll grab the cash and split. Only thing we got to worry about is getting rid of Super Sleuth."

A hand clamped on my arm. I stifled a gasp and allowed my gaze to travel up the arm. The blue fabric of a police uniform stopped at the wrist.

"Joe."

He pulled me away. "What. Are. You. Doing?"

"Eavesdropping. Those two gorillas are planning to do away with me." I yanked my arm free. "Do something?"

"On what grounds?"

"I told you. They want to kill me."

Joe peered around me. "What two gorillas?"

They were gone. I scanned the crowd. "They aren't here. How could they have disappeared so quickly?"

"Come on." He grabbed my arm again and dragged me after him. Joe split the partyers as effectively as Moses had the Red Sea. Several curious glances were sent our way, obviously accustomed to the picture of a clown dragged away by an officer of the law. Nothing seemed to surprise these people.

Once we stood outside, he turned to face me. "What else did you hear?"

"They plan to steal from the town. 'Make a killing' were their exact words. They're using some kind of wristbands."

Joe folded his arms. "The wristbands are legit. So are the fair's prices. Did they say any more about Millie's death?"

"No, but they know I heard them talking. And Big

Sally spoke to some woman about how sad Millie had been the last few weeks."

"Uh-huh. I've heard the same thing. Sounds to me like she may have heard something she wasn't supposed to. There's something fishy about this place." He glared at me. "Be careful, and stay out of trouble. No more looking for it. Who's head of the fair committee this year?"

I chewed my lip. "Mabel or Ruby, I think. Mrs. Hodge is in the group, too. Why?"

"I need to check on this. This isn't the same company we used for the fair the last few years. I want to know where they were before. Do a background check. I doubt Mabel or Ruby did. I'm sure they just booked the lowest bidder."

He stalked back inside, leaving me to dwell on the fact that, once again, I'd managed to make myself a target. And I'd promised Ethan no more detective work. Well, I didn't ask for it. Trouble just seemed to find me. It was like a gift. One I wanted to return.

I moved to follow Joe, and froze. Watching from the murky shadows stood two gorillas. One raised his hand and waved.

8

I sat on the porch swing the next day writing my suspect list while I waited for Ethan. So far, it consisted of two unknown male gorillas and the carnies I'd come into contact with. I lifted my pen and chewed the end. During the summer, I had at least five names. All people I was familiar with. This time, I didn't think I'd find any names of folks who attended the same church I did.

Okay, Lord, this case is going to be harder. And my life's in danger a lot sooner, too. I could use guidance.

Ethan's truck pulled into the driveway. Before he could close his door, I flew off the porch and into his arms. His legs buckled, and we fell to the grass. I covered his face with kisses until he rolled to his side and leaned over me. His blue eyes twinkled, and a dimple winked from the corner of his mouth.

"If that's the kind of reception I'll get, I need to make a habit of leaving more often."

"I missed you." I lifted a hand to caress the rough stubble on his cheek.

"Ditto." He lowered his head and planted one of his searing kisses on me. When he'd left me completely breathless, he pushed to his feet and pulled me with him.

"You've been busy, though, haven't you?"

"Does Joe tell you everything?" Maybe I could get April to tell him to stop. Ever since I'd introduced my cousin to Ethan's sister, Joe had been putty in her hands.

Ethan led me to the porch swing where he sat and drew me under the curve of his arm. He felt wonderful, solid, and safe. I rested my head on his chest.

"I did ask Joe to watch out for you, given your skill of getting into trouble. Seems like a good thing I did."

"You saw the paper?"

"Yep." His hand stroked my hair, lulling me into a peaceful place full of light instead of gorillas hiding in shadows. "Someone stalking you?"

What a horrible way to be thrust back into the present. "They seem to be. Last night at the masquerade party, two people dressed in gorilla costumes talked about 'doing away' with the nosy Summer Meadows." I sat up and stared at Ethan. "I'm getting somewhere on this. I may have stumbled onto this murder accidentally, but someone thinks I know more than I do, or that I'll find out."

His gaze locked on mine before he cupped his hands around my face. "There's no way I can convince you to go away, is there?"

"Where would I go? This is my home." Hope sprang in my chest. "Unless you want me to go somewhere with you?"

Ethan kissed my forehead. "On our honeymoon. You're too tempting to be alone with while we're unmarried."

Had God ever made a more perfect man? I didn't deserve him.

"So, since I can't be with you around the clock, make sure you're with your aunt, uncle, or cousin. April will do in a pinch, but I don't want my sister involved in your gumshoeing."

And my delusions were shot down at his demanding tone. "They haven't tried to hurt me."

"They set a hog on you."

"Could've been an accident." Right. "Someone could

have left the pen unlatched."

"The Ferris wheel?"

"*Was* an accident." Unless you counted the pulled power cord. Or the fact I'd climbed in it in the first place. Okay, maybe it wasn't an accident, but *I* hadn't planned on getting stuck.

"The conversation about doing away with you? Them following you? Laid Back Millie swinging from her shower? Any of this ring a bell?" Ethan stood, his back straight, his chin stubborn and like chiseled marble. "This is not negotiable. I know I can't keep you from going to the fair. You have your booth. I also know you need to work the booth. Eunice can't, and shouldn't, have to cover it alone for the entire week. I'm just saying, don't go anywhere alone." He held both my hands in his. "Is it awful for me to love you so much that I worry about you?"

Ethan could shoot back to the top of my list of perfect people with three spoken words, a kiss, or a steamy look. This time, I got all three.

"Okay. I'll either be with Aunt Eunice or you." He could have the moon if he wanted.

"Great. And God can take care of all of you."

"Break it up, you two. You ain't married yet." Aunt Eunice joined us on the porch. Her gaze swept the driveway. "Where's Roy?"

Ethan rose and gave her a hug. "He should be here anytime. Had to make a stop."

Aunt Eunice frowned. "A person would think getting home to me would be more important."

My uncle's truck pulled in front of the house. Aunt Eunice and Uncle Roy were proud of their twin Chevys. When he stopped in front of us, his grin cut from one ear to the other. Aunt Eunice crossed her arms and glared.

Her face softened a bit when Uncle Roy emerged from his truck with a dozen red roses. Tears ran down her cheeks when he bowed before her as if she were royalty. "I missed you, Eunice. Lord's work or not, a month is too long to be away from my girl."

"Oh, Roy." She grabbed the roses and buried her wet face in their petals. Uncle Roy could show Ethan a thing or two in the romance department. He hadn't brought me anything.

"My turn." Ethan approached Roy and helped him to his feet. "Roy Meadows, I'd like to ask you for Summer's hand in marriage." He clapped a hand on my uncle's shoulder. Did I say Ethan lacked in romance? I thought my eyes would bug out of my head at his old-fashioned way of proposing.

Uncle Roy returned the gesture. "I already gave my blessing, son." He turned to wink at me. "And my condolences. You'll have your hands full."

Ethan knelt before me and fished in his pocket. My hand fluttered to my face like one of those silly beauty pageant winners fanning at misty eyes. He took my hand in his, his touch warm and gentle. "Summer, I know we've spoken about this, but I've never really asked you properly." He held out a black velvet box. "Will you marry me?"

Lord, catch me. I'm going to fall. I grasped the wooden arm rail of the swing.

Ethan opened the box to reveal a gold band with diamonds and roses entwined. My breath came in short gasps.

"Do you like it, Summer? I had it made special."

"Oh, Ethan." My words barely rose above a whisper.

I wished my parents were alive to see this. They would've loved Ethan. "It's beautiful. I'd be proud to be your wife. It's been my dream for as long as I can remember."

He whooped as he rose then gathered me in his arms. He whirled, making my world, and my head, spin. "You are *my* dream, Summer."

———

Aunt Eunice prepared an early dinner before we headed to the fair, and Uncle Roy puttered in his shed. I curled up against Ethan on the porch swing. My heart overflowed with love for him and thanksgiving to God.

After my adventure the past summer, we'd spoken of marriage in our future. Just speaking of it had been enough for me. But Ethan on bended knee after requesting permission from my uncle was better than any childhood dream. I sighed and snuggled closer, breathing in his musky cologne.

With a slight push of his foot, Ethan set the swing in motion. "Happy?"

"I could burst." My cheeks hurt from the stretch of my smile.

He tightened his arm around me. "The thought of something happening to my Tinkerbell scares me. I'm afraid I may not always be there when you need me."

I lifted my head. "Maybe not, but God will. We need to trust each other to Him. You know that, Ethan. You teach Sunday school."

"But I'm also a man." Ethan kissed my forehead. "One who has now been trusted with a valuable gift."

"I'll be careful. I won't go looking for trouble."

"No, but it usually comes looking for you."

He was right. It had a way of finding me, whether I looked for it or not. Was the word tattooed across my forehead, or did I have a sign around my neck that said COME AND GET ME?

The past summer, I'd actively looked for the culprit responsible for burying a fortune in diamonds beneath my Midnight Blue Rose bush, mainly to prove I wasn't the empty-headed, pampered girl everyone treated me as. Once it became obvious my family could be endangered, I'd tried to back off. The culprit hadn't let me. He'd sought me, whispering words of adoration, intending to steal me away from my home and family to make me "his woman."

Ethan hadn't declared his true feelings for me, and I'd backed off to give him space, almost falling for a stranger's flattering words. It wasn't until he and Joe had rescued me from my "admirer" that I realized Ethan loved me as much as I did him.

If I wanted to live long enough to get married, I'd have to solve this case quick. But something deep within my soul told me I needed to do this. With God's help, I'd survive.

"Let's not spoil the evening." Ethan rose and held out a hand to help me. "Dinner's ready, and there's a county fair to enjoy."

"My first as an officially engaged woman." I couldn't wait to show off my ring. The thoughtfulness behind the jewelry's design set wings to my feet. I'm sure they barely brushed the wood floors as we headed in to join my aunt and uncle.

They pulled apart from each other, Aunt Eunice's face

red. Uncle Roy winked at Ethan and pulled out his chair. "Just received a proper welcome home. Couldn't do it outside. The neighbors would've seen."

"Stop it, Roy." Aunt Eunice set a plate of roast beef, potatoes, and vegetables in front of him. "You're embarrassing them."

Ethan laughed and sat, reaching for the second plate, which he handed to me. "You're the one with the red face, Eunice."

She giggled like a schoolgirl and took her place at the opposite end of the table from Uncle Roy. I smiled. The love that still existed between my sixty-year-old aunt and uncle filled me with joy and hope for the future.

Conversation during dinner consisted of wedding plans and my aunt's gushing over my ring. Hopefully, April hadn't seen it yet. I didn't want to miss the expression on her face when I showed it to her. By turning my hand back and forth, I could observe the glints of light flash from my finger.

"Summer, pay attention." My aunt's sharp words brought me back to earth. "Your uncle will work the booth with me tonight so you and Ethan can run off and play. You guys could've called and told us your plane would be late. Then we wouldn't have wasted a whole day waiting."

"I wanted to wait for Ethan. Aren't you glad you stayed home to wait for Uncle Roy? He brought you flowers."

A flush rose in my aunt's cheeks. She reached over to pat Uncle Roy's hand. "Yes, I am."

"We tried calling. Not much cell phone service in Mexico." Uncle Roy kissed her. "I'm gonna get my gun so we can leave."

"For what?" Aunt Eunice's brow furrowed.

"I'm going gorilla hunting."

"Roy, you can't take a rifle to the fair." Ethan wiped his mouth on a napkin and pushed back his chair.

What amazed me was how my uncle could go from kissing my aunt to wanting to shoot someone. I know he wanted to protect me. My heart swelled with affection for the gruff old man, but he was way too fond of settling things with a rifle in the crook of his arm.

9

The second night of the fair bustled with a crowd of people. It seemed as if the entire town, maybe the whole county, saved their visit for Saturday night. Harassed parents shepherded children through the gate and toward the smaller rides and petting zoo. Hand-holding teens made a beeline for more exciting rides and shows. And above it all, the fun house's clown head bobbed and beckoned to those who wanted to be scared within an inch of their life. A catwalk stretched behind the clown's head. It wobbled while it bobbed, and my stomach lurched at the thought of being on that narrow platform.

"They have a cornfield maze this year," Ethan whispered in my ear, tickling my neck. "Want to get lost in it?"

"Don't tempt me." I grabbed his hand. "Let's buy our wristbands."

The giddiness of a teenager grabbed hold of me as tight as I gripped Ethan's hand. Bouncing on the balls of my feet, I strained to see over the heads of the crowd as I searched for April. She entered the gate, her arm linked through Joe's. He wore street clothes. A rare sight.

"April!" I left Ethan to fork over the thirty dollars for two wristbands and waved frantically to my friend.

She smiled and returned my wave then tugged Joe in our direction. As they drew closer, I held out my left hand and grinned as April squealed. "I didn't think Ethan had such classy taste. Good job, big brother."

"Congratulations, buddy." Joe pumped Ethan's hand. "Taking the vows. Big step."

April rolled her eyes and pulled me aside. "I wish Joe would propose. We talk about marriage, but he wants the proposal to be special. When I least expect it, he says. I just want the ring on my finger." She lifted my hand. "It's gorgeous."

"He asked my uncle for permission then got on his knees." I held my hand to the light. "Ethan had the ring designed special."

"Nice." She leaned closer. "What's this I hear about someone chasing you up the Ferris wheel?"

"Not someone. A big fat hog." I had difficulty dragging my attention away from my sparkling treasure and back to her. "It was the most frightening thing ever. A lot of snorting and grunting." I shivered.

"Why'd you hide on the Ferris wheel? Why not the restroom? Any building. You hate that ride."

"I wasn't thinking clearly, all right? It's difficult to think while you run for your life."

"You're so dramatic. It was only a pig. Look, Joe's ready, and Ethan's waiting." She gave me a quick hug. "Stay out of trouble. Let me know if you need anything."

At one time last year, I'd wanted April to be my sidekick, but she'd become too wrapped up in Joe. My fault, since I encouraged them to see each other. Even going so far as to trick Joe into taking April to the annual formal ball.

With a shrug, I turned and took Ethan's hand, enjoying the feel of my small hand wrapped in his large calloused one. *Aunt Eunice is as nosy as I am. She'll be a great sidekick. If she doesn't lecture me to death each step of the way about the possible danger.*

"Let's ride the Scrambler." Ethan's dimple winked.

"That way you'll be spun against me."

"I'll squash you."

"But what a way to go. Come on, Tinkerbell. As your aunt would say, you don't weigh more than a minute. You aren't going to hurt me."

The ride twirled, the world spun in kaleidoscope colors, and I laughed until I cried. The tears dried almost instantly from the wind created as we whipped around. Ethan held me close against his side to prevent our banging together. I could have stayed like that all night, except for the inevitable nausea. Rides had a tendency to make me ill.

"Win me something," I suggested when the ride stopped. "Show me how strong you are. My stomach has to rest."

"The High Striker. Let's go see if this old man still has what it takes." Old man. He'd just turned thirty-three.

We watched for a while as teenager after teenager attempted to bring the mallet down hard enough to send the puck up and ring the bell. Girls encouraged. Boys groaned. One young man built like a football player stopped and handed the mallet to Ethan.

"Come on, Teach. Show us how it's done."

Ethan took the mallet and swung to test its weight. "How'd you do?"

"I haven't yet. Waiting on you." The young man grinned and flexed his muscles. "You might be stronger in the God department, Mr. Ethan, but I'm stronger in the brawn."

"Uh-huh. Get that wooden box built yet, David? I've been gone a month. You had plenty of time." In addition to being youth pastor at our church, Ethan taught woodworking at the high school.

"No, sir. I'll get right on that this weekend."

"I'll make you a deal." Ethan handed me the mallet and offered his hand to the boy. "If I don't ring this bell, and you do, I'll give you full credit, and you won't have to make the box. But I'll see you in Sunday school every Sunday for a month. If you don't strike it, you have to make the box, and varnish it, plus two straight months of Sunday school. Deal?"

"Yes, sir!" David pumped Ethan's hand. "What if we both make it?"

"If we both make it, you can turn in an unvarnished box for full credit."

Ethan took the mallet, then raised it high. He slammed it on the red circle in the center of the platform. The puck rose. The ding of the bell rang over our heads. I clapped and jumped up and down, shrieking like a cheerleader.

"That's one month of Sundays, David." Ethan handed him the mallet.

David laughed, raised his hand to high-five another kid, and raised his mallet. The puck rose three-fourths and fell.

"That's two months." Ethan slung an arm over the boy's shoulder. "Can't wait to see you in church tomorrow morning."

"But I'm entered in the rodeo."

"So am I. The rodeo isn't until two o'clock. You're steer roping, right? That isn't until three."

Ethan punched the young man's shoulder then turned to the prize booth. With a chuckle, he chose a giant stuffed gorilla. "They say a person needs to face their fears."

"How closely?" I pointed toward the space between

two game booths where one of my gorilla friends stood. Ethan shoved the stuffed animal under his arm and with his free hand, grabbed mine and dragged me after him while we gave chase.

Our feet pounded on the dirt-packed surface between the sideshows and attractions. We leaped over stretched cable. We sprinted past Ginger's corral, and she lumbered alongside the fence, keeping pace. Children shrieked with glee and jogged with her.

"Your friend?" Ethan barely panted with our effort, while I could hardly breathe.

"Sort. Of." My lungs burned.

Thank You, Lord, for giving me the sense to wear my gym shoes. Still, at the speed Ethan darted across the midway, I felt as if I really were Tinkerbell flying behind Peter Pan. We finally came to a blessed halt before the entrance to the maze. I bent over to catch my breath.

"He got away. We'll never find them in there."

Somebody screamed, then laughed, and I pulled back. "Good, because I'm not going in there. Not at night. I've seen too many scary movies."

"Don't worry. We aren't going in. Whoever our friend is probably knows his way around. We'd come up against all the dead ends." He glanced at the stuffed animal. "Nothing we can do now. Let's stick this guy in the truck and play some more games. Or would you like to go on another ride?"

"I'd like to check on Aunt Eunice, if you don't mind. See if she needs me."

"Sure." My brave knight took me by the hand again and moved at a much slower pace toward his Ford.

We stashed my furry friend behind the front seat,

then followed a group of people into the arts and crafts building. My spirits soared at the sight of a crowd in front of our candy booth. As we got closer, I realized they weren't there to buy chocolate.

Aunt Eunice's angry voice rose above the mob of on-lookers. Mabel and Ruby stood in front of her. All three women's faces resembled prize-winning tomatoes in color. Ethan shouldered his way through the crowd. I followed in his wake.

My aunt shouted—her face inches from Mabel's. "You stole them. I want them back."

"I didn't take anything!" Mabel put her hands on her hips to imitate Aunt Eunice. "I just got here."

"Then Ruby took them. One of you did. You knew I'd win."

"Excuse me?" Ruby joined the melee. The other two women's plump frames dwarfed her skinny one. "How dare you accuse me—"

Uncle Roy squeezed his bulk between the women. "Ladies, settle down. You're creating a spectacle."

All three women turned on him.

"We don't care if we're causing a spectacle or not." Aunt Eunice narrowed her eyes. "Just chalk it up to an-other sideshow at the fair. Look at the old biddies making a fuss."

"Speak for yourself," Mabel grumbled. "Old, my foot."

"Aunt Eunice." I squeezed my way into the booth. "What exactly is missing?"

Tears welled in her eyes. "My pickles."

10

"I hardly have the heart to go to church this morning." Aunt Eunice plopped into a kitchen chair. Her head fell forward onto folded arms. "Why would someone steal my pickles?"

I wondered the same thing and patted her shoulder before I shuffled to the coffeepot. Even though I'd have my usual frappuccino from the coffee bar at church, I still needed some right now. I couldn't wake up in the mornings without caffeine. Maybe I should switch to cola.

I filled my mug and an aromatic fragrance wafted up with the steam. Closing my eyes in bliss, I sipped before speaking. "Do you really think Mabel or Ruby would sabotage you by stealing your entry?"

"No," she groaned. "And I'll have to apologize. I was upset."

"Do you want some toast?" I popped a couple of slices of bread in the toaster.

My aunt and uncle had been my primary caregivers since I was five—taking care of every tear or scraped knee, and there were lots of them. I tried drumming up some sympathy, honestly, but seven o'clock on a Sunday morning left the well dry.

Aunt Eunice waved off the offer. "I couldn't eat a thing."

The toaster dinged, and I buttered my slices then slathered them with homemade muscadine jelly.

Aunt Eunice bolted from her chair and disappeared into the pantry. "Good thing I set aside a couple jars of pickles for our personal use."

The toast stuck in my throat. I shook my head. "Extras? Then why all the fuss?"

"I felt violated." She emerged with a jar held high. "And your uncle loves my bread-and-butter pickles. He'll be devastated I wasn't able to set much away for us."

"How many jars did you make?"

"A dozen."

Even I could do the math. One lost jar at the fair and one replacement jar still left ten jars. Plenty for my rotund uncle. Things were always one extreme to the next with my aunt.

She set the jar precisely in the center of the table on a homemade doily. "Ain't it pretty?"

"It's a jar of pickles." Aunt Eunice's face fell. Now I'd hurt her feelings. "I'm sorry. You know I'm not a morning person. They're beautiful."

"Hmmph. That's no reason to be rude." She gathered her baby in her arms and stomped from the room.

Aunt Eunice wasn't the only one who needed to apologize to someone. With a deep sigh, I followed her outside, grabbing my purse and Bible on the way.

She sat behind the wheel of her truck, a smug grin on her face. "I'm driving. Your uncle will meet us there."

We entered the church foyer, and I turned toward the coffee bar. Aunt Eunice went to find her friends. I ordered my usual and plopped into the nearest wrought iron chair and café table to indulge in my favorite pastime. Watching people.

Things were more colorful this morning. A handful of the carnies were in attendance, either because they were believers or because they were trying to relieve their boredom. Some arrived in colorful costumes, some dressed like ordinary folk, and others came in their everyday dirt and body odor. They kept to themselves, apparently used to being shunned, even by churchgoers. A group of women actually shrank back when the group passed, stopping a few feet from me. My heart clinched.

As is my norm, I acted impulsively and stepped to the coffee bar. "Frappuccinos for all my carnie friends."

Smiles widened their faces, while incredulous looks replaced the revulsion on some of the parishioners. Soon the coffee bar became a party. Worship music piped through the speakers, and when Ethan finished greeting our fellow arrivals, I introduced him to my friends. My heart swelled with pride as he shook every hand and clapped every man on the back no matter how strongly they smelled.

Washington engulfed Ethan in a hug. "You got yore self a fine woman there, Mister Ethan. A fine woman."

Ethan winked at me. "Yes, I do." He excused himself and made his way to my side. "How are you going to pay for all these drinks?"

"I have no idea." Nor did I care. The smiles on the people's faces made the cost worth every penny.

"I'll help." Ethan pulled me close for a hug. "You are a priceless treasure, Summer Meadows."

From my seat in the bleachers, I whooped and hollered when Ethan charged past on his horse. The participants lined up in the middle of the rodeo ring. He sat a head taller than the majority. My heart swelled. The sun highlighted

Ethan's golden curls like a halo as he waved his hat. He looked so beautiful, I wanted to cry. My cowboy/bronc-riding angel.

The spectators roared as each town member's name rang over the loudspeaker. Some booed with the announcement of participants from neighboring towns and cities. The stands were full. A person couldn't help but get caught up in the excitement.

Rodeo clowns goofed around as the cowboys rode in a circle. One actually had a lasso that he tried roping the riders with.

Aunt Eunice plopped next to me with a huff. "Got my pickles ready."

"She wouldn't rest until another jar sat on the judge's table." Uncle Roy sat down and removed his baseball cap. He pulled a red and white bandanna from his pocket and wiped his forehead. "Since everyone heard the ruckus she made in regards to her pickles disappearing, they let her reenter, late as it is. Judging's this afternoon. Right after the rodeo."

"I'm so glad for you, Aunt Eunice." I gave her a one-armed hug and let my gaze travel the dirt track around the ring. Eddy Foreman and his father stood beside the announcer's box, along with Miss Curvy Platinum Blonde. I was glad Foreman had transferred his attention to someone more receptive.

Big Sally sat at the bottom of the bleachers, her tiny boyfriend next to her. Washington Bean and several of the other carnies who'd visited church leaned against the wooden rodeo railing. Most of them noticed me sitting above them and waved.

"That was a good thing you did this morning," Uncle

Roy said, patting my knee. "The pastor used it in his sermon. Your good deed got incorporated into the lesson he wanted to teach. He taught on compassion and loving our brother."

"I was ashamed, Uncle Roy. When I witnessed some women shrink back in distaste, it hurt. I've been guilty of that myself. Plenty of times."

A roar rose from the crowd. Ethan's student was the first to burst into the ring, giving the best time in the calf roping contest. I cringed as he leaped from his horse, threw the calf to the ground, and wrapped the rope around its legs. Fully aware the act didn't hurt the animal, it still looked as if it did, and sometimes the calf's bawling tugged at my heart.

The next competition was barrel racing. I wasn't familiar with any of the contestants, and my attention wandered. Catching a glimpse of the Ferris wheel out of the corner of my eye, I shivered and made a vow never to ride on one again.

Aunt Eunice leaned over and whispered in my ear. "We ought to be out snooping until it's time for Ethan to ride."

"Snoop for what? We don't know anything."

"That's my point. We ought to talk to the owner of that hog, for one. Find out what set her off."

Chills ran down my spine. "No, thanks."

"And we ought to look around for a gorilla costume. Find the costume, find the culprit."

The people in the stands groaned as a rider fell from her horse, then cheered when she got to her feet. I frowned at my aunt. "We can't go into people's trailers." *Can we?* I'd been contemplating the same thing. Itching to get to the bottom of things. How far could we go in our investigating before we stepped outside the boundaries of the law?

"I don't see why not. We aren't going to take anything."

"Uncle Roy, talk some sense into her, won't you?"

He shook his head. "Won't do any good. She's a hard-headed woman."

Good grief. "I'm not going anywhere until the rodeo is over."

Aunt Eunice folded her arms. "I don't think you're serious about solving this. After the rodeo is the pickle judging. I won't be available to help you then." She dug into her purse. "Here's a new book for you. Since you're so all-fire set on reading them."

"Thanks." I turned the small book over. *A Layman's Guide to Spying.* Wonderful. I didn't have the heart to tell her I'd already bought a book on that subject. After making sure no one watched me, I slipped the book into the denim backpack next to my feet. Well, I did say I wanted a sidekick. It seemed like Aunt Eunice would be an active and willing participant.

I squirmed on the hard wooden bleacher. April leaned against the split-rail fence surrounding the arena and talked to Joe. The entire fairgrounds stretched in front of me, beckoning, and I had no idea where to start looking for answers. Questioning everyone of the appropriate size of my gorilla friend would take days. What did my investigating book advise? Interview prospective suspects. I agreed with my aunt. Time to pound the dirt-packed surface of the midway and ask questions.

The announcer called Ethan's name. I straightened, my eyes fixated on the gate. I gasped along with everyone else when Ethan's mount, a coal black mustang by the name of Diablo, burst into the ring, Ethan on his back. A demon from hell with an angel riding its back. My heart pounded with excitement.

The horse locked his forelegs and bucked, landing with bone-jarring thuds to the ground. Dust hovered knee-deep around him and his rider. Back stiff and arm waving, Ethan stuck tight, and the crowd rose to their feet with a roar when they announced Ethan's time. Eight point three seconds. It would be hard for anyone to beat him.

My hands hurt from clapping. Uncle Roy gave a redneck yell and tears poured down Aunt Eunice's cheeks. Ethan jumped from Diablo's back, banged the dust off his jeans with his cowboy hat, and bowed to the crowd.

The sound of gunfire split the air.

11

My heart stopped. Ethan dove for the ground. Diablo fell to his knees, then rolled onto his side. The horse struggled to regain his footing, only to collapse. The stands erupted in a volcano of noise. Fear as thick as the dust surrounding the rodeo ring clogged my throat.

Screams, yells, curses, and stomping feet swept over me as spectators jostled their way out of the stands. Like freshly beheaded chickens, people darted in each direction. Uncle Roy pulled a fallen woman to her feet and steered her away from us. Another lady cried for her baby.

I stood on the seat and craned to see Ethan. Uncle Roy moved to stand behind me and Aunt Eunice, his strong arms wrapped around both of us. Aunt Eunice slid to her knees.

"Get down, Summer."

"I've got to get to Ethan." I pushed against my uncle. "Let go of me."

Uncle Roy lifted me off my feet. "Not until the crowd disappears. Please, sweetie. At least duck out of sight. The shooter is still out there."

Tears blurred my vision as my uncle shoved me to the floor of the bleachers. From my peripheral vision, I made out Joe, sprinting, weapon in hand, to the rodeo ring. Another officer headed in the opposite direction, presumably from where the shot originated.

When Joe helped Ethan to his feet, I bolted from beneath the protective covering of my uncle's arms, thundered down the steps of the bleachers, then burst into the rodeo ring. "Ethan!"

I hurled myself into his arms. "Are you all right? You aren't hurt, are you?"

"No. I'm fine. I heard the report and dove. Diablo doesn't appear to be as lucky."

The horse whinnied. The whites of his eyes showed. Scarlet stained the dirt beneath him.

I hid my face in Ethan's chest, reveling in the feel of his heartbeat. Breathing in the scent of dust and perspiration. *Thank You, God. I'll never take another one of Ethan's breaths for granted.*

His arms tightened around me as he pulled me behind the protection of the announcer's stand. He cupped his hands around my face. "When I heard that gun, I thought this is the day. This is when I lose my Summer." Tears welled in his eyes.

With those words, the enormity of Ethan's love washed over me as gentle as a spring rain. I was seriously in danger of drowning in his eyes, suffocating beneath the warm blanket of his love. What a way to go.

"I hate to break up the lovefest," Joe said, taking my elbow. "But we've got to get the two of you safely into a building."

"Not the livestock one," I told him. "I won't go in there."

Ethan shot out a hand to stop Joe. "How's Diablo?"

"Lost a lot of blood. The rodeo vet is checking him out. Said it doesn't appear as if the bullet hit anything vital. My concern is for you two."

Joe veered toward the arts and crafts building. Ethan remained glued to my other side, with Aunt Eunice and Uncle Roy trotting behind. Mr. Foreman, the fair owner, met us in front of the building. His son rushed to slam the door behind us.

"Mr. Banning." Mr. Foreman offered a hand. "So pleased to see you're all right. I have no idea what could've happened."

"Someone shot Diablo." Ethan pulled up the nearest straight-backed chair and helped me onto the hard plastic.

Things had happened so fast. I stared at the men milling in front of me. Aunt Eunice fussed over Ethan and brushed the dust from his clothes until he moved her away. Uncle Roy stood with arms crossed and feet shoulder-width apart.

"I wish I had my gun," he grumbled. "I would've got the culprit and blown him to smithereens. Should've brought it, but Eunice wouldn't let me."

"The last thing we need is another nutcase running around with a gun." Joe smiled to take the bite off his words. He turned to the Foremans. "Could you excuse us, please? And mark this building off limits."

"But the pickle judging contest!" Aunt Eunice's eyes widened.

"You can have my office," Mr. Foreman offered. He twirled a finger in his mustache. "It's not far from here, and we can take the back door. Eddy, run ahead and unlock it." He tossed a ring of keys to his son. "And Mrs. Meadows' pickles will still be available for judging. Whether she's present or not."

For the last several months, the tribulations of having us for a family tormented Joe. He always threatened to apply for a job with a different agency. Preferably in a different city than one I lived in. From the expression on his red face, I guessed he was one step closer to the county line. We were the proverbial thorn in his side. I think if Ethan and April weren't part of the group, Joe would've washed his hands of the whole bunch.

With the help of two arriving police officers, Joe ushered us out the back, across a strip of grass, around a coil of electrical cables, and into a trailer. "There's ice water and soda in the fridge. Help yourself." Mr. Foreman closed the door on his way out.

The trailer was decorated clinical shabby. Dingy gray walls, aluminum blinds on the two thin windows, and a battered wooden desk. Two green plastic chairs faced the desk. I plopped into one of these.

"Stay here." Joe stood framed in the doorway. "I'll be back to ask questions as soon as I'm able."

Four pairs of eyes looked down at me. "Why are all of you staring at me? They weren't shooting at me."

"Actually. . ." Joe stepped closer. "I believe they were. They missed. I'll know more later." He turned and left.

My knees trembled, and I thanked God for the chair beneath me. My mind raced over the week's events. Someone wanted to shoot me? "I don't understand. The last time I'd been involved in a murder case, I'd—" *I'd what?*

Sure, I'd been shoved into the trunk of a car and had a gun pointed at my head by a man who fancied he loved me. And he'd shot at me while I ran through the woods, but I'd known he was going to do that. What kind of a coward shoots at a woman when she isn't looking?

My knuckles hurt from the grip I had on the bottom of the chair. Fear and anger swirled in my veins. With a growing sense of helplessness, I narrowed my eyes.

"There's more to this than Millie hanging herself in the shower, not that I believe she actually hung herself. You can't hang yourself from a trailer shower. Even I know the pipes aren't strong enough. This concerns me, and I want to know why."

Ethan glanced at Uncle Roy. His silent gesture told me Ethan knew exactly what went on. We would be having a serious conversation when we got home. "Let's talk about this when Joe returns, okay?"

The temperature inside the trailer grew warm with all of us crowded in waiting for Joe to return. When he did, over an hour later, my aunt's and uncle's heads were nodding. They jerked awake when Joe yanked open the door.

"Well?" I jumped to my feet. "Did someone try to shoot me? What is going on, and don't give me any of that confidentiality garbage."

Joe nodded. "We found bullet casings and footprints in the dust of the catwalk above the fun house. From the angle we figure the bullet came from, it should have got you in the back of the head."

"Why?" An icy hand gripped my heart.

My cousin rubbed his hands across his buzz cut. "Someone has been embezzling funds from Foreman's carnival. That person is running scared. Afraid of you finding out too much information. At least that's what we think at this point."

"I didn't do anything until I got stuck on top of that Ferris wheel."

"Summer, people run scared as soon as you walk in their general vicinity." Joe frowned.

"Ha ha." Crossing my arms, I slouched in my chair. "I promised Ethan I wouldn't go anywhere alone, and today, surrounded by people, I'm almost killed." My heart sank like a stone. That bullet could have struck Ethan as easily as me or Diablo.

"I won't run, Joe. Hiding in a hole is out of the question. If someone thinks I know something, I'm going to find out what that is."

"Summer, I'll lock you up if I have to and throw away the key. Don't think I won't." Joe looked so much like Uncle Roy as he stood there with his hands on his hips that I snorted and fought back a giggle.

Aunt Eunice stepped to my side and put an arm around my shoulder. "And I'm going to help her. A Meadows doesn't run."

"You're only a Meadows by marriage, Eunice," Uncle Roy informed her.

"We've been married long enough that it's the same thing. Don't try to stop me, Roy. You know how I am when I get my dander up. Purely lethal. Joe can't lock us both up."

The warm feelings aroused by my aunt's ferocious defense chilled at the look on Ethan's face. His handsome features could have been chiseled from granite. He worked his cowboy hat in his hands, crushing the brim. A muscle ticked in his jaw. My giant of a man could be gentle as a lamb or ferocious as a tiger. I had a feeling I'd be meeting the angry cat later tonight.

"Is that all, Joe?" Suddenly I wanted out of the stifling trailer and away from the glaring eyes of my family.

"Y'all come over and eat," Aunt Eunice invited. "I've a pot roast in the Crock-Pot. We can decide how to proceed over a rump of beef."

"I'll meet you in our spot," Ethan whispered as he took my arm and helped me from the chair.

Normally, "our spot" was a place to meet for privacy. I found myself less than anxious to be alone with Ethan tonight.

Mr. Foreman waited outside the trailer. His grin spread as wide as his mustache. "Mrs. Meadows, I'm pleased to announce you won a blue ribbon for your bread-and-butter pickles." He handed her a first place ribbon then turned to Ethan. "And for the second year running, I've heard that Mr. Banning had the best time in the bronc riding. Well done, sir. I'm sorry you missed the announcement of your name."

Hard to believe they would've continued the rodeo after the shooting, but as they say, the show must go on. Pride flooded through me at Ethan's win. Diablo had been the toughest of the horses, and still Ethan won. Another glance at his clenched jaw, and my smile faded.

"I'm going to check on my horse. See you later." He gave me a quick peck and stalked away.

___

While Aunt Eunice put the final touches on dinner, I slipped out the back door and made my way to the tree house where Ethan and I had hung out as kids. Since almost falling from the rotting ladder a while back, I hadn't climbed inside.

Ethan stepped from the shadows beneath the tree. He gathered me in his arms and crushed me to his chest. He cried. Silently. His body trembled with sobs.

"Ethan?"

He rested his chin on top of my head. "I know I can't stop you from snooping, Summer, although God help me,

I'd like to. All I can do is ask."

"I didn't go looking for this."

"I know, and I'm more frightened than I've ever been in my life." I tasted the salt of his tears when our lips met. A kiss so tender, gentle tears sprang to my eyes. "You're my world, Summer Meadows. The reason the sun rises each morning, and the meaning behind it setting at night." His breath tickled my lips.

A roar from my left had me scurrying behind Ethan. "What was that?"

"It sounded like a lion." Ethan grabbed my hand.

"A mountain lion?"

"No."

I remembered the roar from the carnival. My insides turned to ice. The only place a cat that size would have come from was the fairgrounds. I squinted through the darkness. "Ethan, there. Hanging from the tree on the other side of the clearing. What is it?"

12

The roar came again, much closer. Startled birds darted from the trees. Ethan sprinted toward the house, pulling me behind. A growl. The sound erupted from somewhere in front of us. Ethan stopped. He pushed me behind him, plastering me between his back and a tree.

"Where is it?" My voice trembled.

"I don't know. It could be anywhere." Ethan squatted then rose with a thick stick in his hand. I stepped forward, wanting to be by his side.

Another roar.

The force of my scream tore at my throat.

Ethan shoved me. My shoulder connected with the tree trunk, and I scraped my way to the ground. Bark against skin. Not a good combination. I couldn't see whether my arm bled, but it stung like fire ants were marching across my upper arm.

Outlined by moonlight, my brave mountain man faced a lion. A large male worthy of *National Geographic*. The lion, not Ethan. Ethan stood with knees slightly bent and shoulder-width apart. The cat threw back his head, its mane waving in the slight breeze. He advanced on huge paws toward Ethan. My breath caught in my throat.

This could not be happening. This wasn't *Wild America*. For a moment, I nurtured the notion that hidden cameras might be filming us and that the massive feline was actually a tame pet. Another growl clarified the reality of the situation.

Ethan and the animal circled each other. I pushed

to my feet. My gaze searched the ground around me. I would not allow Ethan to fight this ferocious beast alone. I grasped a rock the size of my fist.

"Summer, get back."

"You aren't doing this alone." I stepped up beside him.

"If you distract me, we're both dead."

"I'm not going to stand back and watch you get eaten."

Ethan shook his head. "Then back up slowly. And stay behind me."

We moved backward in choreographed steps. The lion mimicked and stepped forward. He stopped, sniffed the breeze, and turned toward the bag hanging from a tree. Ethan whirled and shoved me ahead of him. "Run!"

My tree house sat back approximately half a football field-length from the house. The distance seemed like miles as we hurtled through the woods. Any second, I expected to find myself knocked to the ground by a carnivore going for my jugular.

Uncle Roy met us on the back stoop, his trusty rifle in hand. Joe appeared from around the corner of the house, pistol in hand.

"What is it? The dog's been going crazy. We finally had to lock her in the bathroom."

Ethan wrenched open the door and shoved me inside. "Get inside, Roy! It's a lion."

"We don't have lions around here. Mountain lions, but I ain't seen one of them in years. Nothing big enough to make that noise anyway." He entered the house behind us and locked the door before peering through the curtains. "Of course the Wilson boys swear they saw Bigfoot not more than a week ago, terrorizing their cows. Think it's Bigfoot?"

Joe met Ethan's gaze. "No, Uncle Roy, he doesn't think it's Bigfoot."

"I know you young folks don't believe, but Bigfoot's real. Just because you've never seen him doesn't mean he don't exist." Uncle Roy took a seat in a kitchen chair and placed his rifle across his lap. "People don't see God, but we know He's there."

We all stared at Uncle Roy. As unusual as it was for me, I found myself at a loss for words. I still reeled from the shock of facing the king of the jungle. The prospect of a living, breathing, ape-slash-man creature circling the house definitely did not seem believable.

"What is it?" Aunt Eunice bustled into the kitchen.

"Bigfoot," Uncle Roy told her.

My aunt's hand flew to her throat. "Do you think he's after my pot roast?"

April entered the room with a pitcher of iced tea in her hand. Her eyes widened for a minute, then she giggled, meeting my gaze. Having grown up spending a lot of nights at my house, she was used to my aunt's and uncle's strange statements.

A dimple winked in Ethan's cheek, Joe's face darkened, and I turned away to hide my grin. Joe ran a hand over his face. "It *isn't* Bigfoot. I'm going to call animal control. The carnival's minuscule zoo is probably missing a lion."

Ethan glanced at me. "It's definitely a lion."

"We might as well eat then. Nothing we can do about it." Aunt Eunice opened the cabinet and took down six plates. "Summer, come help. April, you going to pour that tea or keep it all to yourself?"

April commenced pouring and I reached to take the dishes from my aunt. Footsteps padded outside the kitchen window. Massive paws scratched at the door, gouging the wood. Saliva dripped from sharp fangs as the predator stared in the window. I shook my head to clear it of my overly imaginative thoughts. We'd left the cat in the woods. Now was not the time for scary daydreams. As far as I cared, the lion could move on. I took the plates from my aunt's outstretched hands.

When my gaze connected with Ethan's, I guessed he also wondered what the bag hanging in the woods contained. We'd have to let Joe find out for us. No way would Ethan allow me to go. Even if he went with me.

"What's up, you two? Tell me exactly what happened out there." Joe returned from using the phone and sat in his usual chair at the opposite end of the table from Uncle Roy. He ate at our house so often, that seat naturally became his.

"What do you mean?" Afraid I'd fall into the chair from lack of strength in my wobbly legs, I braced my hands on the tabletop and slowly lowered myself.

"I mean, Ethan ran in here sweating and clutching a piece of wood. You were pale as a ghost. We hear a large animal roar and you say it's a lion." Joe speared a bite of roast. "Is it real, or another person in a costume?"

Ethan placed a hand on my arm, keeping me in my seat. What I wanted to do was strangle my cousin. The man never believed anything I said.

"Summer and I came a little closer to the lion than we would have liked. A real live, breathing animal. We know what we saw, Joe." Ethan patted my arm and released me. "There's also a strange bag hung in one of the oaks. I think someone lured our furry friend here. I also don't think he escaped. I bet someone set it free. Much like the hog that chased Summer." Ethan leaned across the table toward Joe. "Someone is playing games, and I don't like it."

Why would someone want to play games with me? Tomorrow, Monday, when Ethan went to work, I'd slip away from the candy booth and start back at the beginning. Millie's trailer.

Joe dropped his fork onto his plate. "I don't like it either, Ethan. I'm not sitting here twiddling my thumbs. The department is actively trying to find out the purpose behind all this. Why the hog chase, why the Ferris wheel ride, and why the attempt on her life today? Now—a lion roaming around Mountain Shadows. Specifically this yard. Coincidence? I don't think so." He wiped his mouth and tossed his napkin to the table.

"Summer does a good deed, which still doesn't make sense to me. Not with the liability involved with her walking an elephant. Then she stumbles across Millie's body and a whole slew of other things. Doesn't add up." Joe pushed to his feet. "Things like this don't happen in other small towns. But then, Summer lives *here*, doesn't she?" He stormed out of the kitchen, leaving the rest of us to stare at each other in silence.

Since my parents' fatal car accident, my cousin Joe had played the part of overly protective older brother. When Ethan and I got engaged, I'm sure Joe hoped I'd become someone else's worry. Instead, it seemed as if the two men got to share in my troubles.

By the time we finished dinner and Aunt Eunice and I were standing at the kitchen sink washing dishes, two officers approached the house with guns drawn. Behind them walked a man dressed in khaki coveralls, carrying a really long rifle-looking thing. Joe joined them on the back porch, Uncle Roy announced he'd stand guard out front, and the officers, Joe, and the Crocodile Dundee guy strode, somewhat reluctantly it seemed, into the woods behind the house.

Ethan walked up behind me and encircled my waist with his arms. "You holding up okay?"

"I am now." I leaned into him, relishing his solidness. Ignoring the grin on my aunt's face, I turned in his arms. "I'm sorry, Ethan. For being a screwup. For being a trouble magnet. You name it." Tears pricked the back of my eyes.

"Summer." Ethan tightened his hold. "I don't want you not to be who you are. I just want you to *be*. Understand?"

I nodded. "Ditto."

"They're coming back." Aunt Eunice pulled her hands from the water. Soapy suds slopped down the cabinets. "They're dragging something. It looks like a body."

April dropped a dishtowel on the counter. "It's definitely a body."

My foot caught on the rung of the chair as I bolted to my feet. Only Ethan's outstretched arm prevented me from falling face first to the worn linoleum. "Let me see. It's too dark. I can't see a thing." I used my hip to push against my aunt.

"Stop shoving. They've gone around the corner."

Like two children at a toy store, we jostled each other as we sprinted toward the front. Ethan chuckled and joined us.

Yanking open the door, I jumped back and screamed as I came face-to-face with the lion. Except this time it was dead. Its dark eyes stared lifelessly at me from the front porch. Next to it lay a shredded, bloody, canvas bag.

Uncle Roy knelt beside the animal. "There seems to

have been another murder. Someone killed this big cat."

Joe scribbled on a notepad. "Good assumption. On first guess, I'd say someone put poisoned meat in that bag then hung it from a tree to attract the lion. Walters said one of his lambs disappeared yesterday, along with a jug of rat poison. What I want to know is. . ." He tapped the pencil against his chin. "If someone lured the lion here to get Summer, why kill it?"

My mind drifted, lost in daydreams, while my fingers swirled shapes in the chocolate. Images of faces appeared in the silkiness. Big Sally, Laid Back Millie, Eddy Foreman, the lion. They were all relative to each other in some way. I just needed to find the link.

The bell over the door to Summer's Confections remained silent. At least business at the fair was good. The candy seemed to disappear out of the booth, leaving money in its place. Making more chocolate had become a necessity. A blessing from God.

Fifties music played softly from the radio, rising above the low clanking of my dipping machine. My gaze kept drifting to the clock. Five o'clock wouldn't come soon enough. I dressed in black for the occasion. I'd help Aunt Eunice in the booth until dark, then sneak over to Millie's trailer. As long as Ethan's volunteer meeting lasted past dusk, I'd be home free.

There had to be something I missed a week ago. Had it only been a week? Not even. Short by a couple of days. I sighed and swirled the letter C on top of a chocolate cream.

One of my prized possessions nestled in the bag I'd set on top of the counter: a tiny pink flashlight right out of a James Bond movie. My lack of proper investigating tools had seriously hindered my crime-solving abilities in the past. The same mistakes wouldn't happen again. I chuckled. I'd be making a bunch of new ones.

At one minute past five, I locked the front door and

jogged to my car. I placed the boxes of chocolate carefully in the backseat, hooked the seat belt across them, then slid behind the wheel.

My palms sweated in nervous anticipation. When I stopped at a red light, Joe's squad car pulled behind me. I froze until I realized I hadn't done anything wrong. Not yet, anyway. I gave him a little wave through my rearview window. He followed me into the fairgrounds.

"What's with the gothic look?" he asked once we'd both exited our vehicles.

"I just felt like wearing black."

"You never wear all black. Said the color depresses you."

"I wanted a change."

Joe reached into his car and pulled out a black ski cap. He grinned as he handed it to me. "If you plan on doing something sneaky after dark, you might want to cover up that red hair."

"It's not red. It's auburn and—" Great. I hadn't denied any sneaky plans.

"Word of advice, my dear cousin." He pointed an index finger at me. "Don't do anything illegal. I will arrest you if I have to."

He'd made those threats before. Besides, what did he take me for? I wouldn't think of breaking the law. Not on purpose anyway.

Aunt Eunice perched on a high stool behind our booth counter. Her chin rested in her hand. On the surface in front of her, displayed on a swatch of black velvet, lay her blue ribbon.

"Drooling, Aunt Eunice?" I set the box of candy on the counter.

"You don't drool over something you already have." She glanced up at me. "Why are you wearing black?"

"Shhh." I pulled her off the stool. "I'm going back to Millie's trailer tonight. Will you watch the booth?"

"I have been all day, haven't I?" Aunt Eunice crossed her arms. "You can't go to that *loose* woman's trailer by yourself. I want to go with you."

"You have to watch the booth."

"Ethan will flip his lid if I don't babysit you."

"Fine. Let's lock everything up. It'll be fine for a few minutes. You can be my lookout."

Aunt Eunice rolled her ribbon in the fabric while I put the chocolate in the near-empty refrigerator. My aunt's face glowed. "This is going to be fun."

I had to admit to a certain amount of excitement myself. And to think I'd originally wanted April as my sidekick. No danger of Aunt Eunice being distracted by the male physique. She liked a roly-poly type of man. Like Uncle Roy. April, on the other hand, stopped helping me solve the diamond mystery with her first glance at Joe.

"Let's go out the back." I peered around our cubicle partition. "Nonchalantly walk with me. Don't attract any attention."

"Right." Aunt Eunice narrowed her eyes. She resembled a shifty-eyed crook. She slouched beside me, then stated in an overly loud voice, "I think I'll head on over to the restroom. Haven't had much of a chance all day. A woman my age can't hold it long."

"What are you doing?" The woman was an embarrassment.

"Creating a distraction."

Well, duh. I sighed and marched faster toward the exit. "I said not to attract attention. Oh, never mind." Like anyone would believe she'd announce to a building full of people her intention of going to the restroom. We were doomed.

A throng of people mingled out back. Mostly carnival workers, although there were a few attendees. Young girls who seemed more interested in the workers than spending time on the rides. Getting to Millie's trailer would take ingenuity.

"We need another distraction. One better planned than the restroom announcement."

"I'm on it." Aunt Eunice marched into the group of people, threw a hand to her forehead, gave a little squeak, and swooned. She collapsed in a surprisingly graceful crumble.

With everyone's attention on her, I ducked behind a trailer. Covert eyeballing of my surroundings showed no one watched me. With a deep breath, I made my way to the target. Yellow crime scene tape still blocked Millie's trailer. A shining beacon that I'd probably be in trouble from my cousin. Well, not if he didn't catch me.

Even with my short height, I managed to get tangled trying to duck under the tape. I'd never been good at the limbo. Too hyper. Never could take my time doing anything. Disentangling myself, I let the yellow ribbon float to the ground.

A turn of the doorknob and I stepped inside. I flicked on my flashlight and directed the beam to each corner of the room. Fingerprint powder covered every surface, even the dishes in the sink. Nothing appeared different from my first visit. One step inside and that annoying floorboard creaked, announcing to anyone inside that he wasn't alone.

Making my way to where I'd found the body, I took

special care not to touch anything. I chided myself about not wearing gloves. Even I should have known that a crime-solver wears gloves when visiting a crime scene. It was written in one of my helpful guides.

Pale moonlight filtered through the red curtains, casting the room in the strangest shade of gray I'd ever seen. I doubted anyone would find that color in a crayon box.

The bathroom beckoned. Shivers ran down my spine, and I considered changing my course of action. What were the chances of finding another body hanging from the shower? I shook off the feeling and proceeded, sighing with relief to see the stall empty.

I ran the beam over the walls, finally settling on the showerhead. Using a nearby hand towel, I grasped it firmly and tugged. It pulled farther away from the wall. I grinned.

No way a struggling body could've hung here and not pulled the plumbing free. Not even someone as small as Millie. She hadn't hanged herself. Someone had placed the body here after the fact.

A creak came from the front room.

I clicked off my flashlight and plastered my back to the wall. My ears strained. My heart thumped wildly. Praying against discovery, I held my breath.

Soft footsteps rasped against the worn vinyl of the trailer floor. I suddenly wished for the ski mask I'd tossed back into Joe's car. If seen, my hair would be a dead giveaway. I mentally kicked myself for using the word dead.

I closed my eyes, took another deep breath, and hurled myself from the bathroom. My feet tangled in a discarded towel and I toppled forward. The fall to the floor sent a spasm of pain through my shoulder. My feet slipped as

I struggled to stand. The footsteps were no longer soft. Someone pounded toward me.

My skidding feet reminded me of a cartoon where the feet move but the character doesn't. Once I managed to get back inside the safety of the bathroom, I slammed the door closed and tried to engage the lock. It wouldn't hold.

The footsteps stopped. The knob turned. With a shriek, I shoved the door open. The impact sent the person behind it slamming into the wall. With a speed born of fear and self-preservation, I sprinted down the short hall and out the front door.

My breath labored, but I fought against it, not stopping until I found shelter behind the arts and crafts building. *Thank You, God.* I searched for my aunt. She sat on a stump surrounded by a mob of caring people.

She played the injured woman to the hilt, grasping her hip and moaning. Once I felt I could breathe without gasping, I made my way to her side. It was now my turn at acting.

"Aunt Eunice, are you all right? What happened?"

"Summer." There were actually tears in my aunt's eyes. "I'll need help getting back to the booth."

"When you didn't come back, I got so worried." Putting a hand beneath her arm, I helped her to her feet. "Thank you all for taking such good care of her." Murmurs of well-wishing followed us into the building.

"You can stop limping now," I said as I released her.

"No, I can't. I hurt my hip when I fell. Must have landed on a rock." She lowered herself gingerly into a nearby chair.

"You aren't faking?" Now I felt horrible. In no way had I wanted Aunt Eunice to actually hurt herself.

"Just tell me this new bruise will be worth it." Aunt Eunice raised eager eyes to mine.

I glanced around to ensure no one paid attention to us. "I know Millie didn't hang herself. Even as small as she was, there's no way she could have hung from the shower without pulling it completely away from the wall." Leaning against the door, I put a hand to my chest. "Someone almost caught me. I've never been more terrified in my life."

"Who was it?"

I shrugged. "I slammed someone into the wall and ran." I groaned. "Ethan is going to kill me. They're going to know someone was in the trailer, and I'll be the first one Joe suspects."

"You do have a way of meddling." Aunt Eunice pushed to her feet. "Let's get back to the booth and pretend we've been there the entire time. Lord forgive me, but I can lie with the best of them if I have to."

14

Ethan and Joe entered the booth. Neither said a word, just stood like sentries, arms folded, legs spread. Their absence of expression reminded me in an odd way of British palace guards. A fine sheen of perspiration dotted my upper lip. Maybe Aunt Eunice could lie, but I couldn't. My face gave me away every time.

Deciding avoidance would be the best protection against a third-degree grilling, I acted busy and rearranged candy in the refrigerator. Aunt Eunice kept up a nervous chatter behind me.

"Hello, boys. Are you here to buy or just take up space, 'cause our space is valuable."

Joe grunted.

"Okay. Well, then, if you ain't buying, you need to move. You're blocking the booth from prospective customers."

I peeked beneath my arm to get a look at the line of customers. No one waited, and neither man so much as twitched a muscle. They resembled very stern statues. Aunt Eunice propped her fists on her hips.

"Look, Joe. Just because you are a member of the police force doesn't give you the right to barge in here and terrorize innocent people."

Oh, boy. Aunt Eunice was going to spill the beans with her attempt at lying.

"Get your head out of the refrigerator, Summer. I need to ask you a few questions." Joe's voice was colder than the air spilling from the appliance.

I turned, banged my head on the door, and bit my tongue. "I'm busy."

"I need to know where you were for the past half hour." Joe unfolded his arms and rubbed a hand over his head.

"Right here," Aunt Eunice answered.

"Then why did Eddy Foreman just inform me you collapsed outside the back door?" Joe sighed.

"I just stepped out for a minute. No law against that, is there?"

"There is if you were covering for Summer so she could contaminate a crime scene."

"I didn't contaminate anything." I closed the door and rubbed the tender spot on the crown of my head.

Ethan closed his eyes and gave a sigh that rivaled Joe's. Joe pressed his lips tightly together. His face turned crimson. He became this shade of red so often, Crayola ought to name a crayon Joe Red.

"Summer Meadows, do you mean to tell me that you did not go into Millie's trailer, ripping down crime scene tape in the process? And do you further mean to tell me that you did not bang the bathroom door against the wall, leaving a big hole?"

Why would he suspect me? Aunt Eunice. She hadn't been exactly subtle with her distraction. Or myself for that matter. Getting tangled in the crime scene tape hadn't helped. My cousin knew me too well. I collapsed in a stool. "I didn't touch anything. The yellow tape got tangled in my hair. Okay, I might have touched that getting loose, but that's it. Oh, and the doorknob." I held up a hand. "But I used a towel to yank on the showerhead, so there shouldn't be any fingerprints."

The color of Joe's face intensified. "You yanked on the showerhead?"

"Look. Instead of interrogating me, you might be more interested in knowing someone else was in there and tried to kill me."

"Tried to kill you?"

"Stop repeating everything I say!"

"I made a simple request. One little request. And just because someone came in, where you weren't supposed to be, by the way, doesn't mean they tried to kill you."

"Joe, take a deep breath before you have a heart attack." Aunt Eunice laid a hand on his arm.

"You knew I was up to something, Joe, or you wouldn't have offered me the ski mask." There. I had him on that one.

"I was joking!" He rolled his eyes toward the ceiling. "Lord, take me now. Take me home right this instant." He turned to Ethan. "You do something with her."

Ethan shook his head. "She's hopeless."

Okay, time to switch tactics back to my life being in peril. "Does either of you care that someone tried to kill me? I know I mentioned this before, but the two of you don't seem bothered in the slightest."

"Fine. But I'm looking for a new job the first chance I get." Joe pulled a small spiral notepad out of his pocket. "Okay, shoot."

"Please don't use that word."

"Get on with it. Did you see the person who tried to kill you? Did they have a weapon? Was it a man or a woman?" He held a pen poised over the pad.

"No, and I don't know. I slammed them into the wall. That's probably how the hole got there."

"You slammed them into the wall. How do you know they wanted to kill you? Maybe they wanted to find out why you were there."

"You're repeating again. They chased me. Anyway, I'm pretty certain Millie didn't hang herself. No way. She's about my size, and I was able to pull the showerhead away from the wall. And that was without a dead weight hanging on it."

"I don't want to hear this. You don't think I've already figured that out? The minute I walked into Millie's bathroom?" Joe glanced at Ethan. "I must have made God angry for Him to give me a cousin like this one."

To my horror, Joe unclipped a set of handcuffs from his belt. "I hate to do this, Summer, but I warned you."

"Ethan?" I leaped to my feet and plastered my back to the wall.

"Joe, put those away." Aunt Eunice, bless her heart, stepped in front of me.

"I've got two sets of cuffs, Aunt Eunice. You're an accomplice. I'm taking you in with her."

Her mouth dropped open. "You have got to be kidding. Roy, do something."

"I can't meddle with law enforcement, Eunice." Uncle Roy patted my aunt's shoulder. "I'll be down to bail you out in the morning. I'll have to use the money we've been saving for a cruise."

"You're going to wait until morning? Our cruise money?" Aunt Eunice crossed her arms. "I ain't staying in no jail through the night. You know the type that frequents those places."

"You mean like you and Summer?" Joe smiled a grin worthy of the most evil of villains. The cuffs clinked in his hands.

Not knowing what else to do, I did the best thing I could think of and bolted for the door. Ethan's arm snaked out and wrapped around my waist. He lifted me off the floor. "No fleeing the law, Summer."

Aunt Eunice grabbed a handful of brochures from the counter and tossed them in our direction. Not much of a weapon, but I couldn't blame her for trying.

"Let go of her!"

"Now, Eunice." Uncle Roy stepped behind her and folded his arms around her waist, pinning her arms to her sides. "These boys are doing what has to be done. It's for your own good."

"Get off me! You'll be sleeping on the couch for a month. If we had a doghouse, you'd be in it." She struggled against him.

"Well, I know where Summer gets her spunk." Ethan's breath stirred my hair. Raising a knee, I mule-kicked him in the shin and got a great deal of satisfaction from his grunt.

By this time, we'd attracted a great number of spectators. Glancing around at the wide-eyed people enjoying the show on our behalf, I stopped squirming. Fine, I'd allow Joe to lock me up. Not one more word would leave my lips in conversation with Joe or Ethan. The thought pained me. Almost as much as the ache in my heart at their turning against me.

So I'd ducked under some crime tape. Big deal. There was a murderer loose, and Joe wasted his time on me and Aunt Eunice. If I *were* speaking to him, I'd give him a piece of my mind.

Instead, I stuck my nose in the air, waited for Ethan to release me, then held out my hands for the cuffs. With a questioning look in my direction, Aunt Eunice did the same.

"Summer, I—" Ethan tried to take my hands, and I turned away.

Maybe I was being unreasonable. Maybe I was acting childish. I didn't care. My heart ached. If my hands weren't busy being secured, I would have clutched my chest. The cold steel of the cuffs cut into my wrists. Did Joe have to clamp them so tight? Where was I going to go? At least my hands weren't behind my back.

Tears welled in my eyes, and I blinked them away. Aunt Eunice sniffled beside me. A glance at Ethan was almost my undoing. You'd think he was the one going to jail, he looked so hurt. Good. A part of me wanted him to suffer on my behalf. The other part wanted to hide from the world in his strong arms.

Joe took me by the elbow and led me through the throng of people. "Uncle Roy, work the booth, would you?" I yelled over my shoulder. We might as well make some money off the crowd's curiosity. An arrest always seemed like good publicity for celebrities; why not me?

My steps halted before the rear door of Joe's squad car. "No way. I am absolutely not getting in the back of this car. Aunt Eunice, tell Joe I know what kind of stuff gets on the plastic seats of squad cars."

"Tell him yourself. I'm not speaking to him."

I stared at her. "Neither am I."

Joe groaned. "I'm standing right here. I can hear you." He strode to his trunk, unlocked it, and pulled out a faded quilt. "Y'all sit on this. I keep it for the lucky days I'm on a nighttime stakeout. Alone and away from people."

I bit my lip against the thank-you that good manners

warranted and stared straight ahead. When he placed a hand on my head to help me duck into the car, I jerked away. My forehead collided with the doorframe. Stars exploded before my eyes. Great. A knot to go with the one on the top of my head. Through tears of pain, I stared out the window to where Ethan stood.

Where was my knight in shining armor? Why did he just stand there instead of rescuing me? Aunt Eunice sniffed again and raised her hands in a good-bye gesture to Uncle Roy. He promised again to pick us up in the morning.

Joe slid into the front seat, started the ignition, then drove out of the fairgrounds. Aunt Eunice glared at me from the other side of the backseat.

"What?" Her unblinking gaze made me squirm.

"This is all your fault," she hissed. "Joe warned you not to break the law."

"You were all for it earlier, Aunt Eunice." I couldn't believe this. Now even my sidekick was against me.

Thankfully, the ride to the small brick building housing Mountain Shadows's police department only took fifteen minutes. The chill flowing from Aunt Eunice could've had icicles hanging from my ears.

We parked, and Joe reached in to help me out, but I shrugged him off. Still smarting from him arresting me, I slid from the car and stalked into the building. Like a common criminal, I bowed my head to not make eye contact with any of the other officers. Men and women I'd grown up with.

Joe released us from the cuffs and ushered us into a small room where a stony-faced woman rolled my fingers across a black ink pad. Then she handed me a wet citrus-scented napkin. I scrubbed at my fingertips while they did the same to my aunt. *Please don't let them take our picture.* I could only imagine what my hair looked like.

My cousin grabbed our elbows again. Laughs and gasps of amazement followed as he led my aunt and me to an empty cell. Three concrete walls and another consisting of bars was home to a plastic bench that ran along two of the walls, one sink, and a seatless toilet. Depression settled over my shoulders like a tidal wave crashing on the beach. I perched on the bench. Aunt Eunice plopped next to me with rounded shoulders. We lifted our hands for Joe to unlock the cuffs.

"I'll be back later for the two of you to sign papers. You've been through enough for now." Gone was the happy-go-lucky man I'd grown up with. This Joe looked carved from wood. Unsmiling and unfeeling. Okay, maybe his statement showed a little compassion toward us, but not much.

The cell next to us contained four women. Two had the largest biceps I've ever seen on a female, and they made crude comments that made me blush. The other two wore so much makeup they looked as if they belonged in Foreman's carnival.

I felt overcome with contrition. The Lord asks us to love our fellow man, or woman, as in this case. Those women were probably some of the nicest people I'd want to know. Then I changed my mind when the comments grew raunchier.

"I'm scared." Aunt Eunice scooted closer to me. "That one big woman is staring at me."

"I'm sorry, Aunt Eunice." My tears fell. "I'm so sorry for getting you into this mess. You're right." I wiped my face on my sleeve. "Joe warned me about breaking the law. My problem is, I don't stop to think about the consequences. If I would've stopped, if I would've taken the time to think things through. . ." My words choked on a sob.

Aunt Eunice put an arm around my shoulder. "You would have done the same thing. Problem with people is, most of them don't think. You oughta change that within yourself."

What about her? I wasn't alone in my breaking the law. "I can't believe Joe actually locked us up." I wiped my eyes on my sleeve.

"More for his peace of mind than anything would be my guess. He's a good boy. Just doing his job. I'm sorry for encouraging you, sweetie. I'm older. I ought to know better."

That's for sure. I shrugged. "You didn't force me, Aunt Eunice." Ethan's betrayal hurt the most. The only thing that kept me from anger was the glance I'd gotten of his eyes swimming with tears. This bench wouldn't feel so hard if my head were on his shoulder rather than Aunt Eunice's resting on mine. The concrete wall would be warmer with his arms around me. If Ethan were here, I could block out the obscene comments from the cell next door.

15

Darkness, backlit by the yellow glow of a night-light, welcomed me when I opened my eyes. Aunt Eunice slept propped against me, an idea I'd jumped at. The thought of lying prostrate on the hard plastic had been unappealing. Who knew what might have made its home among the flecks of peeling gray paint?

How did I come to this, Lord? All I wanted to do was solve this case, find out who followed me in the gorilla suit, and prevent any more people from getting hurt. If I had to bend a few rules to do so, what did it really matter in the grand scheme of things?

Aunt Eunice snorted in her sleep, and I shifted, trying to relieve the weight from my numb bottom half. My arm tingled from lack of circulation. When I tried to raise it to see the time, I remembered they'd taken my watch. My watch, my jewelry, my beautiful engagement ring, all my personal belongings, and shoved them into an ugly yellow envelope.

My fingertips still showed traces of ink from being fingerprinted, the pads darker than the rest of my hand when I held it up in the weak light. Now I had a record. I was officially a criminal. How could Joe do this to me?

He'd threatened to so many times, but I figured he never would. Kind of like crying wolf. And he must have hatched the plan with Ethan. The man who professed to love me hadn't said a word in my defense.

A shadow moved. As if I'd conjured him with my thoughts, Ethan stepped forward and gripped the bars of my cell. Forgetting his betrayal, I leaped from the bench. Aunt Eunice fell over in a slump.

"Ethan!"

He poked his hands between the bars and gripped mine. "Are you all right?"

"We'd all be better, sweetie, if you were in here with us," a voice from the neighboring cell replied.

A muscle twitched in Ethan's jaw.

"I'm fine." And I was. "Can I leave now?"

"I don't know. I've been sitting in the waiting room. I just couldn't go home with you in here."

"Ah, ain't that sweet?" Someone laughed.

"It's not your fault, Ethan. It's Joe's."

A dimple winked from Ethan's cheek, brightening the gloom of my cell. "Sweetheart, it's no one's fault but your own. Joe asked you over and over to stay out of things. He gave you more chances than he would have anyone else." He squeezed my hands. "We're afraid for you. Plus, it's his job. It killed him to drag you here in cuffs. April is livid. She's threatened not to speak to him for weeks."

I couldn't help but think being locked in here with my best friend would be preferable to Aunt Eunice. April and I would laugh about it afterwards, maybe. Make it into an adventure. Embellish the facts and make light of the situation. Aunt Eunice would only find Bible verses that applied, making me feel guiltier than I already did.

A few choice verses on forgiveness came to mind, and I brushed them away. I'd work on that later, when I *wasn't* incarcerated.

"What time is it? Joe took my watch."

"It's three thirty." He rubbed his thumb over the top of my hands. "Look, there's a chair over there. I'll sit where you can see me until you're released."

"Don't be silly. You don't have to do that. Go home and get some sleep."

"I want to go with you." Ethan released me and lowered himself into a straight-backed chair. His silhouette provided a dark contrast against the colorless wall. Knowing he watched over me, my personal guardian angel, I stepped back to my aunt. After resuming my position as her pillow, I nodded off to sleep.

It amazed me the next morning as I strolled toward our candy booth how little the carnies cared that we'd been arrested. They waved, some cheered, but most acted as if arrest was a daily occurrence. I shrugged. Maybe it was.

When Joe released me, he'd made me promise not to go by Millie's trailer, or disappear without letting someone know where I would be, or go nosing around any place that looked dangerous. He might as well lock me back up. However reluctantly, I promised. Another night in jail didn't appeal to me.

The temperature continued to rise in the fabricated arts and crafts building as we celebrated a day of Indian summer weather. Plucking at my sweater, I wished I'd worn a T-shirt. "I'm going to step out for a breath of fresh air."

Aunt Eunice waved a hand to let me know she'd heard and turned back to the customer. The back door pushed open with a squeak.

A light breeze blew between the building and trailers. I lifted my hair off my neck. Hushed voices drifted from around the corner. With the stealth born from a childhood of sneaking cookies from the kitchen after bedtime, I moved toward them.

My eyes narrowed. Washington Bean and another carny I didn't know stood huddled beneath an awning. Their words were too faint to hear. The carny handed Washington some money, and Washington pulled something from his pocket. I stretched my neck, straining to see, and tripped over a wooden crate. After I landed in an undignified heap, I rubbed my smarting shin.

"Miss Meadows, you all right?" Washington bent over me.

I grasped his offered hand and allowed him to pull me to my feet. "Yes, thank you. Another example of me not looking where I'm going."

"You're probably just tired after your experience last night, that's all." He turned the crate over and lowered me onto it. "I know I'm always beat after a night in the slammer."

"How many times have you spent the night in jail?" My heart hammered against my rib cage.

"My fair share, Miss Meadows. Less than some people, more than others."

"Do you sell drugs, Washington?"

"No, ma'am!" His eyes widened. "That stuff will kill you. What you want to know about something like that?"

"No reason." If he wasn't selling drugs, what could it be? Of course, I knew he could be lying. If he was, he deserved an Academy Award.

"Thank you for your help." I stood. "I'd best be getting back to the booth." I turned and limped back into the building.

Once inside, I plopped on a stool and raised the leg

of my pants. Blood trickled from the scrape, staining the top of my socks red.

"What did you do now?" Aunt Eunice planted her fists on her hips. "That needs to be cleaned. You'd better get over to the first aid tent."

"I didn't *do* anything. I tripped over a crate." Now that I'd seen the blood, my leg hurt more. "I'll get a bandage before my pants are ruined."

The walk across the fairgrounds never seemed so long. Exhaustion, the result of a sleepless night, wore at me as if I struggled through thick mud. My shin throbbed, and self-pity threatened. By the time I reached the first aid tent, I was near tears. Sometimes being emotional could be a real hindrance.

When I entered the tent, I almost turned and fled. Instead, I froze in the doorway. A man sat on a tattered couch. He groaned as his hands clutched a foot covered with a blood-saturated bandage. A woman knelt beside him.

"That stupid elephant. She ought to be shot."

"It's fine, Harvey. The ambulance is on its way." The woman laid a hand on his arm.

"It's not fine. I'll probably lose my foot. That's the most cantankerous animal I've ever met. And to think they let little kids look at her. It's only a matter of time before someone gets killed."

"Excuse me?" I didn't dare venture any closer to the man and his blood. "Are you talking about Ginger?"

"You see another elephant around these parts?" The man squinted at me. "Oh, it's you, Miss Summer, the one who walked Ginger here. What do you have, a death wish?"

He shook his head. "I never could figure out why they'd have a greenhorn walk that death trap of a beast." He groaned again and grabbed at his foot. "I ought to sue. You'd think Ginger would have been happy to be fed, wouldn't you? No, sir. Not her. Decided to knock me down and roll me around like a child's ball. Then stepped on my foot. Playing with me, they said. I'll give them playing. Bet Foreman will cancel that particular attraction now, won't he. Oh, my foot. Where's that ambulance?"

A siren wailed in the distance. Its sound rose above the tinny music of the amusement rides. I ventured closer. "I'm so sorry about your foot. Did y'all hear about the lion getting loose? He ended up at my place. About a mile from here."

"Yeah, and that's the strangest thing. His cage was locked up tighter than a drum. I've told Foreman time after time that county fairs don't have wild animals. The man won't listen. Only a matter of time before he gets sued. Mark my words." Harvey clutched at the other woman's hand as paramedics rushed into the trailer. I limped out of the way.

With his free hand, Harvey reached for mine. "Don't do anyone else any more favors, little girl. Think about it. Nothing makes any sense. I've been a friend of your uncle's from way back. Even knew your daddy before he died. Roy's told me what's been going on. Told me to keep an eye on you. I can't do that while I'm gone. Ya hear?"

I nodded and pulled free. His grip had left a blood smear on my hand. With a grimace, I scrubbed it on the thigh of my pants. What did Harvey know about me? Why his spine-tingling warning? I was definitely living in a B-horror movie. If a hag with a wart on her nose showed up, I'd be out of there. With my luck, it'd be a hag with a chain saw.

"May I help you?"

I turned to face an elderly woman in nursing scrubs. No wart. Her kind face put me at ease, and I lifted my pant leg.

"We can take care of that in a jiffy. Have a seat in this room back here."

Twenty minutes later, a clean bandage on my leg, I headed back toward the arts and crafts building. Ginger thundered along the fence of her paddock and trumpeted in my direction. I quickened my limping pace, not wanting to be anywhere near an elephant as unstable as a pit bull.

I halted. Near the restrooms, Washington stood in a whispered conversation with a woman. Money exchanged hands. If I were speaking to my cousin, this might be something worthy to report.

Washington glanced up and locked gazes with me. He smiled, and my blood ran cold. As fast as my injured leg would allow, I rushed back to the safety of the candy booth.

"Took you long enough," Aunt Eunice retorted. She studied my face. "What's the matter? You look pale as a ghost."

Perched on the stool, I rested my elbows on my knees. "Does Uncle Roy know a man by the name of Harvey that works here?"

"Sure he does. Harvey Coons. They were pals in school." Aunt Eunice took a chocolate hot air balloon out of the refrigerator and handed it to a customer. "Harvey never did much with his life. Had a father who drank too much. A mother who took off when he was eight. But

Roy and him stayed friends. Why?"

"I saw him at the first aid tent. Ginger broke his foot." I gnawed my lower lip before continuing. "He said Uncle Roy asked him to look out for me. Then he gave me a warning. Said not to do anyone any favors. Said there's something fishy about me being asked to walk Ginger, and about the lion ending up at our place. It is weird that they asked me to walk Ginger, but I figured, with Sally in the truck following, it was no big deal. Do you think there could have been an ulterior motive?"

Aunt Eunice turned to face me. "Like what?"

"Like maybe Ginger was supposed to kill me?"

16

Aunt Eunice slumped against the counter. "I thought Big Sally seemed like such a nice woman, too."

"Maybe it wasn't her idea. Someone could have suggested it to her. She isn't the brightest star in the sky and with her weight, it *is* difficult to get around. Probably seemed like a good idea. Some people are too trusting." Like me, for instance. "We were lucky Ginger liked me."

"You mean *you* were lucky."

"Gee, thanks." My body sagged from exhaustion. "After last night, all I want to do is go to bed. I had a hard time sleeping on that bench."

"I didn't have any trouble at all. But my back is paining me something awful." She placed both hands on her lower back and arched.

"Let's close up and go home. Get a nap."

"Sounds like a great idea." I locked the refrigerator, grabbed my purse, then followed Aunt Eunice to my car. My eyes were gritty from lack of sleep, and I was grateful I had only a mile to drive.

Once in bed, snuggled beneath a thick quilt, I lay flat on my back and stared unblinkingly at the ceiling. A breeze outside cast shadows through the branches of a tree, and I watched the changing patterns on the plaster over my bed. Never good at taking naps, the bright sunlight streaming through the windows sent sleep to the farthest recesses of my mind. Images of Joe's face clicked across my thoughts like the spool of an old-time movie reel.

A sigh rose from deep within me. The hurt of what

I perceived to be betrayal threatened to fester within me. But sleep wouldn't come without forgiveness. Hurt feelings or not, I'd have to forgive Joe for doing his job. The thought galled me.

I flounced onto my side. The quilt stifled me, and I tossed it to the foot of the bed. When rest continued to elude me, I rose, got dressed, and headed back outside.

Behind the wheel of my car, I blinked against the gritty feeling behind my eyelids. There had to be something better than facing Joe at the station. All those officers staring. Smirking behind their desks. I shuddered and closed my eyes. My head fell back against the headrest.

A rap on the window caused my eyes to shoot open, and a squeak escaped me. Joe peered in.

I pushed the window button and rolled it down. "You scared me half to death, Joe."

"Why are you sleeping in the car?" He was out of uniform. *Thank You, God, I didn't go to the station.*

"I'm not sleeping. I was on my way to see you." I shoved the door open. He jumped back.

"Thought I'd save you the trip." His gaze flickered toward his truck. Ethan grinned from the passenger side. My man knew me so well.

Although I felt manipulated, something that normally caused my hackles to rise, I was too tired to put up a fight. "Y'all come on in. There's coffee left."

They followed me inside without speaking and took seats at the kitchen table. "Since Ethan got you here, Joe, did he happen to tell you why you needed to come?"

"Said you had something you wanted to tell me." Joe twirled an empty mug between his hands. "I figured it had to be important, so I came over on my day off. I'm taking

April to the movies later, so I don't have a lot of time."

God, You aren't going to make this easy on me, are You? I lifted the coffeepot and poured the aromatic liquid into our mugs.

Joe lifted his mug to his lips, and I blurted out what I wanted to say. "I forgive you for arresting me."

Coffee spewed from his mouth. He lifted a napkin from a basket in the center of the table and wiped his mouth. "Excuse me?"

"I. Forgive. You. For arresting me." Feeling immensely better, I sipped my coffee.

"For arresting you? You forgive me for doing my job after I warned you countless times?" Joe shook his head. "You beat all, Summer. You really do. I should have done that months ago."

"For what?" This was not going the way I'd planned.

"The same thing." Setting his mug on the table, Joe leaned forward. "Look. I know you're eager to help solve this case. Just like the jewelry theft and murder in July, but you go about it all wrong. You contaminate every crime scene you come in contact with. You consistently put your life in danger, and you won't leave things alone when I ask you to. This is my *job*. I happen to be good at it. And I could be better if I wasn't saving you every waking moment of the day."

He pushed back his chair and stood. "I'm happy you forgive me. I accept. Now, I've got to go."

I didn't bother to rise. I pictured me soccer kicking his head across the room. Working on my attitude needed to become a priority. *Fine.* "I'm sorry for making your job harder. I know having me for a cousin isn't easy."

Joe laughed. "No, Summer, it isn't." He clapped my shoulder and left.

Nobody asked my permission before burying the diamonds beneath my rosebush a few months ago. Or stashing the money in my tree house. Or breaking into my home. My consent hadn't been given when Nate kidnapped and almost shot me. No more than I'd asked to find Laid Back Millie's body.

Maybe out of ignorance I'd touched things I shouldn't have, not called the police when I should've, and been in the wrong place at the wrong time. Again, these things could happen to anyone. Right? Everyone made mistakes. I was in a learning process.

"What's on your mind?" Ethan scooted his chair close to me and brushed a strand of hair away from my face.

"That didn't go how I planned." I stared into my mug at the light-colored liquid. Should have let it perk longer.

"You thought he'd be grateful. That he'd say thank you."

"Yes. Instead he seemed aggravated." I leaned my head on Ethan's shoulder.

"Come on." He stood and pulled me to my feet. "Let's go into the living room. We'll be more comfortable."

Like a docile puppy, I allowed myself to be led. Ethan lowered me onto the floral-patterned sofa before sitting next to me. He put a pillow in his lap and pulled my head to rest on the chenille fabric. It was heaven against my cheek. My tired body went liquid.

Ethan smoothed my hair, his hand moving from my head to my shoulders in one relaxing movement. "You scare Joe, Summer. You frighten everyone who loves you. The way you get yourself into fixes. Joe may be your cousin, but he cares for you like a brother." His stomach rose with his deep breath.

"I don't ask for trouble."

He chuckled. "Maybe not, but you love it anyway. The attention. The excitement. You caught a bug last July that burrowed under your skin and won't leave."

Ethan was right. The thrill I got from getting close to an answer defied description. And I was improving. The clues came faster this time. The answers easier.

Yet something else nagged at me. Tugged, urged me on. There was another reason solving these crimes meant so much. Not to prove I wasn't stupid, nor to solve a stranger's murder, but I didn't know what it was. And asking God why frightened me.

I stared into Ethan's face. He gave me a crooked smile, melting my heart.

"I'll quit if you ask. I'll buy special crime-repelling bug spray. Right now. This instant. All you have to do is ask."

He leaned forward and kissed me. "I know. And I won't. Doesn't do any good, anyway. Just be careful, and don't break any laws. You put Joe in a tough spot when you do."

My eyelids grew heavier and closed.

I woke to a room cast in shadows. My head still rested in Ethan's lap, and soft snores issued from his slightly open mouth. Low murmurs drifted from the kitchen. I yawned and sat up to stare through the dim light at Ethan's face.

The moon's glow highlighted the stubble on his jaw. To think that someday I'd have complete access to his lips, anytime I wanted, warmed my insides. My gaze shifted to the square of light coming from the kitchen. As protective as Uncle Roy is, it's a wonder he'd allowed me to sleep with my head in Ethan's lap.

"What time is it?" Ethan's voice was raspy from sleep.

"I don't know. My aunt and uncle are in the kitchen. Do you want to join them?"

He gave me a slow, lazy smile. My stomach flipped. "Not really, but we probably should. Before Roy gets his gun."

I'd much rather remain where I was, secure in Ethan's love, relishing his touch, but I knew the wise choice of action. Unfolding my legs, I rose and held out my hand. "Let's join my aunt and uncle. Where it's safe."

Aunt Eunice and Uncle Roy sat nursing cups of coffee. My aunt's gray curls stuck in all directions around her face. Uncle Roy looked glum.

"What's up?" I reached for the coffeepot.

Uncle Roy sighed. "Your aunt just told me y'all's suspicions about that elephant. Sure wish I would've been here. I would have told you straightaway not to walk it to the fairground. Sometimes you ain't got a lick of sense." He raised his head to stare at my face. "You're too sweet, Summer. Too kind. Easily taken advantage of. The world ain't a safe place."

"You would've done the same thing, Uncle Roy. Someone needs your help, you're there. It's as simple as that." I lowered myself into a chair and gratefully accepted a mug of coffee from Ethan, this time brewed to perfection.

"What suspicions?" Ethan asked.

"Eunice and Summer seem to think the carnies asked her on purpose to walk that animal. That someone hoped she'd be hurt—or worse."

Ethan sat in a chair next to me and placed his arm along the back of my chair. "It would have to be a pretty elaborate plan, don't you think? They'd have to stage the accident."

"Not if they just took advantage of things when they happened. Saw the opportunity and took it. Animals can be unpredictable. They aren't all as sweet as our Truly here." Uncle Roy slurped his drink and scratched behind the dog's ear with his free hand.

"Still pretty far-fetched. After staging the accident, they'd have to be certain it would be Summer that found Millie's body. If that was their plan, they wouldn't want her killed or injured."

"What if they didn't want me to find Millie? If I hadn't walked Ginger, I probably wouldn't have." I pushed my coffee away. My stomach churned. Thoughts of my possible demise churned the abdominal acids. Thoughts swirled in a circle, making no sense.

Ethan cocked an eyebrow. "Maybe. But still risky. Animals are unpredictable. There was no guarantee things would work out a certain way."

Aunt Eunice rose from her chair. "I still say there's more to this than meets the eye. As soon as that carnival got to town, Summer's been in one scrape after another. And this time she didn't go looking for trouble."

She placed her mug in the sink. Something out the window caught Aunt Eunice's gaze. She parted the curtains. "But trouble sure did find her."

Three chairs scraped back in unison. Truly's ears rose with the screech of wood against linoleum. Ethan, my uncle, and I dashed to the window.

"Who is that?" Uncle Roy asked. "Bigfoot?"

"That, Uncle Roy, is my gorilla friend." He or she melted into the shadows.

Aunt Eunice stomped to the phone. "I'm calling Joe. A person can't get any peace around here, what with Bigfoot, gorillas, elephants, and lions."

I couldn't help but add, "Oh my."

"It's all just scare tactics," Ethan stated. "It's the same as my students at school. They square off with someone, jerk their body or head at them, have a stare-down contest. Whatever they think it will take to intimidate the other person."

"You don't think I should be worried?" I let the curtain fall back into place.

"I think you should be very worried. That's why I'll be camping out on the sofa." Ethan glared at Uncle Roy, daring him to argue.

I giggled. Last summer the two men had a standoff when Ethan brought in a sleeping bag and spent the night in the front room. Uncle Roy, mindful of my reputation, had forbidden it. Both of them ended up sleeping downstairs.

"Guess I will, too, then. And I'll be sharing my sleeping bag with my rifle." Uncle Roy headed upstairs.

By the time my cousin arrived, Uncle Roy sat in a

straight-backed chair beside the door, rifle across his lap. Joe entered the kitchen and rolled his eyes.

"Aren't you going to go have a look around?" Uncle Roy demanded.

"I've got men covering it. Don't worry. I know how to do my job." Joe headed straight for the coffeepot. "Has your visitor tried making contact?"

"No." I snuggled closer beneath Ethan's arm. "They never do."

Java poured, Joe leaned against the counter. "I hate when the fair comes to town. We have more fights than the rest of the year combined. And why so long? Almost two weeks this year. Mountain Shadows's police are stretched thin enough. I don't suppose I can get y'all to go to a hotel for a few days?"

"Nope," Uncle Roy stated.

"Didn't think so." He lifted his mug again.

This was July all over again. Except this time, my "friend" stayed in the shadows. No one had attempted to enter the house, God forbid they should set the place on fire, and Uncle Roy remained adamant about not being run off his property. Strangely enough, I didn't feel threatened. Not with Ethan's arm around my shoulders, Uncle Roy keeping guard, and God watching from above.

Joe peered at us over the rim of his cup. "I could insist, you know. Make y'all leave."

"I'd like to see you try." Uncle Roy shifted his gun.

"Roy, are you threatening an officer of the law?" Joe's eyes widened.

"No, I'm telling my whippersnapper of a nephew what's what. Short of arresting me, you won't get me to run from my home."

The corner of Ethan's mouth twitched. My family was a never-ending source of amusement for him. Unlike some engaged couples, there was never a problem getting Ethan to visit my family.

"Think of the women, Roy," Joe continued. "They're in danger here."

"They can leave if they want." He stared straight ahead.

"I'm staying." Aunt Eunice stepped beside her husband.

Not to be undone, I raised my hand. "No one has tried to harm me. I'm staying, too."

Joe turned toward me. "You don't call a dead armadillo in your refrigerator or being stuck on top of the Ferris wheel, someone trying to harm you?"

I glanced up at Ethan and smiled. "Just scare tactics." Joe's face reddened, and I continued. "Look, Joe. I appreciate your concern. I've promised you I wouldn't put myself in harm's way. I won't go anywhere alone or question anyone about Millie's death. I'll be boring Summer. The carnival leaves town in a couple of days. We'll just wait it out."

"There's more going on here than someone in a gorilla suit following you!" Joe thunked his cup on the counter. "If y'all want to be stubborn and foolish, fine. God looks out for the fools, the Good Book says. Well, good luck." With those parting words, Joe stormed out of the kitchen. The front door slammed.

What did he mean something else was going on? How did he honestly believe I could stay out of things when he dropped a bombshell of information like that? That's like dangling a meaty bone in front of a dog. He only whetted my appetite. The man played completely unfair.

Ethan stood. His arm slid from my shoulders. "I'd

best be getting home to get my things. Summer, do you feel up to a ride?"

No need to ask twice. "Let me grab a jacket."

Ethan waited on the front porch and greeted me with a smile. "As wonderful as it was, I shouldn't have fallen asleep. I've still got papers to grade."

"I'd love to help."

We crunched across the gravel driveway and made our way to Ethan's truck. He held the passenger door for me, and I slid inside. The interior smelled like him: the musky cologne he wore and a scent as individual as the man I loved. I drew in a deep breath.

I lived three point four miles from Ethan. A country night is dark. Inky black with a blanket of stars in the sky. Not having grown up in the city, I couldn't give a fair comparison, but I'd have to say, the country was the only place for me. "I love it here."

I could feel Ethan's gaze on me. "Good thing. Because I don't want to move."

With my head on the seat, I rolled to look at him. "Would you move if I wanted?"

"In a heartbeat." He started the ignition and backed the truck from the drive.

"You're so good to me."

"I hope you feel the same after we're married. After the hundredth time of the toilet seat being left up, or the toothpaste cap not being put back on."

"You don't put the cap back on the toothpaste?"

"I do. Just testing you."

We hit the outskirts of town. Ethan lived in a small house with April, and he drove down the alley toward his driveway. I gazed out the window. "Wait. Slow down." I straightened.

Washington Bean dug through a Dumpster behind our local bookstore, Grandma's Books.

"Joe's going to have a fit if he finds out we have vagrants in Mountain Shadows." Ethan drove past and parked.

"That isn't a vagrant. He's a carny." I shoved open the truck door and slid off the seat. Keeping the truck between myself and the Dumpster, I kept my gaze glued to Washington.

"Why are we spying?" Ethan stepped to my side.

"Several times I witnessed Washington exchange money, and sometimes something else, with either a carny or a townsperson. Now he's digging through garbage cans. I've also noticed he dresses better than most of the carnival workers I've met. How much do you think a handyman at a carnival makes?"

"Not a lot." Ethan's breath tickled my neck.

"Step back. I can't concentrate."

"Really?" He kissed me below the ear. "Why?"

I flicked a hand in his direction. "Stop. Seriously. Washington is up to something fishy, and I want to know what it is."

"Okay. What do you want to do? Follow him?"

With eagerness, I turned in Ethan's arms. "Can we?"

Ethan rubbed his chin. "I guess so. Sure. It might be fun. But we stay far away. Joe doesn't need to be on my case, too."

"It *will* be fun. I promise." I grasped his hand and darted into the shadows across the alley. The idea of Ethan sleuthing with me had me floating on a cloud of excitement. My skin tingled. Maybe we could start our own business after we married. A crime-solving business called Banning Investigations.

Hunkered behind a pile of cardboard boxes, we waited until Washington closed the lid and shuffled away, his arms loaded with black bags of stuff.

"What do you think he has? He can't have gotten all that out of the garbage. Do you think he's been Dumpster diving all over town?"

"I can't tell what he has, why not, and I don't know." Ethan grabbed my hand. "Stay close to the building. Let's follow him."

"I'd like to see where he lives."

"We aren't going back to the fairground. And why do you want to know where the guy lives? Most likely a trailer with the others."

"I know that. But I'd like to see the inside. See if he's living better than his coworkers. He's selling something, and I'm not sure it's legal."

Ethan yanked me against a brick wall of the closest building. His outstretched arm kept me plastered against the rough surface. Washington stopped, dropped his bags, then searched through a Dumpster behind a small odds and ends shop.

A dog barked and Washington paused in his search. If not for the pale yellow shirt he wore, the ebony-skinned man would have melted into the shadows.

A squad car drove slowly past the alley. Washington ducked behind the Dumpster.

"Definitely up to no good," I whispered. Moving to see around Ethan, my foot brushed against an aluminum can and sent it rattling a few inches away.

Washington spun in our direction. Ethan squatted, yanking me with him. We held our breath and waited. Seconds later, Washington grabbed his bags and dashed down the alley.

"Sorry." I giggled.

"That was fun." Ethan pulled me to my feet. "Let's get my things." We stepped from the shadows and into the glow of a streetlamp.

"Thanks for coming along." I leaned into him.

"I can see why you're hooked. Being the natural nosy person you are, spying is right up your alley."

I opened my mouth to reply when a shout for help sliced through the night.

Sirens wailed.

18

We froze. My ears strained to hear where the cry originated. A car barreled down the alley and Ethan tackled me, knocking me out of the way. My head struck the curb. Stars danced before my eyes. A sharp throb started behind my temple and spread across my forehead.

Through the array of kaleidoscope colors, I noticed the pale face of a woman pressed against the glass of the car window, her mouth opened in a silent plea for help. She looked vaguely familiar. Hopefully, when my headache passed, I'd be able to remember where I'd seen her.

"Are you all right?" Ethan ran his hands over my arms.

"Besides the cracked skull, I'm peachy."

I stared down the alley. Where were the police? If I were a betting woman, I'd bet the cry for help and the sirens were connected. The taillights of the speeding vehicle disappeared around the corner.

My vision cleared, and I allowed Ethan to help me to my feet. My head spun and I clutched his arm for support.

He placed an arm around my waist. "Let's get you into the house. We need to take a look at your head. Hard as it is, you got quite a knock."

"We need to call the police. There's a woman in the car. She's clearly in distress. I think she's being taken against her will."

Ethan half-carried, half-pulled me into his home. April sat with a bowl of popcorn in her lap, watching a chick flick. Tears ran down her face.

"What happened?" She set the bowl on the coffee

table, wiped her face on her sleeve, then positioned herself under my free arm. They helped me to the sofa.

"I'm fine. Just a knock in the noggin. It would take more than that to stop me." My head ached, and my stomach churned. The bowl holding the popcorn might soon have another use.

Ethan chuckled. "Thank God for a hard cranium." He parted my hair with his hands. "Quite a goose egg. We should have you checked out. You might have a concussion."

"I'll get ice." April disappeared into the kitchen.

"Call the police, too," Ethan called after her.

"I'm fine. It isn't the first or last time I've been hit in the head." The room spun, and I sagged against the soft sofa cushions.

"Joe's coming." April slapped a plastic baggie wrapped in a paper towel to my forehead. I winced under her rough nursing.

"Don't go into nursing, girlfriend." I lifted a hand to hold the makeshift ice pack to my bump. "Your bedside manners could use improvement."

"Sorry." She sat cross-legged on the sofa next to me. Ethan lowered himself to the floor. April giggled. "Joe gave one of his famous sighs when I told him you were involved."

"Great."

"It's my fault." Ethan laid a hand on my knee. "I allowed you to go chasing down the alley. And it was me that knocked you down."

I grinned. "Admit it, you had fun."

"I can't believe you got my straight-laced brother to go sleuthing with you." April pulled a pillow onto her lap and wrapped her arms around the striped square.

"I'm not that bad." Ethan frowned. "I know how to have a good time."

"You *are* that bad, and don't suffer any illusions about knowing how to have fun. If it wasn't for Summer, you'd never loosen up."

"Okay, you two." I set the bowl on the table and leaned back. Pictures of the frightened woman flashed behind my eyelids the moment I closed my eyes.

The doorbell rang, followed immediately by the sound of the front door opening. Joe's voice carried through the room. "What happened now?" His question carried the weight of a long-suffering person.

Peering at him through barely opened lids, I answered, "Ethan and I were following a suspicious character. Then a car sped down the alley, and Ethan tackled me to the ground. I hit my head. Oh, and I think the woman in the speeding car was being taken against her will."

Joe stared wide-eyed and openmouthed at Ethan. He reminded me of a bigmouth bass stranded on the shore of a lake. "You let her rope you into this?"

Ethan pushed to his feet. "It was just a carny Dumpster-diving. Nothing to get worked up about."

"And the speeding car?"

"Not aimed at us. We were just in the way. They couldn't see us in the dark alley."

Joe shook his head and turned to April. "Please tell me you weren't involved."

She held up her hands. "I wasn't. I promise."

"Did anyone get the license number?" Joe pulled his notepad from his pocket.

"Too dark." Ethan shook his head.

"What about the woman? Recognize her?"

Ethan shook his head again. "I didn't see her. Summer did."

"I've seen her before. I'm sure of it, but I can't remember where. She could be a carny." I tried to sit up and groaned. My hands clutched my middle, and I grabbed the bowl.

"Are you going to throw up?" Joe stepped back. My cousin had a phobia about vomit. Worse than mine. An upchuck, and we run.

"I'm trying not to."

Pale beneath his tan, Joe set his pen to the paper. "Can you describe her?"

"Pale and blond, I think."

"That's not very helpful."

"It's the best I can do."

He sighed and replaced the paper and pen in his pocket. "You should go to the hospital. You probably have a concussion." Joe bent, laid a kiss on April's forehead, then left.

"I'm not going to the hospital. As soon as the room stops spinning, I'm going to find out who the woman is. She needs us."

Ethan pushed April to the farthest end of the sofa and sat next to me, pulling me into his arms. "That's why you do this, isn't it? To feel needed?"

"To help." And the familiar hunger filled me. Finding Millie dead, presumed a suicide, although I knew someone staged her death, was different. For Millie, I was too late. For this other woman—well, I *needed* to help.

Aunt Eunice told me God gives everyone a gift. I didn't want the only gift He gave me to be candy-making.

I wanted to leave a legacy. To make a difference in the world—in someone's life. What better way than to save her life?

A tear trickled down my cheek. As a child, I'd been unable to save my parents. They'd been going out to dinner, and I'd thrown a fit, not understanding why they'd leave me with a babysitter. My last sight of my mother had been her pale face, smiling at me, and her slender white hand lifted in farewell. I'd pouted, refusing to return the smile or the wave. She'd died in a hit-and-run. The case remained unsolved. I didn't want the sight of another woman's face through a car window to go unnoticed.

Ethan drew a finger across my cheek, wiping away my tear. "Are you sure you're all right?"

"That woman needs our help."

"Joe will handle it."

"No, I need to do this." I sniffled. April handed me a box of tissues. Her eyes swam with unshed tears. "When I set out to solve the diamond case, it was just playing. Trying to prove that I could do more than shop for fancy clothes or make delicious candy. Then things got personal, and I was forced to discover who killed Terry Lee. It wasn't me who solved her murder. Things happened by chance.

"The woman in the car reminded me of my mother. What if I'm the last friendly face that woman saw before she dies? I owe it to her."

Ethan turned to me. His eyes shone, digging into my soul. "Then I'll help you. By your side, all the time, keeping you as safe as I'm able."

Then I remembered where I'd seen the woman before.

19

Uncle Roy argued when I called and told him I'd be spending the night at Ethan's, even though I'd done so hundreds of times growing up as April's best friend. Being an adult and sleeping under the same roof as my fiancé didn't sit well with my old-school uncle. After I made every promise under the sun that I'd be sleeping in April's bed and that she'd be home the entire time, I finally had him convinced everything would be on the up and up.

I lay with an aching head and listened to my friend snore beside me. Footsteps scuffed outside the door as Ethan made his way down the hall to his room.

My heart warmed at his assurance to help me. I remembered seeing the frantic woman laughing and smiling with Eddy Foreman at the carnival. Funny how his name kept entering the picture. He was the right size for my gorilla friend, too.

The days of the fair were winding down. Tomorrow I'd inform Aunt Eunice we were closing the booth. Anyone who wanted to buy candy would have done so already anyway. We wouldn't lose many sales. Then I could concentrate on wandering around, spying, eavesdropping; whatever it took to become a first-rate detective and help this woman.

It occurred to me that I might be too late to save her life. I'd read reports of missing people usually being murdered within the first two hours of their disappearance. If that should be the case, God willing, I'd do everything in my power to make sure her abductor was brought to justice. Joe would have to arrest me again to keep me from this. What other way could I settle the restlessness in my soul?

When I woke the next morning, the throbbing in my head had lessened. April was gone, and the smell of frying bacon wafted through the open bedroom door. I grabbed a flowered robe from a nearby chair and rolled out of bed.

Having been in Ethan and April's home many times, I knew exactly where they kept the ibuprofen and made a beeline for the medicine cabinet. Three little rust-colored pills later, I shuffled to the kitchen with the speed of a snail.

Ethan stood at the stove wearing a ruffled canary yellow apron over a royal blue polo shirt and black dress pants. He brandished a spatula. What an appealing sight. "A man after my own heart." I wrapped my arms around his waist and laid my cheek on his broad back.

He turned. "Good morning, beautiful. How's your head? Are you hungry?"

"Starved. Love the apron, by the way, and my head is much better."

Ethan moved my bangs aside to take a look. "Okay, sit. The apron was my mother's. My more manly apron is dirty." He waved the spatula toward the kitchen table where two plates waited on navy vinyl place mats.

"Where's April?"

"Work."

I glanced at my watch. Seven o'clock. "You're going to be late."

"I've got thirty minutes before my first class. Everything's finished." He slid eggs and bacon onto my plate, then went back for his. "Eat up. I'll drop you at home on my way."

Twenty minutes later I stood on the front porch of my house, staring through the screen at my frowning uncle. "You still a good girl?" He glared at me.

"Good grief, Uncle Roy." My face heated. "What a question. Of course I am. Are you going to let me in?"

He pushed open the screen. "Just checking. A looker like you has to watch out. Ethan's a good man, but he *is* a man."

"And I'm a responsible adult. April is a very suitable chaperone." I placed a kiss on his ruddy cheek. "Thanks for worrying about me. Where's Aunt Eunice?"

"In the kitchen cooking you breakfast."

"I've already eaten."

"Eat again. Don't hurt her feelings."

Great. It's a wonder I don't weigh three hundred pounds.

Aunt Eunice set a plate of pancakes on the table before I took my seat. "Did Ethan take care of your head?"

"Yes." I stared at the stack of pancakes, sighed, and reached for the powdered sugar.

"You shouldn't eat so much sugar." Aunt Eunice sat across from me and folded her arms on the table.

"It's not as much as syrup. That's too sweet."

"What happened last night?"

I recounted the events, leaving out my personal guilt over watching my mother drive away. "I'm going to find out today who the woman in the car was. You sell the last of the candy and return the refrigerator."

"Kind of bossy, aren't you? That knock on the head doesn't give you the right to order me around."

"I'm sorry." I pushed aside my plate. "You're right.

You didn't raise me that way. Do you mind closing up the booth?"

"What's wrong with your food?" The way my aunt's eyes searched my face, I knew she asked in a roundabout way what was wrong with me. She'd always been able to see right through me. I wasn't ready to admit to her that I blamed myself for the way my parents had left the house. Stressed because of an ungrateful child. Not today, maybe never. But, I did owe her good manners and love. Not only because of the sacrifice she'd given in raising me, but because I loved her.

"Nothing." After pulling the plate back to me, I shoved a huge bite in my mouth. "See?"

"Okay. No, Summer, I don't mind closing the booth." A smile tugged at the corner of her lips. "And you shouldn't stick so much in your mouth. You'll choke." A gleam appeared in her eye. "Once I'm finished with the booth, I'll go around asking questions. We'll have to be sneakier about it, though. I don't relish being arrested again."

"You can't be for asking questions." Can you? I speared another forkful of pancake. No. My Dolt book actually suggests interrogating people. They wouldn't recommend a person do something if it was against the law, would they?

⁓

Like a starving child at a buffet line, I stood on the midway and surveyed the milling carnies and fair attendees. Although at least twenty trailers were lined up behind the fun house, I couldn't determine which belonged to Washington.

Eddy Foreman waved his arms, shouting orders to a

ride operator. He seemed as good a place to begin as any.

"Summer!" His demeanor changed. His frown flipped to a smile. His cologne almost overpowered me as he flung an arm around my shoulders. He flipped up my bangs. "What's with the bandage?"

"Just a bump." I took a deep breath, choked on aromatic fumes, and decided to plunge into asking questions. "The other day I saw you speaking with a blond woman. She wore the cutest pair of jeans. I'll just die if I can't get a pair for myself. Do you know where I can find her?"

"Lacey?" Eddy shook his head. "She hasn't shown up for work today. That's her brother I was talking to. He hasn't seen her since yesterday. It's difficult to get good help nowadays, you know?"

He'd been steering me toward the back of the fair, stopping in front of a trailer. Sally held court, lazily fanning her face with a sheet of paper folded accordion style. Her love interest handed her a glass of what looked like iced tea.

"Summer." Sally waved and I slid from beneath Eddy's arm. "Sit right here, sweetie. How you been? See you later, Eddy."

I perched on the edge of a rickety wood-slated stool. It wobbled beneath me. "I'm fine, thank you. And you?"

"Never better." She snapped her fingers. "Woodrow, get my friend a drink. You want some tea? That's Woodrow, my boyfriend. Isn't he the cutest thing?"

"Absolutely." If you liked the miniature type.

He handed me a glass, and his lips twitched in a semblance of a smile, only to disappear as quickly. Mississippi mud-colored hair circled a bald spot on top of the man's head. Eyes of the same color lowered beneath bushy brows. The man was anything but cute, but to each his own.

Another man stepped up behind them. He paused at the sight of me, then ducked out of sight.

"That's Grizzly Bob," Sally explained. "He's not very social, but he's great with the animals. Him and Woodrow are friends. Ain't that right, Snookums?"

Woodrow bobbed his head. "We sure are. How's your drink? Do you need more ice?" He fussed with the pillows behind her back.

Sally patted his cheek. "He's so good to me. A real prize. Woodrow would do anything for me." A hard glint shone in her eye, just for a second, as Sally stared at me. "He'd even die if I asked him to." The cold look disappeared, replaced by a smile. I wondered if I'd imagined it. "How many women can boast of that?"

I sipped the tea. Raspberry, my favorite. "Not many. Sally, have you seen Lacey today?"

"Lacey Love? I don't even think that's her real name. That woman's a harlot. What do you want her for?" Sally tipped her glass and drained the sweet liquid.

"I heard she was missing. I'm just curious." At least I had a name to go with the face that haunted my dreams last night.

"Uh-huh. Word around the fair is that you, missy, are a Nosy Nelly. People don't like that."

I handed my half-finished drink to Woodrow and stood. "Is that a warning, Sally?"

"Heavens, no." She giggled. "I'm just stating a fact. I wouldn't like anything to happen to you. I'm your friend." Sally leaned forward as far as her bulk would allow. "Listen,

Summer. There're all types of people hired to work these carnivals. Most of them are good people, but not all. You keep asking questions, somebody is going to get upset."

Sounded like a warning to me. Suddenly, I didn't feel as comfortable with Sally being my friend. I shivered. "Thanks for the advice. One more thing. I need to ask Washington a question about my booth. Can you point me in the direction of his trailer?"

Sally's eyes narrowed. "Last one on the right. The one that's painted the color of split pea soup."

Did all the carnies get their paint from the "oops" aisle in the local paint store? A rainbow of garish colors surrounded me as I made my way to the end. Baby poop yellow. Orange red. A washed-out blue. Washington's trailer sat right where Sally said it would and was definitely the color of peas. I shivered. I detested that particular vegetable.

Before I could knock, the door swung open and Washington beamed down at me. "Miss Summer. Come in. To what do I owe this surprise?"

Although I burned with curiosity to inspect the inside of where he lived, self-preservation prevailed, and I stopped at the front door. I craned my neck to peek inside.

A chocolate micro-fiber sofa took up one entire wall of the tiny living room. A brass-and-glass coffee table, every inch covered with Precious Moments knickknacks, sat in the center of a faded Oriental rug. Prints of famous artists covered the walls. Definitely not purchased on a carny's pay. Desire to see the rest of his home tugged at me.

"I wanted to let you know that Aunt Eunice and I are closing our booth. With the fair almost finished, we'd like to be able to enjoy ourselves a bit."

"That's fine. I'll dismantle everything tomorrow." Washington's eyes never left my face. "Would you like a look around inside? I've managed to acquire quite a few nice things."

Had he guessed my true intentions?

"Uh. Well, I was, uh, actually wondering how you could afford such nice things on your salary." *Please, God, don't let him think me a snob, but I promised You I wouldn't lie. And the man did ask.*

He laughed. The warm sound washed over me like far-away thunder on a summer day. "I'm the king of Dumpster diving, Miss Summer. Also, I've staked my claim as the carny's shaker. I make quite a bit doing that."

"Shaker?"

He squeezed onto the stoop with me and closed the door before taking a seat on the top step. He patted the narrow space beside him, inviting me to sit. "A shaker is someone who scours the rides at closing time. It's amazing how much money falls out of pockets. Especially near the rides that go upside down. Why so interested? Looking for part-time work?"

My face must have turned the shade of a cherry. "I've noticed you passing things on to others."

His laugh boomed across the alley. "You thought I was dealing!" Washington clutched his stomach. "That is priceless, Miss Summer. Totally priceless. I just sell some of the things I find. Stuff I don't want. Jewelry mostly. I have no need for that kind of thing."

"I'm sorry." Okay, I'm a dunce. A snobbish dunce. There was absolutely no way I would share this particular investigative interview with anyone.

"No need for apologies. I've been questioned by the

cops more times than I can count. There's plenty of money to be found, if a person knows where to look. Most people are just too lazy." He clapped a hand on my shoulder. "You move on now, Miss Summer. I've got work to do. Come by anytime. Might be I could find a pretty little trinket for you."

I rose and extended my hand. "Thank you for overlooking my rudeness."

He laughed again and shook my hand.

I stepped off the stoop and turned. "I'm looking for Lacey Love. Have you seen her?"

"Not since yesterday." He opened his door and ducked inside.

Well, that didn't reveal any new information. Except that maybe I had barked up the wrong tree. Washington didn't appear to be guilty of anything but keeping what others had lost. As far as I knew, that wasn't a crime.

At a loss of where to go from there, I headed back up the aisle of painted trailers. A bubble gum pink one drew my eye. It screamed Lacey Love if anything did.

20

Since no yellow crime scene tape surrounded the pink monstrosity, I felt no compunction about knocking on the door. No one had officially reported Lacey missing. I only hoped I had the right trailer. I didn't want to be surprised by an irate owner arriving home as I snooped. Joe's warning about any further breaking of the law rattled in my head. How do I solve things if I can't snoop?

A man wearing dirty coveralls and driving a beat-up golf cart stopped behind me. "Go ahead and go on in. Lacey won't mind. We got an open door policy around here. She ain't home anyway." And with those words, he sped away as fast as his four wheels would take him.

At least I knew I had the right place. Was everyone around here one big happy family? Then why did people keep disappearing or getting murdered?

The door squeaked as I pushed it open. A musky incense hung in the air of the dark room. Shades covered the windows. Déjà vu struck me. If I found another body in the shower, I'd be out of here faster than a fox after a chicken.

Dishes were stacked in the sink. A half-full can of soda sat on the table. A chair lay overturned on the worn linoleum. The remainder of the kitchen was spotless. Nothing appeared out of place. It was almost as if the woman who lived here had left in a hurry.

Nosy radar antennas quivering, I headed to the bedroom. If I had something important to hide, that's where I'd stash it.

The trailer was laid out identical to Millie's, minus the squeaky floorboard. *Please, God, don't let anyone sneak up on me.* Instead of a door, a brightly striped bedsheet with button tabs over a curtain rod divided the closet from the room. I pushed the fabric aside and pulled the chain on a bare lightbulb above my head.

The chaos belied the neatness of the rest of the woman's home. Clothes hung rumpled on hangers shoved tight together. Shoes lay jumbled on the floor among bulging bags and crushed boxes. Aunt Eunice would've died from the mess. Dismay flooded through me. Where should I start? Especially considering I didn't know what I was looking for.

I decided to start with the less messy section of the closet: the shelf above the clothes. Shoe boxes were piled with no semblance of order. It made sense to start at one end and move down.

The first box held love letters. Once glance at the letter on top set my face on fire, and I hurriedly set the box on the floor. The second held personal mementos like movie tickets and receipts. I lost count of how many boxes of paper, jewelry, hair ties, and other unrecognizable things I riffled through until I found something that made me catch my breath.

Holding a nondescript brown cardboard box in my shaking hands, I stared at a detailed accounting report. I detested math, having dropped out of algebra in high school as soon as was feasible. But even my number-challenged brain recognized the dollar amounts didn't add up. Here was the proof Joe searched for. That something else. Here might just be the proof of embezzlement.

Hot, dusty, and excited, I restacked the boxes on the

top shelf, neater than when I'd found them. I couldn't take the brown box with me, not wanting to be caught with it. I clutched the papers in my hand. I'd read over them in my room tonight before turning them over to my cousin. I wanted to reassure myself I didn't grasp at straws, running to my cousin with something that actually was nothing. Another thing for him to laugh at me about.

The front door of the trailer squeaked. *Not again.*

I clicked off the closet light, let the curtain fall into place, and darted into the bathroom. I folded the papers and shoved them into the best hiding place I could think of—my bra—then flushed the toilet. Joe was going to kill me. I was pretty sure stuffing evidence was walking a fine line on breaking the law, but I couldn't be caught with papers from someone's closet, could I? I'd look and then return them. My cousin would be none the wiser. It's not like I broke into Lacey's home or anything.

"Who's there?" a voice said from the opposite side of the door.

I took a deep breath and stepped out. "Summer Meadows. I needed to use the restroom." The papers in my cleavage scratched and served as a reminder that I could easily end up with the same fate as Millie and Lacey.

The bearded man from Sally's trailer, Grizzly Bob, glared at me. "What are you doing here? Lacey ain't home."

"A man on a golf cart told me I could come in and wait." I held my breath against his body odor. He smelled strangely similar to cat urine. "Said y'all had an open door policy."

"Outsiders don't get the same treatment as carnies. You git out." He pointed a stained flannel-covered arm toward the door.

"No need to be rude." My breath released in a rush. "I'm going."

The man followed me out the front door. I turned and stared into red-rimmed mocha-colored eyes. "You tell Lacey I came by, okay?"

He glared and gave me the tiniest nod. His eyes flicked to my bosom. Did he know I had something hidden, or was it my own guilty conscience? Surely this old, unwashed caretaker of animals didn't find me attractive? I flashed my brightest smile and tossed him a wave. "Nice to see you again."

Grizzly Bob's grunt followed as I headed up the alley. My heart thudded a heavy-metal beat, not slowing until I'd passed out of eyesight of the socially inept man. Bursting to share my discovery, I headed for the candy booth.

Aunt Eunice had marked the last of our product to half price and leaned against the counter, a bored and dazed look on her face. I grabbed her arm and pulled her into a corner.

"I've got something that ought to perk you up."

Her eyes widened. "What?"

I pulled the papers from my hiding place. "Joe mentioned there was more going on here than met the eye. Look what I found in Lacey's trailer."

"Who's Lacey?" She peered over the crumpled sheets. "Did you steal these?"

"Lacey is the woman I saw in the car last night. I'm positive." I held the papers to my chest. "And, no, I didn't steal them." Just borrowed. I had every intention of turning them in.

She grabbed them from my hand. "Joe is going to be furious. And for your information, taking something without asking is stealing. You're going to have to go back to jail."

My heart leaped into my throat. "Here. Never mind, I'll give them to Joe and confess my stupidity."

Aunt Eunice smoothed the sheets flat on the counter. "Whoo-eee! I'm no expert but someone has been taking quite a bit of dough from somewhere. Where did you say you got these?"

"From Lacey's trailer. In the closet." Pride in my investigative skills rose.

Aunt Eunice shoved the papers at me. "Put them back. I don't want to go to jail again."

"Joe will be so excited about us finding them, he wouldn't dare arrest us again." Would he?

"There was no *us* in your filching those papers. At least make a copy and put the originals back."

"Okay." I folded the papers and restuffed my bra. If someone did know that Lacey had taken the papers, they'd be looking for them. If they didn't find the evidence and knew I'd been in her trailer, they'd suspect I had them. For my own safety, I decided I shouldn't disappoint them. "I'll go home and scan a copy right now." What if I was onto something? I couldn't stop the grin spreading across my face.

"Don't forget the Miss Mountain Shadows pageant tonight. You promised to help April with her hair. She passes on her crown. I still say it's too bad you're too old."

"So you've mentioned before." Pageants weren't my thing, but it still pained me to know thirty was the magical age of being considered too old to enter. And my birthday wasn't for a month! I only had April beaten by a couple of months.

I stood before my full-length mirror and twirled from front to back, side to side. Almost thirty, but I thought I still looked pretty good. Good enough to win some county fair princess title, anyway. But April's cute blond curls and big sapphire eyes had won last year's crown. Seemed people preferred that over an unruly auburn mess, highlighted with red or not, and eyes that couldn't make up their mind whether to be blue or green. Having a voice like an angel probably didn't hurt either. I wouldn't have had anything to do for the talent program.

Aunt Eunice always said vanity was a sin. Now I knew why. It depressed a person.

I sighed and headed downstairs to the den. The completed scan of the financial documents waited in the printer's tray. Truly growled from her favorite spot under the desk.

I whirled and spotted a hairy arm as someone ducked around the corner. Heavy footsteps pounded down the hall. I grabbed Truly as she tried sprinting after the intruder.

If there was anything I learned from the past summer's escapades, it was that a person didn't go chasing people who entered their homes uninvited. And not to leave my cell phone where I couldn't easily grab it. I'd left mine on the front seat of my car. Again.

Truly's sturdy body trembled with her growls. With my foot, I slammed the den door. Once Truly was back on the floor, scratching like mad against the painted wood, I engaged the lock. I knew before I lifted the receiver the house phone wouldn't be working. Sure enough, the drone of emptiness reached my eardrums.

Overhead, the scrapes of someone snooping through my bedroom reached me through the ceiling. Glass shattered, and I gnawed my lower lip. He'd better not have broken my new crystal lamp base.

What was he looking for? Surely he realized I'd have the papers they wanted on me. Why hadn't he attacked me in the den? While my back was turned? If Truly hadn't alerted me to his presence, I'd have been at his mercy.

Maybe he wasn't searching at all. But hiding. Waiting for me to enter unsuspectingly into their clutches. I could almost feel his icy fingers lock around my neck and shook my head against my overactive imagination. There was no way I would go upstairs until someone stronger, and braver, said the coast was clear.

Fright tickled at the nape of my neck. It wasn't the first time someone had paid me an uninvited visit, but it was the first time I'd been alone.

Okay, God. Here I am again. In trouble. Asking for Your help. My brain is empty. There are no ideas rattling. Sheer panic has driven all thought away. Could You please yell loud and clear what You want me to do?

The doorknob rattled.

I hurled myself over the desk, scattering papers. The ledgers! I grabbed the original and the copy, stuffing both down my shirt. The sheets poked upward and scratched at my chin. I reached for the nearest thing to a weapon I could find: a sharp-pointed letter opener shaped like a sword, with a fake jewel-encrusted handle. I might have a chance if the perpetrator got within six inches of me.

"Go away! I'm armed."

"Summer, why's the door locked?"

I'd never been so glad to hear my uncle's voice.

"There's someone in the house, Uncle Roy. Someone in a gorilla suit. You've got to get out. Go for help."

"I'll get my gun!" He thundered up the stairs.

I hugged Truly to me. The papers in my blouse crackled. "Well, girl. That wasn't exactly the yell from God I'd envisioned, but Uncle Roy is better than nothing. And he's definitely brave." *Please, God, keep him safe.*

Within minutes, Uncle Roy returned and pounded on the door. "Open up. There ain't no one here."

I placed the dog on the floor and unlocked the door. "Are you sure?" I peered up and down the hall.

"Of course I'm sure. Checked every room. Your new lamp is broke and things are scattered off your dresser, but I didn't see a single person. I think they climbed out the window." Uncle Roy's eyes narrowed. "What's in your blouse?"

"Papers I need to get to Joe."

"Couldn't you think of a better place to carry them? What if the perpetrator decided to go after them? He would've mauled you in places that weren't decent."

"It's the best I could do." I stuffed my hand down my shirt and withdrew the crumpled copies, keeping the originals safe in my cleavage. A manila folder lay on the desktop and I slid them inside. "The phone line must have been cut. The phone's dead, and my cell phone is in the car."

"I'll get your phone and call Joe." Uncle Roy disappeared, and I stepped to the window.

How had my gorilla friend known I'd be home alone?

21

Joe arrived at the house with his usual scowl. I glanced with urgency at my watch. April expected me to arrive at her house in thirty minutes, curling iron in hand. Hopefully, my cousin wouldn't lecture long enough to make me late. Without a word, Joe held out a hand.

I handed him the copies. He wiggled his fingers. How'd he know there was more? My gaze switched to Uncle Roy. He lowered his eyes. Traitor.

"You can't have the original. I've got to put them back." I crossed my arms.

"Summer, you're withholding evidence."

"No, I'm not. I gave you the copies."

"And someone knows you have them. Give them to me."

"Fine." I pulled the papers out of my brassiere and wished I'd thought to make two copies. How was I supposed to solve this case without evidence? Joe grimaced. "Oh, stop being a baby. Be glad it isn't July when they'd be damp with sweat."

"Lord, take me now." Joe stuck the original in the folder with the copy. "And have mercy on Ethan when he marries this one."

"What's that supposed to mean?" I planted my fists on my hips.

"Exactly what it sounds like. You're going to run Ethan ragged with your amateur sleuthing. Not to mention gray hairs like you're giving me. You're making me a laughingstock at the precinct. Now, a straight answer, please. Where did you find these?"

"Lacey Love's trailer." I held up a hand to stop his protests. "Before you get your dander up, I intended on knocking, but someone drove by and told me to go on in. So I wasn't trespassing."

I decided not to tell him I'd been discovered and run off by Grizzly Bob. "Has anyone reported Lacey missing? I'm certain it was her I saw being held against her will in the car last night."

"You don't know it was against her will. She's run off with a man before. And yes, her brother just filed a missing persons report." Joe brushed a hand across his buzz cut. "So, you waltzed into this woman's trailer and just happened to come across these papers?"

"Well, no. I nosed through her closet."

"Summer—"

"If I hadn't, we wouldn't have this proof."

Joe sighed. "Why don't you go through the academy and get a license? Then you could snoop legally."

"That's a good idea." I hadn't thought of that. I'd make a good police officer. Then Joe could be the bad cop to my good one. And I'd get to carry a gun, pepper spray, and one of those cool Tasers.

"I was joking. I'd have to transfer for sure."

"She's too much of a girlie-girl, and too old," Uncle Roy piped up. "There ain't no thirty-year-old rookies."

There's my age again. Why does everyone insist thirty is the magical number for life going downhill? I'd always thought it was forty. Or fifty. Maybe I ought to buy myself a cane before my family stuck me in a retirement home.

"Is there anything else? I've got to get to April's." I lifted the curling iron like Norman Bates brandishing a knife in *Psycho*.

Joe's face hardened. "Are you threatening me? With a hair appliance?"

"It's either the iron or April if you make me late. Which would you prefer?" I lowered my hand and tilted my head.

"Go." He waved me off. "I'll talk to you later."

Free at last, I darted up the stairs, grabbed my purse, then sprinted down and outside to my car. As I drove, I thought about the figures noted on that sheet of paper. One amount had been written in red. Fifty thousand. The amount stolen? Who would benefit the most?

Any of the carnival workers, I supposed. None of them, in all likelihood, made much money. Eddy Foreman wouldn't steal from something that would eventually be his, would he? Washington came to mind clouded by the image of a much shorter gorilla. Sally's boyfriend? Grizzly Bob? I shook my head. Another dead end. Everywhere I turned. I might as well be lost in the maze at the fair for all the progress I'd made.

I parked in the alley next to Ethan's truck. Lost in the cloudy details of the case, I shrieked at a rap on the window. "Ethan. You scared me."

"Sorry." He opened the door. "You getting out? April's pacing the floor waiting on you. You'd think she was entered in the pageant with all the fuss she's making."

I slid from the car and planted a kiss on his lips. "All eyes will still be on her. A woman's got to look her best."

"You look nice."

"Thank you." I ran a hand down the long-sleeved, scoop-necked royal blue dress I'd chosen. "April said as her hairstylist, I couldn't arrive in jeans."

"Why not? You aren't in the pageant."

Did everyone have to remind me?

Still not having seen April's gown, I caressed Ethan's cheek before hurrying inside. April yelled down the stairs that I was late. I checked my watch. Only five minutes. Not bad for me.

She started in as soon as I stepped inside her bedroom. "I want an updo with tiny wisps falling around my face. There's baby's breath on the dresser. You can stick that in anywhere." She peered at me with narrowed eyes. "You can do this, right? Please say you can. It's too late to go to a stylist."

How hard could it be? A few curls. A bobby pin here and there. Sure. I could do this. Granted, it's a long time since high school prom. Confident, I plugged in the iron.

April removed the towel from her damp hair and sat in front of her vanity table. Blond tresses fell to her shoulders. A bit shorter than when we were seniors. Might be harder to pin up. I squirted a generous amount of mousse into my hand.

"That's a lot, isn't it?" April's worried reflection met mine.

"You want it to stay, don't you?" I worked the white mess through her hair, taking care to coat every strand. "Where's your gown?"

"In a white garment bag in the closet. Don't touch it with your messy fingers."

I eased the zipper down on the bag. Inside hung a gauzy creation in bubble gum pink. I couldn't help but compare it to Lacey's trailer. April always had favored that color. "Is it strapless?"

"Spaghetti straps. Long with a short train. I'm queen.

I've got to look the part."

At the bottom of the bag lay April's tiara. A rhinestone-covered crown. With a glance over my shoulder, I plucked it up and placed it on top of my curls. Oh, how I would have loved to possess this jewel.

"Put it back. I've just had it cleaned."

With a sigh, I followed her orders. "When did you get so mean?"

"When you knocked off a stone the last time you played with it. Come on, time is wasting."

"Relax, April." My fingers kneaded her shoulders. "You're so tense."

"I'm nervous. I'll be the center of attention."

"The new queen will be the center of attention." The green light glowed on the curling iron and I singed my first strand of hair. I plucked the severed piece from the metal barrel, burning my finger. It was in the back. Maybe she wouldn't notice. I sniffed. A little singed hair but not too bad. I grabbed a bottle of perfume, sprayed a few squirts, then spun the stool and placed myself between my friend and the mirror.

"Now who's being mean?"

To distract her, I informed April of my discovery in Lacey's trailer.

"Wow, Summer. You're getting good at the mystery thing."

"You think?" Before we knew it, her head was a riot of ringlets. I pulled the curls back, securing them with about a million bobby pins, and set to work with the hair freeze spray. Then, with random abandon, I poked in the baby's breath. I spun April to face the mirror. "Ta da!"

She bolted to her feet. "Oh my gosh! Oh my gosh." Tears welled.

"You like it?"

"I look like Shirley Temple with weeds growing out of my head. What did you do to me? You've ruined me." She turned to glare. "You did such a good job for the prom."

"That was 1995. With the dress and the crown, you'll be gorgeous." A bit dated, but gorgeous. I darted to the closet, yanked out the gown, and dropped it at her feet. "Sorry." I lifted it and proceeded to yank it over her head.

"Stop. You'll make my hair worse. I have to step into the gown." April removed the dress from my clutches. "What is wrong with you? Oh, I should have known better. Look at *your* hair."

"What's wrong with it?" I surveyed my mane in the mirror.

"Never mind." April let her robe fall to the floor and stepped into the gown. She was a vision of loveliness. At least in my opinion.

I jammed the crown on her head. "There."

"Ow!"

"Sorry." Really, I couldn't fathom what had gotten into her. She'd never been this grouchy in all the years I'd known her.

"You just wait until your wedding. See what I don't come up with to wear."

Thank You, God, that I'm picking out the bridesmaid gowns myself. Aunt Eunice would sew them from a pattern of my choosing. And they wouldn't be pink.

Taking her by the hand, I sat her on the edge of the bed. "Girlfriend, there's more on your mind than this pageant. Spill."

"You're right." She grabbed a tissue from a nearby box and dabbed her eyes. "Joe took me out to dinner last night to an expensive restaurant. Made a big deal of it. I really thought he was going to pop the question." She looked up at me. "What's he waiting for?"

"He's probably scared, the big ninny. How my cousin became a cop is beyond me. He's frightened of the tiniest things. Don't cry. You'll ruin your makeup." I perched on the bed beside her. "Do you really hate your hair?"

"No. It's a bit wild, but it's okay. The crown helps squash it some." April took a deep shuddering breath. "Let's go. I can't be late. My shy boyfriend is playing bodyguard for the pageant entrants. I've got to keep an eye on him. An evil-eyed, stay-away look, or those queen wannabes will be all over him. And he'd better be watching me and not acting like a police officer."

I didn't have the heart to tell her, I'd already put Joe in a bad mood.

22

Ladies." Ethan swept his arm toward the alley. "Your chariot awaits. Tonight you're not short-stuff or Tinkerbell, but queens of royal blood."

"Oh, Ethan." April wrapped her brother in a hug. A silver Hummer sat next to Ethan's truck.

"This is a big deal for you, little sis. I thought you should arrive in style. I'll be the chauffeur and there's dinner afterward. Joe said he'd be able to get off early tonight. Once the pageant is over, he's a free man."

Did I mention what a wonderful man I was engaged to? Country boys definitely ruled in the romance department. I tossed him a smile.

Ethan held April at arm's length. "What did you do to your hair?"

"Summer styled it." April put a hand to her head. "It's all right, isn't it?"

"Uh—" He glanced at me. I glared a warning. "Sure. Beautiful." Before she could question him further, he opened the back door and helped us inside.

Obviously, being the hairstylist of a pageant queen had its perks. The seats were upholstered in the softest leather and hugged our bottoms in luxury. Between us, Ethan had placed a bottle of sparkling cider in a bucket of ice. That man of mine thought of everything.

"Ready?" Ethan slid behind the wheel.

"Ready." April pulled the bottle from the ice. "Where did you get this vehicle?"

"It's a rental. You can get anything if you know where

to look. Cars are easy."

She handed the bottle to me to open. "I'm renting a convertible one of these days. Driving to California. Coasting up and down Highway 1. Seeing the giant redwoods."

I popped the cork. Obviously I was also April's handmaiden. When she had to perform duties as my maid-of-honor I'd have her so busy, she wouldn't have time to think. I chugged my first glass of cider, sputtering on the carbonation.

"Maybe for your honeymoon," Ethan tossed over his shoulder.

April squealed, sloshing her drink across my lap. Great. Wonderful. I dabbed at the spot with a nearby napkin.

"Do you know something I don't?" April clutched the back of Ethan's seat.

My gaze met Ethan's wide-eyed one in the rearview mirror. He'd said too much.

"Uh, no. Just speculating."

Unfortunately, our smooth ride didn't last long. Driving a mile takes mere minutes, and before I'd gulped my second drink, Ethan pulled our chariot behind a white tent erected for the evening's ceremony.

In a trailer behind the tent, twelve nervous young women giggled and fussed. They jostled for space before mirrors just big enough to reflect their faces. April gave a short speech of what the new queen's duties would be. Her words were intended to calm the trembling herd. Instead, a couple of girls gasped. Another shrieked, and one fanned a hand at shining eyes. I ducked out of the trailer, not wanting any more to do with impending hysterics.

I turned and bumped into Mr. Rick Foreman. "Excuse me."

He twirled his mustache. His eyes focused over my shoulder. "Perfectly all right. The girls doing okay? Wonderful. Gotta go." The man practically ran to get away from me. Did his distraction have anything to do with the fact that he was short a lot of money?

Shivering from the dampness of my apple cider-soaked dress, I stepped through the back entrance of the tent. Almost every seat was occupied. Fathers, brothers, and lovers clutched tons of flower bouquets. Mountain Shadows took pride in their young women, and tonight it showed.

I scooted around the edges of the room and took a seat in the back. My gaze studied every person who walked in and out, those sitting in hard plastic chairs, and the few men who chose to stand in the rear. Somewhere on this ten-acre plot of land walked a thief and a murderer. Someone knew who killed Laid Back Millie, who had Lacey Love, and who stole from Mr. Foreman.

Another picture of Lacey's face plastered beseechingly against the car window brought back the memory of my mother's sad face as she waved good-bye at my stubborn five-year-old self. Aunt Eunice would ask why I dwelled on something that happened twenty-five years ago. I wouldn't have an answer.

My parents' death was my fault. If they had left before my temper tantrum, as planned, they wouldn't have met the drunk driver. Was it my reasoning and not the need to prove myself that was driving me to want to solve this case? What did I hope to accomplish? Nothing would bring back my parents.

The accident wasn't your fault, child.

God's whisper in my ear brought tears to my eyes. If

only I could stop this feeling of guilt.

Seven o'clock drew near and a dull rumbling from the spectators filled the tent. Time for the pageant finalists to step onto the makeshift wooden stage. An elderly, balding man dressed in a shiny polyester leisure suit stepped before the microphone as the evening's emcee.

He welcomed the crowd, recounted the evening's schedule, and moved aside to sing in an amazingly good baritone as the entrants sashayed on stage. A roar rose from the crowd with redneck yells and whistles as favorites stepped into place. The contestants resembled a vibrant rainbow.

My gaze roamed over the crowd. None of the carnies were in attendance, thus not my gorilla friend. At least not in costume. I tapped my foot in impatience, waiting for the winner to be announced and crowned. I didn't think I'd find the embezzler beneath this white canopy.

Joe stepped beside me, a white poster board in his hand. Sweat beaded on his brow, and he wiped his face with a damp handkerchief. He glanced at me. "Warm in here, isn't it?"

"Not really. We're standing beside the open flap, in the evening, in September." I studied his flushed face. "Are you sick?"

He shook his head and took a deep shuddering breath then collapsed in the empty seat next to me. "Nervous."

"About what? Aren't you supposed to be working?"

April stepped to the microphone, stopping any answer Joe may have given. Her beautiful face glowed as she opened the gold envelope she held and called out a name. A weeping brunette in an emerald-colored gown darted forward. A young boy raced on stage. The crowd erupted in laughter at his haste. The boy held a plush velvet cushion in both hands on which sat a new, sparkling crown.

With a smile, April lifted the crown and placed it on the new queen's head. The girl stepped lively to center stage as roses were tossed at her feet.

Joe bolted to his feet and held his poster over his head. April's eyes narrowed as she focused on the words, then her shriek rivaled the new winner's. I craned my neck to read the words, "April, will you marry me?"

Not that I thought it cool for my cousin to steal the new queen's thunder, but you couldn't beat his theatrics. The crowd burst into applause as April screamed, "Yes!" Happiness for my best friend welled in me, starting my tears anew.

Ethan slid behind me, wrapping his arms around my waist. He planted a tender kiss on the back of my neck.

"You did know," I challenged as I folded my hands over his.

"Yes. Almost spoiled the whole surprise. Joe thought it would be a dead giveaway if he drove the Hummer, so I volunteered. He wanted tonight to be special."

April leaped from the stage and, holding the hem of her dress in one hand, raced toward Joe. He stepped into the aisle and braced himself as she threw herself into his arms.

People crowded around the new queen, who clapped her hands in glee at the romance, while others gathered around April and Joe.

Ethan took my hand and led me from the tent. "Joe told me about the papers you discovered."

I wrapped my arms around Ethan's neck and snuggled against the chill in the air. "I didn't do anything illegal;

well, not too much."

"He also told me that Lacey, the woman you saw, is officially missing."

What was he getting at? "Yes."

Ethan tugged on his left ear. "I know I've said this a million times, but—"

"I know. Be careful."

"People are dying. Money is a big motivator for murder."

"Not something I possess a lot of."

"No, but you're a born snoop. It makes people nervous."

April slammed into us from behind, almost bursting my eardrums with her elation. "He did it! He finally did it!"

Finally, did it? They'd only been dating since the summer. A few weeks longer than Ethan and me. Of course, we'd known each other since we were kids. "You'd better not get married before me."

I grabbed her hand to gawk at the rock on her finger. A beautiful, simple princess cut. Perfect for April. I grinned at Joe. "Good taste, cousin. How's that nervousness now?"

"Moved on to terrified."

April punched his arm. "Oh, stop. Marriage to me won't be that bad. It's Ethan that needs to look out."

I was really getting tired of being the brunt of jokes. Over Ethan's shoulder, I spied my gorilla friend lurking in the shadows between food booths. "Look."

Ethan clapped a hand on Joe's arm. "Ready to give chase?"

"I'm not in uniform." He patted his jacket. "I don't have my weapon."

With fists planted on my hips, I stood before him. "What? You can't chase down a suspect without your trusty gun? You're going to let someone who broke into my house get away? Besides, I never carry a weapon. That doesn't stop me."

"Fine." In true Scooby Doo fashion, me resembling Velma and April a fine Daphne, the four of us sprinted after the suspect, who left us in his dust. He disappeared among the outbuildings.

"Wait." April let the train of her gown fall, and she collapsed against the shabby siding of the women's restroom. "I can't go another step in this dress."

Joe and Ethan faded into the shadows. To our right, a dark figure turned a corner.

"Stay here, April. I'll be right back." With caution in each slow step, I followed. All the way around the building, I saw no one. Not even April where I'd left her.

Apprehension rose in me, choking and stifling. I'd been so nasty to her earlier, out of my own jealousy and ill-feelings. Doing the only thing I could think of, I sprinted around the building and sobbed her name. It didn't take long to dash a circle around the small restroom. Still no April or a sign of the gorilla. So I ran again, wildly, around the same building, finally collapsing, winded against the wall April had leaned against earlier.

A sob blocked my throat. Where was she? Had she been kidnapped? I bent over, hands balanced on my knees, and gasped for breath. Tears landed on the top of my hands.

A shadow fell over me. I glanced up. Dismay completed the process of strangling me. Towering over me stood the gorilla.

It's amazing what fear can drive someone to do. Or anger. I dove at the person, wrapped my arms around his waist, and took him to the ground. A spurt of satisfaction ran through me. I may be tiny, but I was mighty. Like a super hero. And I did this for my best friend.

The gorilla moved to shove me away, and I clutched at the costume. I rolled, coming away with the head. I screamed, holding the furry face. Grizzly Bob glared down at me. His wiry hair stuck out in all directions. He snatched the costume head from my hands, whirled, and dashed out of sight.

April stepped from the restroom and stared at me. I lay on the dirt-packed surface and avoided her glare. Instead, I gazed at the stars overhead. Pleasure as warm as the chocolate I covered candies with washed over me. I'd taken down a full-grown man. Granted, he hadn't stayed down, but I wouldn't let a little detail like that steal my happiness.

Nothing made sense. Here I lay, right beneath the gorilla's clutches. Instead, he had grabbed his head and run. Did the gorilla have nothing to do with Millie's death or Lacey's disappearance? Was it not related to the disappearing funds?

"Summer?" April's forehead wrinkled. "Are you okay? Why are you lying in the dirt?"

"I went looking for you."

"I went to the restroom."

"I see that now." I propped myself on one elbow and glared at her. "I ran around this building like a chicken with my head cut off. When I couldn't find you, I figured Grizzly Bob did."

She held out a hand to help me to my feet. "Who's Grizzly Bob?"

"The gorilla."

"I'm confused."

"Welcome to my world."

Feet pounded in our direction. I threw myself across April and plastered us both to the side of the building. She shoved me away. "What *is* wrong with you? It's only Joe and Ethan."

I must look a sight, but better than April. Her hair had come loose from the pins and stuck up in all directions, causing her to look remarkably like the bride of Frankenstein. I had used a really strong mousse on her hair. A rip from the ground to her knee marred the beautiful gown. As rapidly as if I were swatting at stinging mosquitoes, I slapped at the dirt on my dress.

Joe and Ethan stopped about ten feet from us and gawked. My cousin clamped his lips together. Probably to keep from swearing at us. Once upon a time he'd used language rivaling a pirate captain's, but since coming to Christ, he'd sworn off curse words. Difficult, with me as his cousin.

"What in this green earth happened here?"

I held up a hand to signal April that I'd do the talking. The words flowed. If anyone could make sense of the babble spewing forth, then good for him. My sentences and thoughts tumbled over each other like a creek rapidly rising over rocks.

"You ripped off someone's head?" Joe would pick out just that one part, wouldn't he?

"Grizzly Bob's. Or rather, the gorilla's."

"After he attacked you."

"Well, maybe he didn't attack me. It was more the other way around." I glanced at Ethan. He gnawed the corner of his mouth in an attempt not to laugh.

Joe rubbed both hands vigorously over his face. "And where was April?"

She stepped forward. "In the restroom. I had no part of any of this. I came out and Summer was lying in the dirt, staring into the sky with absolutely no sense."

"Sounds like her." Joe pulled April close before transferring his attention back to me. "To make a long story short, you tussled with the man in the gorilla suit, who turned out to be a guy named Grizzly Bob. You tackled him to the ground, ripped off his head, and he gets up, takes his head back, and disappears."

I crossed my arms. "That's about it."

"Great. Let's go to dinner." Joe steered April toward the waiting Hummer.

Ethan slung an arm around my shoulders. "You beat all, Summer. I would've loved to have seen you tackle someone."

"I was brilliant. Y'all didn't see anything?"

"Nope. And now that you know the identity of your friend, I doubt you'll see any more of that gorilla slash Bigfoot."

"Uncle Roy will be disappointed."

23

I arrived at the fairgrounds Saturday morning with every intention of watching the hustle and bustle associated with the teardown and removal of the rides and portable buildings. Instead, carnies stood huddled around Ruby, Mabel, and Aunt Eunice. The only member of the committee missing was my neighbor, Mrs. Hodge. Since her son Richard had been shot by Joe while the man had been trying to kill me, Mrs. Hodge stayed pretty much to herself. The ordeal of her son trying to involve her in his scheme of stealing diamonds had almost been more than she could bear. Eddy Foreman paced between the two divisive groups, waving his arms over his head.

I squeezed through the packed bodies. "Aunt Eunice, what's going on?"

"Seems the carnival can't pay for the use of the land. The committee," she pointed at Ruby and Mabel, "is holding their property as payment. Buildings, rides, animals, etc."

"Where's the senior Foreman?" Most of the buildings were a permanent fixture from fairs over the years, so that part didn't bother me. Having to house wild animals did.

"Seems to have disappeared." Aunt Eunice crossed her arms across her ample bosom and tilted her head closer to mine. "Ruby and Mabel confronted him yesterday, he went to his safe to pay them, discovered it empty, and nearly had a heart attack. No one has seen him since."

"This case gets more curious by the minute."

Shouts rose in the air as the carnies realized there

most likely wouldn't be money for their salaries. Big Sally approached us, leaning on a cane and breathing as if she'd run a mile. The crowd parted like they let royalty pass.

Woodrow toted a wooden bench that he placed in front of the mob. Sally sat, her bulk drooping over the edge. She held up a hand to quiet everyone.

"Everyone calm down. Let Eddy have time to sort this all out." She smiled at me. "I'm sure Summer won't kick us out on our rears. She'll let us stay until this matter is resolved."

Well, sure I would. We didn't use the land for anything but the annual fair, but it would've been nice to be consulted. I nodded at the questioning glances from the carnies.

"What about the electricity you've been using?" Mabel wanted to know.

"And the water." Ruby's head bobbed like the tiny sparrow she resembled. More so beside the plump Mabel and massive Sally. "Who's going to pay for these things?"

"We've got the earnings from last night." Eddy pulled a handkerchief from the back pocket of his blue polyester pants and wiped his brow. "It ought to cover the utilities, but that's about it. Rather than worry about the money, someone ought to call the police to find out what happened to my father. This fair is his baby. He wouldn't have left voluntarily. And Grizzly Bob is gone, too."

"He feeds the animals," someone yelled. "I ain't touching that elephant."

"It's like the rapture of the carnies," Aunt Eunice whispered. "The way they keep disappearing."

"Shhh." I retrieved my cell phone from my pocket and punched in Joe's number. When he answered and I explained why I was calling, his sigh vibrated through the air waves. "Please hurry, Joe. The mob is getting restless, and Aunt Eunice is volunteering me to take care of that elephant."

"I don't even want to know why. I'll find out when I get there." Click.

"Ginger trampled Harvey," I pointed out to the others. "I don't feel qualified to take over her care."

"Honey, she likes you." Sally shifted her bulk. The bench creaked beneath her. "She didn't care for Harvey, nor Grizzly Bob much, come to think of it. You're the best choice."

"You're her trainer."

"I can't do what I once did." A hard glint shone in Sally's eyes, belying her smile. "We can't let the poor thing perish from hunger and lack of exercise, can we?"

Whoever said a fair was fun was not at the top of my popular list. It's been one headache after another. I couldn't help but remember the warning regarding Ginger that Harvey had given me. Maybe Ethan would feed the beast. Then fear for my beloved flooded through me. The gray saggy-skinned giant did seem to hold a fondness for me. The elephant, not Ethan. "Where's the bucket?"

"I knew you'd see it my way." Sally waved a hand until a teenage boy sprinted to my side, a battered plastic pail, the kind you buy bulk food in at a club warehouse, in his fist. "Feed's in that building over there. Water spigot is next to the paddock. She's all yours." Sally struggled to her feet. "I'll sit close by and give you instructions if you need 'em."

"What about the liability?" Mabel's round face creased with worry. "Insurance?"

Sally waved her off. "We don't worry about such things between friends."

Friends, huh? We may have started out on friendly terms, but something about Sally was starting to bug me. *Watch over me, Lord, as I embark on another foolish errand.*

The bucket banged against my jean-clad legs as I marched toward the small shed that held Ginger's feed. All I wanted was to make a difference in the world. Maybe save a few lives. Leave a legacy, other than making the finest chocolates this side of the Mississippi River. Something people would remember, and God willing, rid myself of the burden of guilt I felt over my parents' death. Taking care of a temperamental elephant didn't fit in with the plan.

Sighing, I pushed open the sagging wooden door. I recognized this building. Years ago, it had served as a pump house to a pioneering homestead of my great-grandfather's. Remnants of the rock wall still took prominence in the eight- by ten-foot shack. What would he think now, seeing his once profitable cotton acreage as home to a group of carnies and misfit animals?

Dust shimmered in the rays of sunlight filtering through the cracks of the walls. I sneezed. A mouse darted across my feet, startling me. I choked back a scream and dropped the bucket. I giggled recalling Ethan's aversion to mice.

After lifting the bucket, I dipped it in the barrel that contained some fragrant grains and couldn't help but remember the bloody gardening glove I'd found in a bucket of birdseed during the summer.

I squinted against the noon sun as I emerged from

the dim building with a much heavier bucket. Sally hadn't told me how much to feed Ginger. As my arms strained with the load, I hoped one bucketful would be enough.

I approached Ginger's paddock praying she was in a good mood today. The beast's trunk went straight for the water.

"If you spray me with water from that trough, I'll bang you upside the head with this bucket." Ginger trumpeted her reply, and I set the bucket by my feet. Next to the paddock a pile of hay was heaped. Using a nearby pitchfork, I tossed a forkful on the ground next to the feed.

So far so good. Her manner seemed consistent with that of a docile Hereford.

Uncle Roy roared onto the fairgrounds with a blare of his 1952 Chevy truck horn and a shout hello. The melodies of Dixieland burst from beneath his hood. A field mouse ran between my legs, and I screamed.

Pandemonium broke loose. Ginger tossed her head, blasted her own horn, and crashed through the wood railings of her paddock, knocking me to the ground. Guess she wasn't much for Southern anthems.

My side collided with the wood, and I lay in the dirt, hay, and trampled grasses and struggled to breathe. This was it. For the second time I thought I'd die trampled beneath the feet of a monstrous beast. I rolled under the lowest rail, out of Ginger's way.

Ethan lunged from the passenger side of the truck and shoved his way through the throng of hysterical people. I watched him come, like the moving reel of a slow motion picture.

Ginger knocked Sally backward and she shrieked.

Uncle Roy, exiting the truck, slid back in and slammed the door. Aunt Eunice waddle-darted—I'd never seen her move so fast—to the arts and crafts building. Mabel and Ruby froze, looking oddly like female versions of Laurel and Hardy. Eddy Foreman darted here and there, shouting orders and waving his arms. The rest scattered like a flock of chickens chased by a fox intent on carnage.

My ribs ached from the knock against the fence. With one arm hooked over a rail, I pulled myself to my feet. Ginger obviously had no intentions of harming me. Her goal seemed to be the green Chevy. I pointed. "Ethan, help Uncle Roy."

Ethan stopped his dash toward me and spun. In horrific Kodak color, Ginger charged the truck, ripping off the door Ethan had left open. Uncle Roy's eyes gleamed white, seeming as large as dinner plates, when Ginger turned for another charge. Ethan grabbed the pitchfork from where I'd tossed it and sprinted toward the enraged animal.

Lowering her head, Ginger butted the Chevy, knocking it to its side. Screams rang through the air, followed by shouts as carnies grabbed any weapon they could find and joined Ethan's rush toward the elephant. The Chevy flipped again, now resting upside down.

Joe's squad car pulled into the melee, lights flashing, siren wailing. Ginger trumpeted and thundered through the throng of approaching peasants armed with farm tools and sticks. With tosses of her head, she threw the men like a child's toy soldiers.

Joe emerged from his car, gun drawn. He pointed his weapon into the air and fired several rounds to no avail. He moved to the backseat and withdrew a shotgun. "Get back!" He aimed and fired.

Ginger changed direction. Her hooves shook the ground as she charged my cousin.

Harvey, bless his soul, hobbled past me with a huge tranquilizer gun. "That peashooter won't penetrate her hide."

Holding an arm firm against my side, I stood beside him. "So, you'll put her to sleep?"

"Oh, yeah. Unfortunately, it won't be permanent. Grizzly Bob keeps this gun for such a time as this."

The boom had me covering my ears. The dart hit. Ginger faltered and staggered. The next shot felled her with a mighty cloud of dust rising around her still body. She lifted her head and gave a feeble bleat. Harvey had taken her down just feet from Joe.

I rushed as fast as damaged ribs would allow toward my fallen friend. Despite the near miss of Joe and Uncle Roy, I—Uncle Roy! I changed direction.

Ethan knelt beside the truck and I limped to his side. "Get an ambulance!" Ethan shoved his cell phone in my hand. "That elephant caused a lot of damage. They might want to send two."

"Roy, Roy, Roy," Aunt Eunice chanted with each pant as she rushed toward her husband. "Tell me he ain't dead!"

Ethan stopped her. "He's alive. Just hurt, and the truck is smashed bad enough I can't get him out."

She fell to her knees. "Roy, honey. Can you hear me?"

"Of course I can hear you. Ethan told you I wasn't dead."

"You're bleeding." Tears coursed down my aunt's face.

I bent for a closer look. Uncle Roy must have grabbed

his hunting knife from the glove compartment before being rolled. It stuck out from his chest in the middle of a spreading stain of scarlet.

24

The hospital waiting room felt like a sardine can, stuffy and cloying with the perfume of elderly ladies. Beneath the scents hung the unmistakable odor of antiseptic. Gray walls, maroon vinyl furniture, and a desperateness signifying the need to flee from the room hovered over my concern for Uncle Roy.

Ethan, uncharacteristically gruff with several well-wishers, found me and Aunt Eunice a seat. I'd never been prouder of my protective man. Once he'd made us as comfortable as possible, he dashed down the hall after the doctor.

Aunt Eunice and I had been praying for a lifetime, it seemed, and while my spirit felt at peace, my body quivered with nerves. My hands shook and tears slid so regularly down my cheeks, I felt they forged a raw canyon. My makeup was long gone.

Ruby and Mabel perched on a shiny vinyl sofa like a sparrow and a plump dove. They'd been acting like bitter rivals since both courting the same widower. Yet here the two sat, praying against the enemy with my aunt and for my uncle. Uncle Roy said, despite their outward antagonism, the two were the best of friends.

Harvey, the mighty elephant killer and saver of the day, slumped in a chair, his casted foot propped on a stool. Eddy Foreman, the only other carny in attendance, paced. Probably worried about liability, the little weasel. The gold chains around his neck caught the reflection of the fluorescent lights.

If Uncle Roy should die, my guilt would be complete. The thought lodged the ever-present lump more firmly in my throat. I vowed to walk away from the case of the carnies and never look back. My obsession with nosiness was affecting those around me.

April rushed into the room, glanced in Joe's direction, then knelt before me. "How you holding up?"

I shrugged.

"I brought you a coffee." She handed me my favorite: a venti mocha frappuccino with whipped cream.

"Thanks." The drink froze my trembling hands and when I sipped it, icy heavenliness soothed my parched throat. Then I was able to speak. "Uncle Roy stabbed himself, April."

"Not on purpose. Joe told me what happened. Don't be melodramatic." She took my hand and pulled me to my feet. "Let's walk."

Aunt Eunice waved me away when I made a move to remain in my seat next to her. "Go on. I'll send someone for you when the doctor comes."

April led me to a lush garden the hospital maintained for waiting families. A light breeze rained petals from a flowering tree upon our heads and colored the brick pathway under our feet. April sat me on a carved marble bench donated in memorial to somebody's loved one. I traced my fingers over the raised name.

My friend put her hand over mine. "Roy is in God's hands, Summer. Same as whatever is bothering you."

"What makes you think something's bothering me?"

Her hand moved to my shoulder. "I'm your best friend. I can tell. When you want to talk about it, I'm here. Have you given it to God?"

No, I hadn't. Growing up spoiled, with most of my wants satisfied and all of my necessities, I had not developed the practice of going to God with my needs. And I wasn't prepared now to go before the throne and lay something of this magnitude, something as strong as my feelings of guilt, before the Creator of the universe.

"Something is driving you, girlfriend. Making you take on these cases better left to Joe and the police."

"I want to leave something behind, April. I want to make a difference in people's lives."

"Go on missionary trips with the church."

I shuddered. The thought of sleeping in a non-air-conditioned tent, surrounded by bugs, was not my cup of tea. Camping without a shower and blow dryer for three days every spring was as rustic as you would find me.

"Okay. Get more involved at church. Teach Sunday school, help with the women's ministry. There're loads of opportunities where you could make a difference." April moved her arm and pulled my head to her shoulder. "I know what your problem is."

"You do?" She smelled like sunflowers and spring.

"You don't want to do anything that might require more effort than you're willing to give. You, Summer Meadows, are lazy."

"What?" I straightened. "How can you say that? I own my own business. Candy making is backbreaking work and often requires long hours."

"But that's what *you* want to do. That's *your* dream. And these mysteries you're so bent on solving, they're the same. Something you thought might be fun. They aren't taking you out of your comfort zone and getting you to do something God wants you to do." She held up a hand to stop me.

"I'm not saying they're wrong, just that maybe, just maybe, you need to ask God what He wants you to do."

"Ethan supports me." And I could guarantee crime-solving often took me out of my comfort zone. "You're my best friend. Of everyone, I thought you'd be my strongest supporter."

"Because Ethan's not dumb enough not to. If he's helping, he can keep an eye on you. It doesn't mean he approves. And I am your best friend. That's why I care."

"You're way off, April. Acting like my own version of Nancy Drew has nothing to do with having fun." *Well, maybe a little.* I thought about taking her advice. Things would be much easier if I just let go of the reins and let God have control of my life. Let Him take me where I should go. But what if He said no? I shook my head. I wasn't ready yet.

"Well." April stood and smoothed her skirt. "I know there's more you aren't telling me, but this is what I see. Come on. Let's get back before we get into an argument."

I slipped my hand into hers, and we passed through the glass doors, swinging our arms like we did when we were children. "Thanks, April. For a moment, you made me forget why we're here."

"You're welcome. But I still told you what I thought."

"That you've always done."

When April and I entered the waiting room, the doctor stood in front of Aunt Eunice. She motioned for me to join her. I released April's hand and went to my aunt, resting my hand on her shoulder.

"Mrs. Meadows, your husband will be fine. The knife missed any vital organs."

"Praise God," Aunt Eunice said. Tears streamed down her cheeks.

The doctor smiled. "And he's suffering from contusions and crankiness, but he'll be able to go home in a few days."

I sagged with relief. Ethan burst through the waiting room door and made a beeline to my side, wrapping his strong arms around me. He kissed the top of my head. When the doctor had gone, he sat, pulling me into his lap. For the first time that day, my tension began to melt.

"Roy is strong. Wouldn't let me leave his side. We prayed until he went under anesthesia." Ethan met Aunt Eunice's gaze. "Eunice, he told you not to worry and apologized for not letting you in the room. Didn't want you to see him looking weak. He's in recovery now. In a couple of hours, you'll be able to go back and see him."

She gave a shaky chuckle and pulled a soggy tissue from her bra to dab at her eyes. "Stubborn man."

My cell phone rang out the melody to *Willy Wonka*. With a sheepish smile I mouthed "I'm sorry" and stepped away from my aunt.

"Hello?"

"You've got to stop her." The voice was muffled, as if spoken through a wadded towel. I thought it was a woman but couldn't say for sure.

"Who is this?" I whispered, cupping my hand over the phone's mouthpiece.

"She's going to know I called you. I had to take the chance. You've got to stop her. I only recently found out. Oh. Someone's trying to get in!"

"Call the police." My voice rose and Ethan's gaze jerked to mine. "Tell me who you are. Who are you talking about?"

Ethan stepped beside me. He raised an eyebrow in question. I shrugged and he leaned nearer in an effort to hear. Joe planted himself, arms crossed, in front of me.

"I can't do that, dear. Be careful. You've got to stop her."

"Is this Mrs. Hodge?" The endearment was a dead giveaway, and since I'd solved the case in July regarding her peeping Tom, she always called me when she needed something. "Call Joe!"

"He's bu—" The monotone dial tone droned in my ear.

"Who was it?" Joe reached for the phone and flipped through my incoming calls.

"I'm not sure. Mrs. Hodge, I think. Whoever it was is in trouble."

He snapped my phone closed. "We have a phone number. Let me call it in."

"There isn't a lot of time, Joe. The line went dead. Mrs. Hodge is an old lady in no condition to defend herself." I clutched Ethan's hand. "Her boyfriend isn't much stronger."

"Let's go pay her a visit while they run the phone number." Joe handed me my phone, slid his walkie-talkie from its holder, then led the way to his SUV.

We made the drive to Mrs. Hodge's house in silence.

The tires crunched the gravel driveway at Mrs. Hodge's small Victorian. My heart stopped when I glimpsed the busted front door.

Stay in the car." Joe slid from behind the wheel with his hand on his weapon. I reached for the door handle as he made his way to the front porch.

"Joe said to stay put." Ethan's lips pressed in a thin line.

A rapid volley of shots rang out. The windshield shattered. Glass showered Ethan's head like diamonds in the sand. Joe sprinted from the house and took cover behind the thick trunk of a massive oak. Bullets gouged the bark of the ancient tree.

"Find out where my backup is! I called them ten minutes ago."

Ethan fumbled for the radio, then lifted the receiver to his mouth. "Officer needs assistance. I repeat—"

Thankful I wasn't one of those shrieking females who lost their mind in a crisis, unless chased by a demon pig, I dove to the floor as another barrage of shots flew past. When the gunfire quieted, I peered over the back of the seat. Joe took a step out from behind the tree. A single shot caught him. My cousin spun like the ballerina in a child's music box before he fell.

"Joe's been hit!" I fumbled with the lock, shoved the door open, and fell to my knees in the gravel. The impact sent shock waves through me. "We're sitting ducks. Get me out of here."

"Officer down. Officer down! We're on Highway 64, Hodge's house." Ethan dropped the radio. "Bumbling country cops. Sorry, didn't mean that."

He yanked me to my feet and slammed me against the car. "Make for the trees and keep the car between you and the house. I've got to get Joe."

"Don't leave me. Please." So much for nonhysterical female. I clutched at his shirt front. Even weaponless, Ethan's presence made me feel safe.

His eyes searched my face. "Okay, come on." In a crouching run, Ethan led me into the thick woods surrounding Mrs. Hodge's house. We circled wide, slapping branches away from our faces and shoving through dense foliage, until we were mere feet from where Joe lay.

"Stay here," Ethan said.

No worry. There was absolutely no way I wanted to present myself as a target. I'd been shot at before. That time I'd been running, not squatting behind a bush. On second thought, I'd choose the action anytime rather than the inactivity of hiding.

"God help us. God help us." I whispered the prayer as Ethan darted to the oak Joe had sought shelter behind. I continued to pray when he reached for Joe's feet and dragged him into the bushes. Fear wiped my mind clear, allowing only the three words that I chanted: God help us.

"I'm fine," Joe told us. "Get away."

"We aren't leaving you. I've called for backup. Any minute, buddy. Hold on." Ethan peeled away Joe's shirt to reveal the gunshot wound. My stomach lurched, and I clamped my eyes shut. "Summer, put pressure on his shoulder. This isn't mortal. I've got to stand guard."

I shuffled over and pressed my hands, one on top of the other, over my cousin's wound. Bile rose against my continuous swallowing. *I won't be sick. I won't be sick.*

Joe groaned.

"Sorry." I pressed harder. My hands turned a shade of crimson I would never wear on purpose. I worried about the elderly Mrs. Hodge while I struggled to keep my cousin's blood inside him where it belonged. Where was her boyfriend, Pete? Her son, Richard Bland, had been the murderer and diamond thief from the case I'd solved months earlier. Alone, she'd turned to me when she needed help. How long had it been since I'd visited? One week? Two? Guilt rose in me.

Dried brush crunched about twenty feet from us. Still crouching, Ethan turned and pointed the gun in that direction. My pulse pounded in my ears so loudly, I didn't hear Joe speak. His lips moved but nothing issued forth. "What?"

"Go. They're coming. You and Ethan get out of here."

I met Ethan's gaze as Grizzly Bob stepped out from behind the trees. I shifted my eyes to stare down the barrel of the man's weapon.

"You should have stayed out of things, Miss Meadows," he said, his voice gruff, gravelly. "Should've just let us go about our business. But no, you're a meddlesome woman. Millie was bad enough, then Lacey. We had us a nice little group until they got nervous."

Ethan moved to stand.

"Stay put or I'll put a bullet through this little woman's brain. Drop the pistol."

Ethan placed the gun on a pile of dead leaves.

"Now scoot it this way."

My hands trembled as I fought to keep pressure on Joe's wound. "What now? Are you going to shoot us all? You shot a police officer! What did you do with Mrs. Hodge?"

"Stop with the questions. She's another worrisome

woman. The world is better off without the bunch of you."

My heart sank at his words and rose again at the far-off sound of sirens. Bob turned, and Ethan lunged. He caught the older man around the knees. Gunfire blasted the branches above our heads as the two men hit the ground. I lay across Joe to shield him from the falling debris.

They tussled, each grasping the weapon. If the barrel dropped with Bob's finger on the trigger, Joe and I'd be riddled with bullets. Not the way I'd envisioned dying. I much preferred the falling-asleep-in-bed-as-an-old-woman approach. Ethan would be holding my hand, spouting words of love.

Two squad cars, followed by an ambulance, roared onto the property. "Over here! Over here!" I waved my arm and prayed they'd spot me through the bushes.

The vehicles stopped as close to the line of trees as possible. Four armed officers, ducking and using whatever cover was available, rushed across the yard. Three of the officers ordered Bob to release his weapon while the fourth tackled him and wrestled the gun from his hands. I stood and glanced in dismay at the blood covering the front of me. "You hurt?" One of the officers asked.

"No, but Joe is. And there may be a couple of bodies inside the house." I turned and threw myself into Ethan's arms.

"Come on, baby."

I pulled away. "No, I've got to check on Joe."

"He's in good hands. We'll only be in the way." Ethan led me back to Joe's car, where he took a blanket from the backseat and wrapped it around me.

"Thanks. Guess I was right about the embezzlement."

Ethan laughed. "A piece of paper with a number in red doesn't constitute embezzlement. With the money gone from Foreman's safe, either he took it, or it's robbery."

Embezzlement sounds bigger, doesn't it? I sighed. "You're right. Who else do you think is involved? Bob mentioned 'us' as in more than one."

Ethan pulled me to his chest. "It's time to step out of it, Summer. At least four people are dead, if Mrs. Hodge and Pete are lying inside. It's not a game."

"We don't know that Lacey is dead." I peered up at his face. "We've got to find out what happened to her. I need to find out."

We were interrupted by the sight of two body bags being rolled on gurneys. Tears welled in my eyes. "Poor Mrs. Hodge. One blow after another in her life." Another emergency technician followed with a blanket-covered Joe. I took a step toward him and grasped his hand. He smiled. "Ethan and I will follow you, Joe."

I'd been too busy to visit Mrs. Hodge as often as I would've liked, believing the woman no longer needed my company since Pete courted her. I choked back a sob.

An officer approached us. "Your cousin is going to the hospital. Let me take your statements, and you can follow."

"We came in Joe's car," I pointed out. "What about Lacey Love? Did you find her?"

The officer frowned. "I can't divulge that information to you at the moment."

He'd just told me all I needed to know. I'd failed her. Sobs erupted from deep within me, rising with the violence of a volcano. Besides Lacey's killer, I was most likely the last one to see her alive. Just like my parents. Now, Mrs. Hodge and her boyfriend joined the list of victims.

The officer glanced at Ethan. "I'm sorry. I wasn't aware you two knew the victim."

"I—didn't." I buried my face in Ethan's chest. "Well, not Lacey, but I knew Mrs. Hodge."

"Why don't you two come down to the station later, and we'll take your statements there?" He waved over an officer who looked like he belonged in high school. "Officer Sweeney will drive you." With an obvious sense of relief, he turned over the care of us to the younger officer.

We made the trip to the hospital in silence, broken only by my sniffles. I rode burdened beneath a mountain of guilt and ineptitude. Ethan's arm around my shoulders did little to comfort me. My pain came from inside. From my inability to solve this mystery and save lives.

How many more people would die while I fumbled my way through the case?

I made my way to the chapel. In this country city, the hospital's chapel wasn't much larger than some people's master bedrooms, but it was quiet. Aunt Eunice knelt before the wooden altar, not rising as I entered. God didn't care what size the room was anyway.

The wooden pews were polished to a high sheen, and a simple oak cross hung above a podium. I chose a seat a few benches from the front and collapsed. My forehead rested against the pew in front of me.

Prayers for my uncle and Joe rose within me, not getting any further than my clamped lips. How could I pray when guilt threatened to choke me? Tears poured down my cheeks to land with splats on my folded hands. Empty-headed, ditzy, goofy were all adjectives used at one time or another to describe me. Guilty and empty—never. I swallowed against a sob. I was tired of hiding my guilt. I wanted release from my burden. My throat ached from the effort of restraining my grief.

Someone had left a Bible on the pew, and I reached for it. April once told me of a time when she'd desperately needed a word from God and asking, had let the Bible fall open. The pages fell on a verse that suited her needs to perfection. I shrugged and held the book by its binding, letting the pages ruffle open.

The words of 1 John 3:20 leaped at me from the onion skin pages. *Whenever our hearts condemn us. For God is greater than our hearts, and he knows everything.*

Yes, my heart condemned me. Yes, God is greater and

knows all things, but how did I forgive myself?

Aunt Eunice straightened and glanced over her shoulder. "Summer? You all right, sweetie?"

I shook my head. My aunt pushed to her feet and bustled to my side, scooting in next to me. She pulled my head to her bosom where it had rested many times over the years, through millions of tears and hundreds of childhood heartaches.

"What is it? Maybe I can help."

"Joe was shot today when we drove to Mrs. Hodge's house. Mrs. Hodge and Pete are dead. Grizzly Bob killed them."

Aunt Eunice stiffened. "Joe's dead?"

"No. A shoulder wound, but it's all my fault! Just like Mom and Dad and Terri Lee and Lacey Love and…"

Aunt Eunice stroked my head. "You're quite a powerful person, aren't you, dear?"

That stopped me in my tracks. Powerful? Hardly.

I pulled away from her and focused through my tears on her face. "What?"

Aunt Eunice took my face in her hands and brushed my cheeks dry with her thumbs. "To have done all that. You started young, too."

"I don't understand."

"That's obvious." She pulled a tissue from inside her shirt and handed the soggy scrap of Kleenex to me. "Sit up, blow your nose, and listen to me. I don't profess to completely understand God and all He does, but your moping around lately has got to stop. If I'd had any idea you felt responsible for your parents' death, well. . .I don't know."

I stuffed the used tissue into my pocket. "I threw a

temper tantrum that last day because they were going to a party without me. Mom waved and tried to smile, but I'd stressed her out so much, she couldn't. I didn't return the smile or the wave. Dad roared out of the driveway. If I hadn't have put so much pressure on them and made them late, they'd still be here."

"You don't know that. Summer, you were five years old. Not responsible for your actions. A drunk driver killed your parents. Not you. And you've carried this around with you for twenty-five years?"

I nodded. "I didn't realize it until lately, but that's what's driving me to solve these cases I get mixed up in. A chance for rectification. To undo a wrong I've done. I've failed so many people."

"I knew you were spoiled, but I had no idea you had such a lofty opinion of yourself." Aunt Eunice picked up the Bible from where I'd let it fall. Confusion clouded my brain. If this was my aunt's way of making me feel better, I'd choose to stay a wreck.

"Do you believe what this book says?"

"Of course."

"All of it? Or just parts? What verse did you read just now?"

"First John 3:20."

"Uh-huh." Aunt Eunice thumbed through the book until she found the verse. Her lips moved silently as she read. She closed the Bible, keeping her finger inside as a marker. "I guess that verse must be a lie, considering you're still sitting here feeling sorry for yourself."

I scratched my head, frowning. "I don't understand what you're getting at. Nothing in the Bible is a lie. God doesn't lie."

"Really? So you just don't believe it." She lifted her chin. "Tell me what the verse means."

"That God knows everything. That He is greater than our hearts."

"But what does it *mean*? Did you read the verse before that one? What about the ones after?" She reopened the book and began to read. " 'This then is how we know that we belong to the truth, and how we set our hearts at rest in his presence whenever our hearts condemn us. For God is greater than our hearts, and he knows everything. Dear friends, if our hearts do not condemn us, we have confidence before God and receive from him anything we ask.' " She lifted her gaze back to mine. "What have you asked for, Summer?"

I opened my mouth, then clamped it shut. Nothing. Out of my sense of shame, I hadn't felt worthy to ask for anything.

Aunt Eunice set the book down and gathered my hands in hers. "God knows our hearts, our motives, our every piece. God will not condemn us." Her lips spread in a slow smile. "And he isn't going to hand over control of the universe into these soft hands of yours. You aren't responsible for the death of these people. Your parents or anyone else. Your desire has been to help, not hurt."

"How did you get so wise?" For the first time in a long while peace began to fill me, tiny crevice by crevice, and the burden of guilt I carried lifted an inch.

"Do you know who I was praying for before I fell asleep on that very uncomfortable pew?"

"Uncle Roy?"

"No, he's going to be fine. I was praying for you. I knew the moment you walked through those doors you carried a whole mountain of hurt." She cupped my cheek. "Now let's go check on that cousin of yours."

"I'll be there in a minute, okay?"

"Okay." Her hand rested on my shoulder for a second before she rose and left.

Alone, I sat. No tears, no shudders, just the ever-present lump in my throat as I absorbed the healing words my aunt had spoken. I'd accepted God's salvation at the age of thirteen, but never had He seemed as real, as loving, as He did this very minute. Thirty years old and I'd finally grown up.

Ethan waited for me outside the door. I stepped from the peace of the chapel to the warmth of his embrace.

"Are you all right?"

I nodded. "Wonderful. It took me a while to take myself off the pedestal I stood on and let God take over. How do you put up with me?"

"Blinded by love, I guess." Laughter rumbled in his chest.

"Ha, ha. How's Joe?"

"Not bad. Doctor said the bullet went straight through." Ethan slid an arm across my shoulders. "Ready to go home?"

"Very." My mind returned to Grizzly Bob and the missing carnival funds. Did he kill the people and take the money or was none of it related at all? Was the case solved? If so, where was Mr. Foreman? Was he involved or an innocent victim? I gnawed my lip. With Joe laid up, there was no one at the station I could go to for answers. My nosy personality left me unsatisfied. I knew there were still parts of the story left untold. Despite my resolve to stay out of the investigation, I had too many unanswered questions.

I yawned. Tomorrow, after I gave my statement to the police, I'd go back to the carnival grounds and speak with Big Sally. She seemed to be the hub of the carnival and a close friend of Grizzly Bob's.

27

Folks huddled in small clusters of three or four when I arrived at the fairgrounds the next morning. An autumn chill hung in the air, and people's breath puffed like dragon smoke. What could be dismantled had been. The other buildings and rides were unplugged and boarded up. Because my family owned the land these people rented, my first stop of the day should be Eddy Foreman's. I shuddered and pushed open the car door.

Even my footsteps sounded muffled as I made my way across the dirt-packed ground. Last year, once they'd finished the breakdown, the carnies threw a party. The air had been full of gaiety. Lack of money definitely put a damper on things.

I rapped on the door of Eddy's trailer. As usual, he seemed happy to see me and still wore his signature polyester. "Summer!"

"Eddy." I peered past him. He appeared alone although several empty beer cans littered the battered coffee table. Eddy could learn some tips on cleanliness and interior decorating from Washington.

"Come in, please." With a swipe of his arm, he cleared a section of the green sofa of old newspapers and offered me a seat.

"Thank you." I shoved aside the curtains, allowing any passersby a clear view of the inside of Eddy's trailer. "Want to keep everything above board and proper, don't we?"

He guffawed. "You do beat all, and to think I offered you Millie's job."

"Just think." I still hadn't gotten over the mortification of *that* experience. "How do you get by with it? The prostitution, I mean?"

"Prostitution? Only suspected, not proven." Eddy winked. "What my employees do on their free time has nothing to do with me. Besides, your cousin was about to put a halt to everything anyway. We don't get invited to many towns for a second run."

Imagine that.

"So extracurricular activities are easy to slide past the authorities." He plopped on the other end of the sofa. "To what do I owe the pleasure of your visit? Business or pleasure?"

"Definitely business." The thought of visiting him held absolutely no pleasure for me. I felt dirty just sitting in close proximity with the man. "Have you located your father?"

"Unfortunately not. He seems to have disappeared into thin air. He's gone, the money's gone, but his car is right where he parked it." Eddy ran a hand through his heavily pomaded hair. "With Lacey turning up dead and Grizzly Bob in jail, I fear the worst for my old man."

I gnawed my lower lip. Things didn't look good for the kind owner of the carnival. Eddy looked genuinely upset over his father's disappearance, but I wasn't going to cross him off my suspect list yet. I decided on the direct approach. "Eddy, has anyone been embezzling funds from the carnival?"

"Embezzling? You'd have to talk to Lacey. Well, you can't, can you? I guess that leaves Woodrow. He's the fair's accountant. Lacey was his assistant."

"Could they have been stealing from you?"

Eddy shook his head. "I trust my employees, Summer. Completely. Most of them have been with Foreman's Fair and Carnival for years."

"So you and your father didn't have some type of system to make sure people stayed honest?"

"We're a small business. Besides the meddling of the IRS, we trust each other. There's never been an issue until the other night. No, I don't think embezzlement is a problem. It's an act of out-and-out theft and kidnapping. Find my father, and we'll find the money."

"You think your father took it?"

"Someone did. It's missing, and so is he."

We rose at the same time. The heel of my boot caught on the frayed edge of the sofa and I tilted forward. Eddy caught me and pulled me close. My hands splayed across his exposed chest. Perspiration glistened from among the coarse hairs. The fumes from the beer he'd been drinking washed over me, and I swallowed against the bile rising in my throat.

"I'm lonely, Summer, with Lacey gone. Stay for a while."

Averting my face, I tried to step back. For a man who was only five-foot-seven, his strength amazed me. "You don't appear grief-stricken over the loss of your girlfriend."

"Lacey was everyone's girlfriend. You're different. One woman; one man."

"That's right, and I'm taken." The well-placed heel of my boot exerting pressure on the top of his foot made him release me. "I'm sorry for your loss, Eddy, and I'll do whatever I can to help you locate your father, but I'm off-limits. Understand?" I marched to the door and turned, my manner softening. "Like I said, don't worry about where y'all can stay. I'm not going to run you off my land."

He rubbed his hands across his face. "We have somewhere to be in a couple of weeks. I'm afraid I won't have enough employees left to get us there."

"God provides, Eddy. Spend some time getting to know Him instead of the bottom of a can of beer." When did I get so self-righteous? "I'm sorry. That came out wrong. You let me know if there's anything me or my family can do to help."

"You got a few thousand dollars?"

"Sorry." I took a deep breath and decided to blurt out what had been on my mind the last few days. "I was in Lacey's trailer a few days ago and found a sheet of paper with numbers and an amount written in red. Fifty thousand dollars."

Eddy laughed. "She was saving to buy a house. Lacey wanted out of the carnival business. Wanted to settle down and have a family. That's the amount she wanted to save."

"Oh." I jerked the door open and stepped outside. I was officially an idiot. Why did I have to make things seem more sinister than they were? Embezzlement! I shook my head. Looked like I was mistaken, and with Grizzly Bob in jail, this case was closed. More deaths than we'd had back in July, and I still had no motive for Bob's murdering spree. It seemed the trail I'd been following led nowhere.

Maybe the authorities could get Bob to tell them why he'd shadowed me dressed as a gorilla. Or why he'd killed Laid Back Millie and staged a suicide. Then there was Lacey and the disappearance of Foreman. An endless circle of questions with no answers.

My gaze roamed the almost deserted fairgrounds. A melancholy haze seemed to hover over everything as if not only the carnies and animals mourned, but the structures themselves.

What am I missing, God? With Joe out of the picture and Grizzly caught in the act, the police would look no further for answers. With my mind clear from the fog of guilt, I knew it was only a matter of time before things clicked together into something that made sense. Having Grizzly Bob caught and Mr. Foreman still missing. . .I shook my head. No, there was still some searching to be done.

My steps turned toward Sally's trailer. The woman didn't hold court outside her trailer today. Instead, the unmistakable sounds of heartbreaking sobs drifted to me from a partially open window. My hand paused in midknock, reluctant to intrude on someone's grief.

Woodrow spoke from behind me. "Go in, Miss Summer. Sally could use a friend right now."

My hand fluttered to my chest. "You scared me, Woodrow."

"Forgive me." He nodded toward the door. Once inside, he brushed past me and knelt in front of Sally. "Dearest, you have company."

Sally held out a hand to me. "Summer!" The woman's red-rimmed eyes focused on me. A smile split the folds of her face. She appeared happy to see me. Why did I feel her greeting was forced?

The feeling didn't dissipate when she patted the sofa beside her. Her weight caused the piece of furniture to tilt. I took a seat, leaning away from her and hooking my arm over the edge of the sofa to not slide against her and the pile of soggy tissues between us. Woodrow held out a glass of lukewarm tea.

I now faced a dilemma. Let go of the sofa and take the tea, which would result in my sliding into the woman's lap, or decline the tea and risk being considered rude. I chose to slide, spilling some of the tea in my lap as I did so. A sour smell rose from Sally's unwashed body the closer I moved to her. My hip plastered against hers. She slung one meaty arm across my shoulders, and I felt I'd suffocate beneath its weight.

"Oh, Summer." She pulled me closer, much the way a mother hugs a child. "I've lost my dearest friend. Besides Woodrow, that is. I don't see how I can go on. Now I have the unpleasant task of deciding how to avenge my loved one's death against the murderer. There's only one person responsible, and that person still walks."

"But Ginger isn't dead."

She raised her head and speared me with a red-rimmed gaze. "I'm talking about my son."

Uh-oh.

28

O dor washed over me, causing me to feel as dirty as Sally smelled. With the ease of an eel, I slipped free of the woman's hug and leaped to my feet. I set the glass of tea on top of a pile of books on the crowded coffee table. In slow motion the cup fell. I lunged too late and smacked my shin against the edge of the glass tabletop. Amber liquid splattered my favorite boots.

"Wait, Summer." Sally stretched a hand toward me. "Stay. Enjoy a snack with us. We've managed to lay our hands on the most delicious jar of bread-and-butter pickles. You must try some."

"No, thank you." I forced a smile to my lips. Goose pimples prickled my flesh, and I crossed my arms. "I've really got to be going."

"What's your hurry? You paid us a visit for a reason." Sally wiggled her fingers at Woodrow. "My medication, sweetie. The liquid and the capsules." Her gaze slipped back to me. "I live my life in pain, Summer. Both mental and physical. Can you understand what that is like? Of course not. You're bright, thin, beautiful. Life is like a bowl of cherries for you, isn't it?"

"I prefer a box of chocolates."

Sally giggled. "And you're a movie buff. Splendid."

Woodrow poured a small glass of liquid from a whiskey bottle and handed the drink, along with three small red tablets, to Sally. She chased the pills with the liquor, sighed, and laid her head back against the sofa. "Why don't you get to the point, Summer? I'm extremely tired."

"I came to see how you're holding up after what happened to Ginger and Grizzly Bob."

"Bob? What's that fool done now?"

"He's a murderer, Sally." My hand fumbled for the doorknob. "He killed an old couple and wounded a police officer. He's in jail."

"Well, we're all murderers of a sort, aren't we? In tidy prisons of our own. Some of us are just ignorant to the fact. Living in their pretty little houses, with their pretty little lives." Sally's hand crushed the fragile glass she held. Scarlet drops fell on the pile of snowy tissues beside her. "The one responsible for hurting my beautiful Ginger will pay. Don't worry your lovely little head about that. But that's not the justice I'm focusing on right now."

I shoved the door open and ducked back out into a drizzly, rainy day. Directly across from me, the fun house clown's head towered over the grounds as if in agreement with Sally's threat. I needed to warn Harvey, then pay a visit to Joe in the hospital.

I glanced over my shoulder. Woodrow peered through the curtains. To hide my ever-increasing feeling of fear, I waved and increased my pace toward the other end of the fairgrounds. A breeze picked up as I walked, leaving me cold and clammy.

I knocked on the door of what I believed to be Harvey's trailer. No response. I peeked in the window to see the lights off and a neat orderliness to the living space. Nothing seemed out of the ordinary, but I couldn't help wondering if he had gone missing, too, adding one more name to the missing person's list. Two, if you count Harvey's wife. I shrugged. With luck, the couple was shopping in town, and my imagination was working overtime.

Once behind the wheel of my car with the doors locked, my rapidly beating heart returned to normal. The small groups of carnies who'd braved the increasingly cloudy weather to work on the carnival's tearing down had disappeared, seeking drier places to congregate. A quick glance at my watch told me Ethan still had a couple of hours of work before he'd be home. I started the car and drove to the hospital.

Aunt Eunice and her friends Ruby and Mabel stood outside the front entrance. The three were engaged in an animated conversation of friendly rivalry over whether or not we should have contracted Foreman's Fair and Carnival for our annual fair. I shook my head. Those three would argue over the shade of gray of today's sky if nothing better presented itself. Aunt Eunice waved me over.

"What do you think, Summer? There's been nothing but trouble since this group arrived." Ruby's tiny frame trembled in the cold. "Your aunt Eunice won't see reason and make those people leave."

I released a frustrated burst of air that puffed out my cheeks. *Guide my words, Lord.* "There's no guarantee in life, ladies, that any other carnival would have had better luck. Y'all contracted them. What was your reason?"

"They were the cheapest bid, and we thought it would be nice to have a little something extra with our county fair." Mabel announced. "I told Ruby you get what you pay for. We need to clean up Mountain Shadows and tell them to go."

"The land belongs to me, not Aunt Eunice or Uncle Roy. I've already said they could stay until things are resolved. I won't go back on my word. They have nowhere else to go until they get their money back."

"Eunice said you'd be that way." Ruby hugged her purse to her chest. "You always were a headstrong girl. I thought maybe once you got with that nice boy, Ethan, you'd get your head on straight."

My Irish temper flared. "I'd rather have my head on crooked than be a self-righteous old busybody with a cold heart. Have you forgotten that Christ asked us to consider the least of these? That in giving them just a glass of water we've quenched *His* thirst?"

"Summer!" Aunt Eunice's eyes widened.

"I'm sorry, Aunt Eunice, but you need to keep a tighter rein on your friends." I spun on my heel and shoved through the double doors of the hospital. The fact that Ruby and Mabel were correct about the heap of problems we've had since the fair came to town hadn't been lost on me. I just had a problem with the women's way of wanting to handle the trouble. In a gesture of goodwill, I poked my head back out the door.

"I'll ask Joe what we should do."

My boot heels clipped against the tiled floor as I marched past the nurses' station. Lucky man. They'd given him a single occupancy room. His eyes were closed, so I flopped into the chair next to him.

"I'm not sleeping."

"Oh, good. I need to talk to you." I scooted forward and perched on the edge of the seat.

"Otherwise you wouldn't be here." He opened one eye to peer at me.

"Be nice. I came to see how you're doing. And I brought you chocolate." I pulled a box containing a dark chocolate lion from my purse.

"Uh-huh. Spill."

"How certain are we that Grizzly Bob is our man?"

Both of Joe's eyes were now open. "We caught him in the act of shooting me. You and Ethan were next."

"I know, but there are still a lot of holes. Like, where's Mr. Foreman and the money? And why does Big Sally have Aunt Eunice's missing pickles? I saw them with my own eyes. Sally has threatened to make someone pay for murdering her son and—"

"Whoa!" Joe pushed the button to raise his bed. "Slow down. You're running off at the mouth like a tsunami."

I balanced my elbows on my knees and leaned forward. "Did you know that Sally drinks whiskey and takes pills? Together? She's insane, Joe. I saw a side of her today that I've never seen, and I have to admit, it frightened me. Gone was the jolly fat woman."

"Lord, take me home now. Save me from this woman."

"Aren't you curious?"

Joe reached for the plastic cup of water on the bedside table and took a sip. "Start at the pickles. You lost me on that one. Then move on to Sally's son being killed. That's new to me."

I refilled his cup from the salmon-colored pitcher. "I paid Sally a visit. To give my condolences for Ginger and Bob. She offered me some bread-and-butter pickles. Remember Aunt Eunice's disappeared right before the judging?"

"And what makes you think they belonged to your aunt? Lots of people can stuff cucumbers in a jar and call them pickles. They could also have been a gift. Maybe you should ask Eunice if she gave them to Sally. Or Ruby or Mabel did."

"What about Sally's drinking and popping pills? What

about her threatening to get even for her son's death?"

"She wouldn't be the first person. When's this murder supposed to have taken place?"

"She didn't say. Drugs are expensive. It could be a motive for murder and robbery. You should've heard her talking, Joe. Very spooky."

He stared at me as if I'd lost my mind or had worms crawling out of my ears. "Grizzly Bob admitted to killing Lacey, Pete, and Mrs. Hodge. You personally ripped the gorilla head off him. In time, he'll crack and tell us where Mr. Foreman's body and the money can be found. The case is winding down, Summer. Leave the carnies alone."

I slouched against the back of the chair. "Something tells me there's more."

"Do I have to arrest you again?"

"What about Harvey? He wasn't at his trailer."

"So? Besides, Harvey doesn't live with the carnival. He only hires on when one comes to town. He and his wife live down Forrest Road."

"Then why haven't I met him?"

Joe laughed. "He belongs to the same hunting lodge as your uncle. You don't hunt."

No time today. "Ruby and Mabel want to know what you intend to do about the carnies."

"Me?" His eyes widened.

"Okay, what do you want me to do? I already told them they could stay until either the money is found or Eddy's father is."

"Well, they can't stay forever."

"No, but having them there makes it convenient for solving this case, right?"

"The case is finished. Leave it alone."

"I can't. With you laid up, there's no one to see that justice is done."

"I'm not the only officer on the force. I can have you locked up."

I stood. "Stop threatening me. Do what you have to. I'll do what I have to. Right now I'm going to meet Ethan for dinner. Stop me if you can. Bye." I clapped him on his uninjured shoulder, winked, and strode from his room.

29

My favorite royal blue wraparound blouse and black pants hung on the outside of the closet waiting for my date with Ethan. With the fair taking up so much of my time, it'd been a while since we'd spent romantic time together. Despite that, I couldn't help but wonder whether Ethan would want to go on a stakeout with me. My *Handy Dandy Guidebook to Spying* beckoned from my bedside table.

I snatched the book and let it fall open. The pages fell on "Ten Ways to Think like a Spy." Number one, act like you belong. That's easy. I own the land the fair sits on, so I belong there as much as anyone else. Number two, have a purpose. I did, didn't I? A desire to get to the bottom of things. So far so good. Number three, blend in. A bit harder now that everyone knows me, but not impossible, right? I could feel my mind become sharper, like a trap ready to ensnare the suspect.

"Summer? Ethan's here." Aunt Eunice's voice ripped me from my covert studies.

"Be down in a jiffy!" I tossed my spy book into the small tote bag I used as my spy case—when I remembered to stick it in my purse, that is. Most of the time the black leather tote remained in the top drawer of my nightstand. Not tonight. I shoved everything into my purse. The bag contained my tiny flashlight, a notepad and pencil, and the sweetest little recorder that fit in the palm of my hand. I had my eye set on a camera next. The electronic store had one that would be perfect.

With the fair over, I was certain I could now put an end to the sinister dealings at Foreman's Fair and Carnival. Whether Joe agreed or not, I knew with absolute certainty things were not over. Call it a detective's intuition.

I let my jeans and turtleneck shirt fall to a puddle on the floor and grabbed the clothes hanging on my closet. Once dressed, I pulled a brush through my curls, tied my hair back in a ribbon, grabbed my purse, then darted down the stairs.

"Sorry I'm late. Time got away from me." I planted a kiss on Ethan's cheek.

"No problem, Tink. I'm used to it and you're worth waiting for." Ethan slid an arm around my waist. "See you later, Eunice."

"Bye, you two." Aunt Eunice disappeared into the kitchen.

"Ready?" Ethan smiled down at me.

"Ready."

Once we'd eaten and discussed all the everyday things that lovers talk about over dinner, I decided to broach the subject of a stakeout while Ethan was pleasantly full and enjoying the aftereffects of his steak.

"Ethan?"

"Yes?" His dimple winked. "So, are you ready now to tell me what's been on your mind all evening? Don't tell me nothing. I know you."

How did he do that? How did he always know? I filled him in on the details of my visit with Sally. "So, I'd like to do some spy work."

"You don't know the first thing about being a spy."

I dug in my purse for the guidebook and slid it across the table. Ethan laughed. I sat straighter and clenched my teeth. He picked up the book and skimmed through the pages.

"I'm asking you to go with me, Ethan. I could go by myself, but I'm trying to respect your wishes." I gripped my hands around my glass.

"I appreciate that." He handed the guide back to me and crossed his arms, leaning on the table. "Joe is certain Grizzly Bob is the culprit. I'm sure Sally's words are just that. Words of pain. But, if I can squeeze in a little time holding you, I'd be willing to sit in the dark, in the cold, on a stakeout with you."

"Really?"

"For my own completely selfish reasons, of course."

I dropped the book back into my purse and raised my hand for the restaurant bill. "Of course." The glance he gave me melted my insides, and if the look was from someone else that I'd be sitting in the dark with, I'd be seriously concerned for my virtue. But not my strong-willed hero. He'd keep things on the straight and narrow, despite myself. Ethan paid the bill then steered me outside to his truck.

Fifteen minutes later he stopped before the open gates to the fairgrounds. No one stirred. The grounds sat in quiet shadows. Muted light glowed from behind drawn curtains. My gaze scanned the night, searching for a place where we could park unseen.

"Pull behind the arts and crafts building," I whispered. "We'll have a clear view of Sally's trailer."

"Why are we whispering?" Ethan turned the wheel.

"Because that's what spies do."

"Right."

I soon grew bored and my eyes weary from straining to catch movement from Sally's that didn't come. Ethan glanced at me and grinned.

"Ready to give me a kiss?" He pulled me close and planted a kiss on the tender spot beneath my ear. I shivered, losing myself in the sheer bliss of his lips. "Your uncle would shoot me if he caught me nuzzling you in the dark."

"Most likely. But what a way to go." My words threatened to be swept away in the breathlessness of his kiss, and I lost myself in the arms of my soul mate. I turned my head to meet his lips. If this was what a stakeout with a handsome man and the world's best kisser did to someone, I'd join the CIA in a split second. As long as Ethan could be my partner.

The door to Sally's trailer opened. "Wait." I planted my hands on Ethan's chest and pushed. "Look." Woodrow stepped out, glanced both ways, headed down the corridor between the buildings, then disappeared in the shadows.

I eased my door open. "Come on. Let's follow him."

"I'd rather stay here where you can keep me warm."

"Come on." I tugged at Ethan's hand. He slid along the seat after me and closed the door with a muffled thud.

"Shhh." I held a finger to my lips and glared.

"Sorry."

I pulled him behind me in the direction Woodrow had gone. We caught up with the man outside one of the carnies' trailers. Ethan and I darted behind one of the restrooms and peered around the corner. How I wished I had that camera I'd been yearning for.

Woodrow used his elbow and broke the window. He glanced around at the sound of glass shattering, then knocked out the rest of the pane before climbing inside.

"This doesn't look good." Ethan loped toward the broken window and pulled me with him. "Something else shattered inside." Ethan shoved me around the corner.

"I can't see anything," I hissed. I shoved closer. From beneath Ethan's arm, I caught a clear picture of Woodrow climbing back out the window, a plastic bottle of pills clutched in his hand. "He's buying or stealing drugs. I knew it. I told Joe this was all about Sally being an addict."

"You did?" Ethan glanced down at me.

"Well, words to that effect."

"Uh-huh."

Once Woodrow had sneaked back toward Sally's trailer, Ethan and I stepped out, being careful to keep the man several yards ahead of us. Raised voices reached us before we approached the partially open window of Sally's home.

"What took you so long? I'm dying here. You know I need my medication, Woodrow."

"I hurried as fast as I could, dear."

"Not fast enough. You know the pain I'm in. Hurry, hand me the bottle."

My height was not an advantage to peering in windows. A quick study of the nearby ground yielded a battered milk crate. Ethan placed it beneath the sill, and I stepped up, keeping myself between the aluminum siding of the wall and the protection of Ethan. This position promised a clear view of the living room and kitchen where Woodrow prepared a drink for his lady.

"Oh no." I glanced at Ethan.

Woodrow pulled a bottle from beneath his jacket and dumped a healthy portion of white powder into the glass of whiskey he'd just poured. He then shook out three of the red pills he'd given Sally earlier. "He's going to poison her."

My foot slipped.

The crate banged against the side of the trailer.

Woodrow whirled. The glass in his hand crashed to the floor where it shattered.

I fell backward, taking Ethan to the ground with me. The air left my lungs with a muffled whoosh. A scrap of fabric from my blouse hung from an exposed nail on the window frame.

"Who's there? Woodrow, go see who it is." Sally's bellow burst from the open window. Her shrill girlie voice had been replaced with gruffness.

"Come on." Ethan scrambled to his feet, hefted me in his arms, then darted around the corner of the trailer.

"We've got to stop him, Ethan. He's going to kill her."

"Shhh." He clapped a hand over my mouth.

Woodrow's shadow, complete with the silhouette of a hand clutching a gun, stretched around the building.

The spy book never mentioned what to do if we get caught." My heart beat with the pace of a thoroughbred, each thud like mighty hooves against the racetrack of my rib cage.

"We aren't caught yet." Ethan kicked a nearby rock. It knocked into a storage building opposite us. Unlike in the movies, the sound did draw Woodrow's attention in the opposite direction.

"Is that you, Miss Meadows? 'Cause I'm wondering who else would be sneaking around our place at this time of night." Woodrow's voice took on a singsong rhythm.

I shivered, not only against the night chill, but with the eeriness of the position I found myself in. The tone of his voice, his attempt at playfulness while trying to kill me, cast the situation in a surreal nightmare. I clutched Ethan's arm. My fingers dug into the flesh of his bicep.

"Noisy, meddlesome woman. My life is full of wretched females who can't leave a man alone. Can you hear me? Can you see me?" I couldn't remember a time when Woodrow had spoken more than a few words at a time. Now the man seemed to spew words like a fountain.

If I had to be stalked by a madman, I thanked God for Ethan being with me. I tended to lose my head in extreme circumstances. Ethan disentangled his arm from my grip and steered me ahead of him around another corner.

Breathe, Summer. Deep breaths. Too deep. Danger of hyperventilation. Spots swam before my eyes. I swayed and Ethan steadied me.

"There's the truck." Ethan gave me a shove, and we dashed across the alley. My hands fumbled with the truck's door latch until Ethan reached around me and opened it. Keeping low, he scooted to the driver's side, climbed in, then turned the ignition.

"That was a rush." Ethan grinned at me as we spun gravel out of the fairgrounds.

A nervous giggle escaped me. "Wasn't it?" I laid a hand on his arm. "We need to let the police know that Woodrow is stealing from the pharmacy and planning to murder Sally."

"We don't know the powder is poison. It could be part of her medication." Sometimes Ethan's logical mind overshadowed his ability to see the possible what-ifs.

"What about his chasing us with a gun?" I tilted my head, glaring through the dimness of the truck's cab.

"There is that." Ethan remained silent until we pulled in front of my house. He turned to me. "Summer, this evening was fun. Adrenaline-rushing, in fact."

"But?"

He pulled me to him and cradled my head on his chest. "I'm a teacher. You make candy. This is above our heads. No matter how much fun we have, we need to be responsible and let the police handle things."

"Joe's laid up in the hospital."

"Why can't you hear what I'm telling you?" Ethan set me back, one hand on each of my shoulders. "God, help me. Woman, you scare the living daylights out of me. I love you so much it frightens me. The thought of losing you—" He let go and ran his fingers through his hair. The moonlight coming through the windows highlighted his curls with silver, and my hands ached to follow the path his had left. "Eunice told me about your feelings of guilt about your parents."

"Oh." I loved this man with all my heart, but my aunt telling him something so confidential still felt like betrayal.

"I want you to be able to come to me with struggles like that." His pain sounded so raw his words bled across the small cab.

"It's not so bad anymore, Ethan. I've given it up to God."

"Then why are you still so driven to solve this?"

"I thought you were having fun."

"I was. Not so much when I saw the gun. You scare me. Back there, at the campground, you trembled in my arms. Fear oozed from you, yet here you sit, raring to go again." He leaned back, resting his head on the back of the seat. His gaze rolled to mine. "What am I going to do with you?"

"Marry me?"

"What, you don't want to wait until next fall? And don't change the subject." The porch light blinked on. "Looks like your aunt doesn't want us sitting in the truck any longer."

"When will she realize I'm almost thirty and stop treating me like some wild teenager?"

Ethan chuckled.

I punched his arm. "And don't say it's when I stop acting like one."

"Okay, I won't say it."

I punched him again and he jerked me close, his lips claiming mine. For the next several minutes I forgot about the Sallys, Woodrows, and gun-wielding gorillas of the world. It wasn't until the porch light blinked on and off in rapid succession that I pulled free from the intoxication of Ethan's kisses.

"Tomorrow is Saturday. Feel like making a trip to Forrest Road and visiting Harvey?" I smoothed a wayward curl back from Ethan's forehead.

"You'll go either way, right?" He kept his arms around my waist.

"Not if you really don't want me to."

"What's out there?"

I told him about Sally's threat regarding Ginger. "And she's threatening revenge against someone who supposedly killed her son. I can't think of anyone else to question. Especially since Harvey already warned me about being in danger. I'm assuming he meant the elephant."

"Okay. I'll pick you up at ten."

He opened the truck door and slid out, pulling me with him. "This conversation isn't finished, Tink." I closed my eyes when he placed a kiss between my brows.

I sighed. "I have to go through with this. Yes, I've given the guilt to God. It won't be something that is solved in a day. I'll have to make the choice each morning when I wake and each night when I go to bed. I've lived with that burden for so many years, Ethan, it feels like a part of me. I'm standing on God's promises, but I made a promise, too. I made a promise to a scared woman whose face I glimpsed through a speeding car's window."

The flickering of the porch light increased in intensity. "Kiss me again. Give Aunt Eunice a heart attack."

Ethan smiled and lowered his head. His kiss lit up the night until I feared for my heart. The squeak of the screen door signaled that Aunt Eunice had gotten tired of waiting. "I love you."

"I love you. See you in the morning." I caressed his cheek and turned to meet my virtue-saving aunt.

"What are you thinking, necking in the driveway?" Aunt Eunice folded her arms. "What will the neighbors think? I raised you better than that."

"You, Aunt Eunice, are a gem. A true gem. I thank God for you." I hugged her and marched into the house.

"What happened to your shirt? If that boy got too rough, your uncle will have words to say to him."

I glanced at the bottom portion of my blouse. Ethan's kisses had kept me warm enough, I'd forgotten the missing section. The fabric fluttering from the window of Sally's trailer announced to everyone that someone had been peeking in her window.

31

Ethan and I sat in the cab of his truck and stared at the swinging screen door of Harvey's house on Forrest Road. Everyone wasn't as conscientious as my aunt and uncle, but I had a hard time believing the banging of the door wouldn't attract the attention of someone inside.

I swallowed against the rising knot in my throat. "Do you think we're going to find more bodies inside?"

"I hope not." Ethan reached for his cell phone. "But I do know we aren't going inside without the police."

"Can we at least explore the surrounding area?" My gaze scanned the thick forest of trees around the property. "Maybe we'll find some clues. The police won't let us inside once they get here."

"Look, Nancy Drew, in real life people don't go barging around crime scenes." He chuckled and clapped a hand to his forehead. "For a moment, I forgot I was speaking to Summer Meadows. Now *she* definitely gets enjoyment out of messing up crime scenes."

"Ha ha. Very funny." I crossed my arms and slouched against the seat. "We can't just sit here."

"Why not?"

"I—well. . . Give me a minute. I'll think of something." A cry drifted on the morning air. I straightened and rolled down my window. "Did you hear that?" It was a definite plea for help. Before Ethan could utter another *God help me,* I bolted from the truck.

"Summer, wait." I hadn't closed my door before he appeared by my side and gripped my arm.

"Someone needs us. Listen."

"I hear." We paused. My ears strained to detect the direction the cry came from.

"This way." I grabbed Ethan's hand and sprinted for the trees.

He yanked me back. "Stay behind me." Ethan clipped his phone back to his belt. His hand hovered over the black leather case like a cop with a gun. He caught me looking and grinned. "I might need to grab it quick. Besides, you ran from the truck before I could place the call."

He led me fifty feet into the woods. We stopped beneath a large oak and stared up at a tree house. Harvey's wife and a boy approximately eight years old peered down at us.

"Thank the Lord. Please tell me you're the good guys. I can't stay up here for another minute. Every bone in my body aches to high heaven." The woman chattered as she shifted and climbed down the rope ladder. Her plump behind strained against the cotton pants she wore. I bit back a chuckle as she jumped the last rope knot, landing in an undignified heap at our feet. "I'm not made for climbing trees anymore." She stood and dusted herself off. "I'm Ester and this is my son, Harvey Junior."

"Where's Harvey?" I asked. The boy climbed down much nimbler than his mother.

"I haven't seen him since the fiasco at the fairgrounds." Tears welled in the woman's eyes. "I'm worried about him."

As she should be from what Sally spouted off. "Why are you hiding in the tree house?"

"We're hiding from the gorilla." Junior stepped forward. "I tried to get my rifle, but Mom made me run out the back door and hide up there."

"A gorilla?" Did everyone in this part of Arkansas think they could solve their problems with a gun? Redneck clichés ran through my mind of flannel-shirted, tobacco-chewing hillbillies grasping rifles. I almost expected a three-legged dog to romp around our feet. I shook my head to clear it. "When?"

"Last night." Ester headed back toward her house. "Y'all come on in. I want to see what damage has been done. And it wasn't a real gorilla, mind you. Someone in a suit."

Of course. My gaze met Ethan's. Grizzly Bob was already behind bars. At the thought of two people hiding behind a gorilla mask, taking turns stalking me, a cold sweat collected beneath the sweater I wore.

"What time last night?" Ethan took my arm.

"Late. We were already in bed when the dog's barking woke us. Maybe midnight?"

"Later than that, Mom," Junior said. "I stayed up to watch cartoons on cable. Maybe two o'clock."

Ester rolled her eyes. "He don't listen very good. But with Harvey gone so much, I don't have the strength for heavy discipline. The boy plumb wears me out at times." She led the way up the porch steps and into the house. Complete disarray greeted us in the form of clothes scattered across furniture, cabinet doors hanging open, and dishes left in the sink and on counters.

"Looks like they were searching for something. They've destroyed your house." I stepped farther into the kitchen. "We need to see whether anything is missing."

"Nah, this is how it always looks. I'm not much of one for housekeeping, either. I like the lived-in look. As for stealing, we don't have anything worth somebody taking."

The dreaded flush crept up my neck. Open mouth, insert entire leg. Ethan fought back a grin.

"It doesn't look like anyone's here now." Ethan headed for the back of the house. "Let me have a look around, make sure everything's fine. You should probably call the police and let them know you had an intruder."

He reappeared moments later with a shivering Chihuahua in his arms. "Here's your fearless protector. Found him hiding under the bed."

"Momma's little Snookums!" Ester hugged the dog to her bosom. "If you find Harvey—Lord, we pray You keep him safe—tell him to get his rear end home."

"Will do." Ethan ushered me out the front door. "Do you want us to call the police for you?"

Ester waved us off. "I'm gonna call 'em now."

I glanced back at her over my shoulder while Ethan and I walked across the yard. "She doesn't seem too concerned, does she?"

"She's used to her husband being gone." He opened the truck door for me. "It's the way of life for women who marry carnies. They either go with them or stay behind."

"I'd be scared spitless if my husband was gone and someone wearing a gorilla suit came to my house."

"You've had worse."

"And I was terrified each and every time." I slid inside the truck. "Two gorillas, Ethan. That's why they always seem to be wherever I am. Woodrow had plenty of time to drive out here last night after we left. We need to check on Sally. She could be lying dead right now."

Ethan shook his head. "He suspects you of peeking in his window. If you show up, he could confront you. We'll go to the station and tell them our suspicions."

Does he always have to play things so safe? A sigh escaped me. "I really enjoy you as my sidekick, Ethan, but you sure do hold me back."

He took my hands from my lap and folded them with his. "Let's pray for Harvey's safety and then head to the station, okay?"

I nodded and bowed my head, struggling to focus on Ethan's simple prayer of protection and discernment. Instead, my mind raced like a whirling twister. The few clues I'd gathered sucked up like debris and turned muddy, hard to see through. Were Woodrow and Grizzly Bob working together? What part did Sally play in all this? I didn't believe her to be completely innocent or clueless.

And what motive could they all have? That's the part where I got lost. I couldn't believe the acts of violence were because of money. Too simple, and I couldn't see the relation between the victims, other than the fact they all worked for Rick Foreman, who was also missing.

Lord, make things clear, please. Ethan's amen jerked me back to the cab of his truck. Shame flooded through me. I wasn't even a decent enough person to stay focused during a prayer for someone's safety.

Words my aunt spoke to me last July echoed through my mind. I am spoiled and selfish! How can anyone love me, much less God? I vowed to do better. To make myself worthy of His love. Starting with saving Harvey. I'd failed with so many others, but this time I would triumph.

I stayed lost in my self-accusation while Ethan drove us to the police station. It took fifteen minutes for someone to greet us and another ten before they were able to tell us who was acting chief while Joe lay in a hospital bed. Eventually, an officer who didn't look old enough to be out of the academy strolled up to us, his face wearing the telltale signs of stress in lines around his eyes and mouth.

"I'm Lieutenant Downs. You're looking for me?"

Ethan shook the man's hand. "We'd like to speak with you about what we are assuming could possibly be an attempted murder."

"Assuming?"

I rattled off the events of last night. The officer's frown deepened.

"You were peeking in someone's window."

Did Joe impart his wisdom of repeating what I said to his officers? "Yes. We'd like for you to send someone to check on Sally."

Lieutenant Downs scratched his forehead. "I don't have the manpower. Eddy Foreman is putting pressure on us to find his dad, we still haven't found Lacey Love's body, Mrs. Hodge and Pete were murdered, Grizzly Bob is talking a lot of nonsense, and now Harvey's wife called and said a gorilla visited them last night. That's not taking into account that her neighbor swears she saw Bigfoot cut across her property last night. Until we get a call, giving us more to go on than your assumption, well, my hands are tied. Why don't the two of you go out? Give us a call if you find anything."

"Uh, well, I kind of left a piece of my blouse hanging on a nail outside Sally's window. They'll know we were spying. Or at least someone was." Did the guy really tell us to go on our own? Maybe Joe could stay in the hospital awhile. I'd have more freedom.

Downs shrugged. "Like I said, my hands are tied. If you'll excuse me." The man turned and marched away, shouting orders at a rookie drinking from the water fountain. "We don't have time for that! Get out there and start solving this case."

Ethan glanced down at me. "Want to go see Joe?"

"Definitely."

—

Joe sat propped up in bed staring mournfully at a bowl of chicken broth when we entered his room. "Hey." He didn't even look up. "I'll be your best friend if you bring me a double cheeseburger."

Ethan laughed. "You are my best friend. You look like a puppy dog that's just had its bone stolen."

"I'll be godfather to your future children."

"Already done." Ethan lowered himself into the vinyl chair beside the bed. Joe turned his head and scowled at him.

"My, my, we're a bit cranky this morning." I pulled a hard chair next to the bed and handed Joe a bag from the nearest fast food joint. "Stop whining. We brought you lunch."

"Did y'all come here to cheer me up? You're doing a poor job."

"Whose bright idea was it to put Lieutenant Downs in charge?" I crossed my arms. "The man is clueless."

Joe switched his gaze to me. "Mine. I'm still in charge; he's helping by being my eyes and feet."

I filled my cousin in on the happenings of last night and this morning. His face reddened until I feared for his blood pressure.

He redirected his scowl back to Ethan. "I thought I told you to keep her out of trouble."

Ethan shrugged. "Other than tying her up, I felt going along with her was the safest thing to do."

"Right. So what is it you two super sleuths want from me? If you hadn't noticed, I'm a bit indisposed."

"And feeling sorry for yourself," I added.

"What we want, Joe. . ." Ethan leaned forward, ". . .is some advice. Obviously Downs isn't going to check things out at Sally's. Should we?"

"If you really think her life is in danger, you should go, because I don't personally think there's anything to worry about her getting hurt. But I need to warn you." Joe shoved aside his rolling tray. "Harvey isn't missing. He's hiding. Came to see me yesterday. Said his life was in danger, and his family would be safer if he took off for a while. I'm not sure Sally is an innocent victim here."

It reassured me to know the feelings rising in me weren't part of my imagination. "Did Harvey happen to mention to you that he thought there was an ulterior motive for Sally asking me to walk Ginger to the fairgrounds? Because just yesterday, you were under the impression this case was solved."

"Yes, and I'm beginning to agree with him. This isn't about money; I'm willing to bet my career on that. There's something more, and if I wasn't tied to this bed, I'd be finding out."

"Then we'll have to hit the pavement for you." Ethan rose and clapped a hand on Joe's shoulder. "We'll keep you informed."

Joe's hand rested on top of his friend's. "Thanks. You two be careful." As we walked from the room, he muttered, "I can't believe I'm letting my scatterbrained cousin loose on a murder investigation. I *am* desperate. Ethan, don't let her out of your sight."

32

"So, do we wait for cover of darkness or go now?" I linked my arms through Ethan's.

He raised his eyebrows. "I thought you were worried about Sally."

"Not as much after hearing Joe echo the same thoughts flitting through my mind. I still think Woodrow is up to something, though."

He looked taken aback.

"It isn't you someone's trying to kill." I yanked open the car door and slid inside.

"No, it's the woman I love." Ethan moved behind the steering wheel.

I burst into tears. Digging into my purse for a Kleenex, I blurted out the awful feelings of guilt and unworthiness I'd been carrying around inside me. I wiped my nose and filled out the details with my thoughts of selfishness and the inability to turn my burden over to God, then finished with my desire to save Harvey. With the knowledge of his being safely hidden away, I admitted to feeling a little let down. I didn't know where to go from there.

The tender smile Ethan gave set me to hiccuping. "The thoughts and feelings you're experiencing aren't a surprise to God. He knows the number of the hairs on your head, which is quite a feat." He patted my unruly mane.

I pushed his hand away. "Then why am I still having such a hard time?"

Despite my halfhearted attempts to keep him at bay, he pulled me into his arms. "Until you come to terms with the fact you weren't responsible for the death of your parents, until you've forgiven yourself, you're going to struggle with accepting God's forgiveness."

"You sound like Aunt Eunice."

"Wise woman."

I giggled and wiped my nose with the soggy Kleenex. "I'm just feeling sorry for myself. It's getting a bit old having people try to kill me."

His chest rumbled with laughter beneath my cheek. "I imagine it is. Let's get something to eat before we head to the fairgrounds. Woodrow knows we're suspicious. I don't think he'll try anything else anytime soon."

"Those books I bought on being a detective haven't helped much, have they? Maybe I need to go back to the bookstore."

"Come on, Nancy Drew. I'm hungry."

In the restroom of the diner, I splashed my swollen eyes with cold water. After checking beneath the stalls to make sure I was alone, I stared at my reflection in the mirror. "Okay, God. I heard once that sometimes, well, probably most of the time, we have to actively give up our burden. So, I give it up. My guilt, my shame, the whole shebang. It's Yours. I don't want it back. If I try taking it back, knock me upside the head. Not too hard, but enough to get my attention."

It took several long minutes, but the load on my shoulders started to lift. My spirit began to soar. I realized I'd probably have to do the handing-over thing again tomorrow and each day after that until I got it right, but the peace I felt at the moment made the future handing over seem like child's play. I knew I wanted the feeling to last and would be willing to do my part for God to keep the reins.

"You look better," Ethan remarked as I slid into the booth across from him.

"I had a little talk with God. Amazing how that makes you feel, isn't it?"

"Absolutely. I ordered you a double cheeseburger, same as me. Is that all right?"

"Wonderful." I couldn't seem to wipe the face-splitting grin from my face. Biting into the jumbo burger almost accomplished the fact, but it wasn't until Woodrow stepped beside the table that my smile faded. Funny how the sight of a gun tucked into someone's waistband has that effect.

"Ms. Meadows. Mr. Banning. You two need to come with me. No yelling, no crying out for help, or I'll shoot one of these people who are innocently enjoying their dinner. I would regret doing that."

"How did you know we were here?" I grabbed my purse.

"Small town. I've been following you since you left the hospital. Let's go."

What happened to the meek man who hid in Sally's shadow? My gaze met the steely one of Ethan. A muscle ticked in his jaw. Uh-oh. I recognized the look. My gentle giant was angry. He tossed some cash on the table.

Woodrow ushered us ahead of him to the parking lot. "You drive, Mr. Banning. Your lovely fiancée will sit between us with my pistol aimed at her side. Do I need to shoot her in the foot to show you how serious I am?"

Ethan shook his head and yanked open the driver's side door. "You're being very clear with your intentions, Mr. Bell."

"Ms. Meadows." Woodrow motioned for me to open the passenger side and slide in. Our captor followed suit. "Now, isn't this cozy? Drive to the fairgrounds, Mr. Banning. My love awaits. She has quite a story to tell."

"So you didn't kill her." I could have bitten my tongue as Woodrow's face turned a fire engine red.

"Why do you think I want to kill the woman I love? I'm doing all this for her."

"Why? Why Millie and Lacey? Where's Mr. Foreman?"

"Millie and Lacey were Grizzly Bob's doing. Not mine. I've no idea where Foreman is. Ran off with his money most likely. Probably figured out we were aiming to relieve him of it. Women have very loose tongues, wouldn't you agree, Mr. Banning?"

Ethan clenched his jaw and continued driving.

"They figured out what you were up to, didn't they?" It *was* about money. So cliché. "If it's money you want, why me?"

"I'll let Sally explain that, my dear. We thought we'd kill two birds with one stone upon arriving in Mountain Shadows, so to speak."

Ethan jerked the wheel, knocking Woodrow against the door. The man didn't loosen his grip on the gun. "Do that again, and you'll be carrying your pretty little woman, minus a few toes, into the trailer."

For the first time in my life, I wanted the drive down Highway 64 to the fairgrounds to take forever. In a town the size of Mountain Shadows, it couldn't. Ethan stopped the truck behind Sally's trailer. We sat silent, as twilight approached.

"What are we waiting for?" If the man wanted me to hear something, then I wanted things to move. All I received for my question was a jab in the ribs with the gun.

Another first for me, sitting there not speaking. A huge accomplishment of which, under different circumstances, I would've been proud. I stole a glimpse at Ethan's profile. His jaw still twitched. His gaze remained straight ahead, and I could almost detect the wheels working in his head as he tried to figure a safe way out of our predicament. I squeezed his hand and received a reassuring squeeze in return. He'd find a way out of this. I knew he would.

Once darkness fell, Woodrow slid from the truck and motioned for us to follow. "Let's go. She's waiting and making her wait too long isn't wise."

"Well, we wouldn't want that now, would we? We waited until dark. What was that all about?"

Ethan gave me a sharp look at my wisecrack.

"Don't make her angry, Miss Meadows. The dark is the best place to hide when you don't want to be seen. Isn't it?" Woodrow shoved his pistol into the small of my back. I winced against the sharp pain, certain I would be sporting a pretty purple bruise tomorrow. If I lived through the night. I gave myself a mental shake at the path my thoughts took.

"I wouldn't speak unless she asks you to. Sally hasn't been in the best of moods since Ginger was shot."

Good grief. They act like the elephant died.

We mounted the steps in silence. Ethan opened the door and entered first, I went second, followed by my shadow, Woodrow. Sally sat on the sofa, thick ankles propped on the coffee table. She waved us toward a couple of kitchen chairs lined up in front of her.

"I'm sorry you're here, Mr. Banning. It's Summer I want. You're an inconvenience really." The mood felt surreal; the little girl voice spilling from the mound of woman opposite us. Her eyes glittered like the reflection of the moon on dark ice.

I raised my hand. Sally crooked an eyebrow. "Yes?"

"Uh, Woodrow told me not to speak until spoken to, but—" I lowered my hand and folded it with the other one in my lap.

"Get on with it. Time is wasting."

"I have to admit to some confusion, Sally. What exactly is it you want from me?" Dread filled me as I waited for her answer.

"My dear, I'm afraid you are not able to give me back what it is I want." She turned to Woodrow. "My pills, Woodrow."

He scurried to do her bidding. A glance over my shoulder showed me he still kept the gun trained on us despite it hampering his progress. When he returned to hand Sally the glass of amber liquid and red tablets, she turned her attention back to us. "A pity about Mrs. Hodge. But the woman really shouldn't have tried getting involved. She'd already done so much. Summer, does the name Richard Bland mean anything to you?"

My breath caught. Richard Bland, or rather Richard Hodge, had courted me in July, using the name of Nate, after he discovered I'd located the diamonds he'd stolen. After kidnapping and attempting to murder me, he'd been shot and killed by Joe. "Yes, I remember Richard. Not his real name, as I recall."

"No, that was his real name. His birth name. Mrs. Hodge was his adoptive mother. Bland is my name. Richard was my son. I had to give him up. Couldn't justify dragging a baby around from fair to fair. Made a tidy sum off the transaction."

"You sold your baby?"

"Happens all the time. Doesn't mean I didn't love him. I expected Mrs. Hodge to take better care of him. She sent him away to a mental hospital." Sally spit. "What kind of a mother is that? But my boy was smart. He escaped. But you know all about that, don't you?"

I couldn't help but think craziness ran in Sally's family.

She shrugged. "Anyway, so you see, dear, you were directly responsible for the death of someone very precious to me. Now, what do you think I should do about that?"

33

Ethan bolted to his feet.

Woodrow sprang across the coffee table, pulling a black rectangular object from his pocket. Before I could blink, Ethan lay still on the floor, groaning.

"Silly man." Sally struggled to her feet. "We didn't want to hurt you. Woodrow, have Summer help you drag teacher man out to the storage shed. Make it quick. He'll be able to move soon. You don't want to have to zap him again."

With a wave of his pistol, Woodrow motioned for me to grab Ethan's feet. "I'll get this end."

"I will not help you lock him up!"

"Would you rather I shoot him?" Woodrow cocked his head. "That's Bob's area. I'd prefer to lock them up and run, but maybe I can be persuaded."

"You're going to kill us. I'm not stupid." I planted my fists on my hips. "We can identify you."

"Fine." Woodrow shook his head. "Would you like to watch as I shoot him?" He aimed the gun at Ethan's head.

"No, please." I reached for the gun, withdrawing as Woodrow twitched his trigger finger.

"Then grab his feet."

My gaze locked with Ethan's before I wrapped my hands around his ankles. He weighed a ton. And neither Woodrow nor I was big or brawny. Our inability to lift Ethan had him thumping down the wooden steps of the trailer, which was sure to leave marks on his gorgeous physique. Woodrow opened the door to a rusty metal shed and dragged Ethan inside, where he zapped him again.

"You're going to send him into cardiac arrest." I stared down at my jerking fiancé. A deep burn started in my stomach, then rose. My neck heated. My hands itched to form around Woodrow's skinny neck. It took every ounce of willpower I possessed to keep myself in check. Turning on the man would only get me and Ethan killed. As long as I breathed, there would be an opportunity to escape.

"I can't have him moving until I'm ready to deal with him." Once Woodrow shoved me back outside, he turned to lock the padlock. "It's your fault he's in there. Everything is your fault. Sally's son, Ginger's banishment to the wild, Sally's increased use of drugs. Everything."

I took advantage of the momentary attention diversion and slammed him against the wall, taking a great deal of satisfaction from the grunt that escaped him. I grinned and sprinted around the building. I tried door after door of abandoned buildings and found them all locked. Sheer desperation sent me to the one building I wanted most to avoid.

The clown's head seemed to mock me, bobbing and grinning its maniacal smile, as I darted down the track into the dark recesses. I knew we should have torn down the old building years ago, but it made a convenient haunted house for Halloween and got reused for the fair every year. I breathed a prayer of thanks to God that Woodrow hadn't relieved me of my purse. Obviously the man didn't suspect Summer Meadows of having a backbone. Few people did. I'd dwell a moment on that painful thought when I got out of there.

I withdrew my tiny pink flashlight and my cell phone.

One glance at the phone's dark face, and I swallowed against sobs. Again, I'd forgotten to charge it. I might, at times, have a spine of steel, but I also have a memory incapable of remembering the mundane.

How long until Woodrow discovered where I'd gone?

"Miss Meadows?"

Question answered. I increased my dash down the tracks, dodging the unmoving cars. The heel of my boot caught on a rail, and I sprawled across the iron tracks, banging my head on the plastic image of a monster wielding, thankfully, a rubber axe. As many times as I'd conked my head the last few days, it was a miracle I wasn't in a coma. My purse disappeared beneath the closest car. I groaned.

I'd hated this place since the summer I'd turned thirteen and Joe had ridiculed me until I sneaked in after dark. Then, like the wonderful cousin he'd been, he'd left me there to find my way out. Ethan had been my knight in shining armor then. *Please, God, let him get free and rescue me this time.* Or maybe, against insurmountable odds, I would rescue him.

I shivered. An unreasonable fear swamped me every time I stepped near this laughing, creaking idea of some maniac's sense of fun.

Getting to my feet, I placed a hand to my head and winced. A dark sticky liquid shone on my palm when I withdrew my hand. Wonderful. I blinked against the wetness.

"Are you in here, Miss Meadows? What a fun place to play a game of hide-n-seek, wouldn't you agree? Makes me feel like a child again." His voice sounded eerie in the tunnel. Its consistent tone of playfulness sent ripples of fear down my spine. "Sally decided she has no further use for you. She only wanted to torment you. Make you suffer a bit like she has the last few months. Mess with your family. She does like to play games. Then she'll kill you in cold blood as you did Richard. The game is over, Miss Meadows. Except for the game we're playing. This one is much more fun. If I had my way, I'd conk you over the head and go to Mexico. But, I need the missing cash for that."

The man's crazy. *Help me, God.* I thought the old coot wanted Sally dead. Then why this macabre chase through the fun house?

"It really shouldn't have come to this." The man's voice seemed to come from my right. I ducked down a hall to the left.

"The accident in front of your house was my idea. That led to the ingenious plan of you walking Ginger to the fairgrounds. It should have resulted in your death then, which would have spared us all this. But we wouldn't have had this wonderful opportunity to play. Who knew that stupid animal would take a liking to you? She'd hurt plenty of people before. People more skilled than you at handling animals. If everyone wasn't afraid of Sally, the animal would most likely have been killed a long time ago. . . ."

Mirrors of all shapes and sizes surrounded me, illuminated by the moon's rays through a skylight. More than twenty pale, wild-haired Summers surrounded me. Some tall, some skinny, some short, some fat. I whirled, searching for the exit. The room spun around me, making me dizzy.

"Don't you like the moving floor, Summer? It's a riot with the young people."

My legs wobbled as if I were trying to make my way across the deck of a bucking ship. I fell to my knees. My gaze searched for a way out.

No track ran through to show me the way. A weird combination of thrills bent on providing a nightmare to anyone who sought one. With hands splayed in front of me, I ran my palms over the cold, flat, two-dimensional figures of myself, searching for an opening, a crack in the glass, anything.

Lord, show me a way. Please don't leave me, having found a new, honest relationship with You, only to die in the dark by a madman's bullet.

One of the panels swung free at my touch, exposing an opening. With a sob that bordered on hysteria, I threw myself into an even darker tunnel. The mirror closed. A groan reached me from the corner. "Who's there?" My eyes strained through the inky blackness, broken only by the minuscule beam of my flashlight.

A man sat tied to a wooden chair, a dirty rag shoved in his mouth, bound by duct tape. I rushed to his side. "Mr. Foreman?" His eyes beseeched me to release him. He sagged against his bindings. "Have you been in here all this time? Did Bob put you here?" He nodded.

"Do you know where the money is?"

Mr. Foreman slid his gaze toward a chest in the corner. Wonderful! I would let Joe know as soon as I got out of here. I searched the surroundings for something to cut the zip ties that bound him. Nothing.

I spun at the noise of fumbling fingers on the other side of the mirrors. My heart accelerated to the speed of a race car. *Think, Summer.* "Mr. Foreman, nod in the direction of the maintenance room. There is one, right?"

He inclined his head to my left, bless his heart. "I'll be back. I promise." I shone my flashlight around the room until I discovered an opening in the back wall. Another tunnel led to my left, continuing the mad pursuit of terror and someone's idea of fun.

This tunnel led me to a makeshift graveyard. Skeletons and zombies leaped from behind tombstones like deranged corpses. I choked back a shriek.

Through the walls, I heard him. "Mr. Foreman. How nice to see you again. Bob must have stashed you here, then got arrested before he could finish the job. Did that two-timer get the cash for himself? I'm rather surprised to find you alive. Once I've dealt with my current problem, I'll be back to deal with you. Maybe together we can find where Bob stashed the dough. Oh, well, such is life. My guess would be that Miss Meadows came through here, didn't she? Well, I'll leave you to your business. I've a game to win. Then your hidden cash to locate. Busy, busy."

The man gained on me. I raised a hand to my wet face. Tears now mixed with the blood.

A fallen tombstone, with the familiar *May he rest in peace*, lay next to my feet. I hefted the wooden shape in my hands and stood with my back plastered against the wall where I knew Woodrow had to emerge. I held the prop like a baseball bat. When Woodrow stepped through the door, I hit him. He fell to the ground, the stun gun flying from his hands. I wanted to search his pockets for the real weapon, but he groaned. I hadn't knocked him unconscious. As he cursed and struggled to his feet, I fled the room.

"So, my dear, the game continues." His voice followed me down yet another corridor. "Now, when I find you, I'll have no choice but to shoot you. Sally wanted to do the deed herself. I still haven't figured out why she didn't want to shoot Mr. Banning along with you. She said she had no grudge against him. Oh, well. I'd wanted to play more, but, alas, that is no longer a possibility. You're proving more resilient and sharp-minded than I'd figured. Good job. A worthy adversary. A welcome change from the empty-headed Millie and Lacey."

Where was the maintenance room? My flashlight? I'd dropped it when I'd bashed Woodrow. A tiny beam of light shone around the corner. He'd found it, putting himself at a definite advantage.

I trailed my fingers down the wall as I ran, searching without sight for a gap. My chest burned with the effort to breathe normally. Sobs stuck in my throat, making each breath more difficult. I vowed to begin an exercise program as soon as possible.

God, please!

Then I found it. A door that, during the day, probably seemed part of the tunnel. I shoved against it, falling into a room full of tools, a workbench, and, *thank You, Lord*, another door. I grabbed a pair of wire cutters from the desk and burst outside. I took a deep breath. Ethan! I dashed toward the shed where Woodrow had locked up Ethan.

The door stood open, hanging from a busted hinge. He was gone. A volcanic rage exploded within me, and for the first time in my life, I had the desire to take someone's life. I doubled over with the pain from my sobs, glancing again at the shattered hinge.

Wait.

Woodrow had the key. He had no need of breaking

through. We weren't alone in the deserted fairgrounds. I whirled at a sound behind me. Ethan leaned against the restroom wall, a bit unsteady on his feet, but alive.

"Ethan! Oh, Ethan." I almost knocked him over as I hurled myself into his arms. "How did you get out? Who?"

"Miss Meadows?" Woodrow's voice drifted to us on the breeze.

"We've got to hide. He's coming."

"You're bleeding." Ethan brushed aside my bangs.

"I'm fine. Come on." I slid beneath his right arm to support his weight and led him back into the restroom. I spied urinals mounted on the wall and dragged Ethan to the single stall at the back of the building. I couldn't help but think of Aunt Eunice. Even under these circumstances she'd be astounded that I'd gone into the men's room. "Sit here. I've got to go back. Mr. Foreman is tied in the fun house."

"No, Summer. There's no need." Sounds of a scuffle reached us through the walls. A boy's shout. A thud. A curse. A yell of triumph.

A dimple winked in Ethan's cheek. "Some of the football team is here. Seems they were up to a bit of mischief themselves. I heard them through the walls of the shed and yelled for help. They busted me out. And, since no teenager nowadays is without a cell phone, I had them call the police."

"Mr. Banning, you in here?" Ethan's student David, along with two other boys, dragged a weak and battered Mr. Woodrow into the restroom. David handed the pistol to Ethan. "It wasn't hard to sneak up and overpower the little weasel. He didn't have a chance against us jocks."

Ethan stood. "I appreciate that, boys, but I asked you to call the police. You could've been shot." He stuffed the gun in his waistband.

"We did call." Sirens wailed in the distance. "See? But we couldn't resist having a little fun with him."

I handed David the wire cutters. "There's a man tied up in the room behind the fun house mirrors. Can you find him?"

"Sure. We've spent the night in there plenty of times. Scary place. Lots of fun."

I laughed. "Yes, it is." My hand clasped in his, Ethan and I made our way out of the restroom and into the blinking lights of two squad cars.

A female officer walked behind a cuffed and cursing Sally, ignoring the woman's pleas about being ill. Two more officers burst into the restroom behind us and dragged out a still unconscious Woodrow.

Although my body would protest with pain tomorrow, and I'd have one humongous headache, I felt lighter than I had in months. My faith strengthened, the ability to get myself out of tight jams, and the love of the best man in the world lifted me above the atrocities of the last few weeks.

Ethan's arm rested across my shoulders. "Woman, you do get into adventures, don't you?"

"Life with me won't be boring."

"Definitely not."

I peered at his face. "I don't want to wait until next fall to get married, Ethan. I want to get married in the spring. A new life. A new beginning."

He lowered his head to kiss me. "Sounds good to me. How about April Fools' Day?"

Having grown up in the foothills of the Ozarks, small-town life in Arkansas holds a special place in Cynthia Hickey's heart and is the setting for most of her writing. She is the Detention Monitor at her local school and likes to hear nothing better than a student saying they'd like to write a book someday. Besides writing, she enjoys reading, making DVDs from family photos, and hanging out with family.

You may correspond with this author by writing:
Cynthia Hickey
Author Relations
PO Box 721
Uhrichsville, OH 44683

A Letter to Our Readers

Dear Reader:
In order to help us satisfy your quest for more great mystery stories, we would appreciate it if you would take a few minutes to respond to the following questions. We welcome your comments and read each form and letter we receive. When completed, please return to:

Fiction Editor
Heartsong Presents—MYSTERIES!
PO Box 721
Uhrichsville, Ohio 44683

Did you enjoy reading *Candy-Coated Secrets* by Cynthia Hickey?

Very much! I would like to see more books like this! The one thing I particularly enjoyed about this story was:

_____
_____
_____

Moderately. I would have enjoyed it more if:

_____
_____
_____

Are you a member of the HP—MYSTERIES! Book Club?
Yes   No

If no, where did you purchase this book?

_____

Please rate the following elements using a scale of 1 (poor) to 10 (superior):

___ Main character/sleuth   ___ Romance elements

___ Inspirational theme   ___ Secondary characters

___ Setting   ___ Mystery plot

How would you rate the cover design on a scale of 1 (poor) to 5 (superior)? _____

What themes/settings would you like to see in future **Heartsong Presents—MYSTERIES!** selections? _____
_____
_____
_____

Please check your age range:
- ○ Under 18   ○ 18–24
- ○ 25–34   ○ 35–45
- ○ 46–55   ○ Over 55

Name: _____

Occupation: _____

Address: _____

E-mail address: _____

Continue your mystery adventures at the Heartsong Mysteries blog!

SpyglassLane.blogspot.com

- Read original mystery short stories
- Enter exclusive member contests
- Play the weekly Mystery Theater game
- Learn more about your favorite authors

AND SO MUCH MORE!

Heartsong Presents—MYSTERIES!
PO Box 721
Uhrichsville, OH 44663
(740) 922-7280
www.heartsongmysteries.com

Heartsong Presents

Any 8 Titles
for $32!
A 20%
Savings!

Great Mysteries
at a Great Price!
Purchase Any Title for
Only $4.97 Each!

HEARTSONG PRESENTS—MYSTERIES!
TITLES AVAILABLE NOW:

(If ordering from this page, please remember to include it with the order form.)

MYSTERIES!

Heartsong Presents—MYSTERIES! provide romance and faith interwoven among the pages of these fun whodunits. Written by the talented and brightest authors in this genre, such as Christine Lynxwiler, Cecil Murphey, Nancy Mehl, Dana Mentink, Candice Speare, and many others, these cozy tales are sure to challenge your mind, warm your heart, touch your spirit—and put your sleuthing skills to the test.

Not all titles may be available at time of order.
If outside the U.S., please call
740-922-7280 for shipping charges.

SEND TO: Heartsong Presents—Mysteries! Readers' Service
P.O. Box 721, Uhrichsville, Ohio 44683
Please send me the items checked above. I am enclosing $_____
(Please add $4.00 to cover postage per order. OH add 7% tax. WA add 8.5%.) Send check or money order—no cash or CODs, please.
To place a credit card order, call 1-740-922-7280.

NAME _____

ADDRESS _____

CITY/STATE _____ ZIP_____